APRIL'S FOOLS

by Peter Cooper

authorHOUSE®

AuthorHouse™ UK Ltd.
500 Avebury Boulevard
Central Milton Keynes, MK9 2BE
www.authorhouse.co.uk
Phone: 08001974150

First published by AuthorHouse   4/19/2010

ISBN: 978-1-4520-0168-5 (sc)

This book is printed on acid-free paper.

Acknowledgements

Many thanks to everyone who supports King of Hearts Creative Outreach.

Special thanks to…

Sam Thompson who encouraged me to publish;

my son Phil for his proof-reading skills;

my wife Audrey for lots of things;

and to Aliti, the real 'Emily Darkchilde' for lending me her fictional name.

And thanks to you for buying this book. If you didn't buy it, but only borrowed it, then don't read this part.

Peter Cooper

1.

Ben April was beginning to lose concentration when the principal announced that it was his turn to speak. He had been looking across the people seated on the stage at the members of staff at this unusual little college, and he had caught a glimpse of a particularly attractive young lady, which had distracted him until he heard his name. He looked up quickly at the principal, Professor Michael Kennington, who was ushering him to take the stand and do his bit for his subject on the first day of the new term – the first day of the new college, in fact.

He stood up quickly, nearly upending his chair as he did so. As he walked briskly to the wooden lectern, he noted that, almost out of his eyesight, his colleague Bryn Jones, who had been sitting next to him, was holding onto the newly displaced chair and putting it back where it belonged.

He looked out over the crowd of 'eager young faces', or whatever the principal had just called them, pausing to take a breath before he began talking, just as he had been taught. It was hardly a great hall full of eager young students – more like a small hall half-filled with kids who couldn't get in anywhere else. Professor Kennington had great visions of his college becoming famous because of the success of these sixty-or-so budding practitioners of various arts, but Ben was not at all impressed by what he was looking at. Oh, well...

"My name is Ben April, and I am a magician," he said. Then he paused, as if he had just had a new thought. "Sounds a bit like Alcoholics Anonymous, doesn't it?" The audience chuckled a little, but most of them were probably still dozing after the previous long-winded monologue, or 'monotonologue' as Xander Herron would later call it. Ben paused again. "I wonder why they call it 'Alcoholics *Anonymous*'? The first thing you do is tell everyone your name." Still little response.

Ben decided to waste no more of his razor-sharp wit on this bunch of losers. "I'm going to be running the magic lessons. We'll be learning some magic tricks, of course, but we will also be studying past masters of the art, and looking at stagecraft and how to present the tricks we learn to make them entertaining. I asked Mr Kennington to let me have a few words because I thought you might sign up to my class because you think it might be an easy option. You know, beats working. Well, it's about performing, like a lot of other lessons here at the college, and it's about hard work to perfect our art. After the first six sessions in my class I will evaluate every student. I imagine I'll throw some of you off the course. You know, of course, that if you don't do enough classes, you are asked to leave the college."

He looked around the group of students again. He was instantly sorry he'd said that. He had intended from the beginning that he would lay down the law about discipline in his class. He didn't want people who just wanted to know how tricks worked; he wanted people who were serious students. However, he hadn't meant to put people off coming to his class. And the young people in front of him weren't a bunch of losers. What the principal had said in his speech about aspirations and potential, what Ben had heard of the speech anyway, was true. He knew that every young person there could amount to something.

Honest.

He turned and nodded, rather feebly, to Michael Kennington, then returned to his seat. Bryn held his hands up in readiness to clap, but as nobody else had started applauding, he thought better of it and put them down again. Kennington gave him an odd look as if he had not understood a word of what Ben had said, then he got up to the podium to introduce the next tutor who wanted to advertise their subject.

After a few more introductions the students were dismissed with nothing to do for the rest of the day but look round the college premises and sign up for any extra classes they needed to fill their quota. Ben had only three students assigned to his class so far, but he was sure he'd have a last-minute deluge because his was more a curiosity group than serious study, and not necessarily something people would have thought through before their arrival here this morning, as much as he would like it to be different. Even the principal, Michael Kennington,

2

who had personally invited him to join the team for the new venture, must have known that it would be like that.

The college was an old converted Georgian mansion in its own grounds, well looked-after by an enthusiastic team of volunteers and one paid groundsman. Less than half of the sixty-four students lived on the premises, the rest were day students who lived in the local area. There was a small housekeeping team to look after the boarders, some of whom were as young as 17 and were away from home for the first time. They, along with a small number of live-in staff, Ben included, lived in pleasant rooms on the east side of the great house, while all of the classes happened on the west side in several rooms of various sizes, upstairs, downstairs and in the basement. The best room for the dancing was on the ground floor, as the basement beneath was largely protected from the noise by a solid floor. That was a good thing, because that was where Ben was going to be situated.

The old house was a large, elongated building, surrounded on three sides by extensive grounds and various outbuildings once used by the gentleman farmer that had owned it many years earlier. These buildings were now in a state of disrepair, some used for storing tools of yesteryear, some for keeping the more modern equipment used to keep the grounds in order, some not in a good enough condition to keep anything. The principal's vision was to grow the college so big that there would be money to change these decrepit old outbuildings into further classrooms for more students. The big house itself was in a surprisingly good state, and well looked-after by the team of workers who took a pride in keeping the house and grounds looking good, for it was the pride of the local village, Lockley, just two miles down the winding country road.

Professor Michael Kennington's vision was to change the fusty old school into a bright and interesting place to be. He wanted the school to become famous for producing quality stars of the different arts, possibly famous singers or dancers, comedians or even, you never know, magicians. He started by changing the name from Lockley Art College to Lockley College of the Arts. He still retained a traditional art teacher (and you couldn't get more traditional than Bryn Jones), but he built up a further team of teachers of associated arts. He had even thought of bringing in a tutor for ventriloquism, but the cost of the American specialist he had asked was too high. Ventriloquism was a dying art in this country, but very popular over there. Maybe next year.

Ben sat in his classroom and looked around at the place. It was about the average size for a classroom, with about twenty desks and chairs all lined up and ready for action. As half of the classroom was effectively underground (the house was built on a slope), the light to the room was provided in part by the thin row of high windows up by the ceiling, and mainly by numerous theatrical-style spotlights and lamps, some of them free-standing and reasonably mobile to adjust to whatever set-up he might want. A sizeable storeroom adjacent to the classroom stored his extensive stock of magical props, including equipment for sawing a woman in half which he had never used. Perhaps the desks could be moved out, and maybe the space at the back of the class could be rearranged for a small stage to be put in. He looked up at the ceiling. It was a little too low to build too high a stage, but he could always book one of the two theatre areas elsewhere on the premises for big show rehearsals. Anyway, if he ended up with nobody other than the three who had signed up, he wouldn't need a stage area down here.

He looked at the names of the three students who had already signed up for the class, then at the twenty empty seats. After his performance in the opening speeches, perhaps three would be the limit. Assuming that none of them dropped out after hearing what he had to say. Somewhere, in the back of his imagination, he had thought that the students would be flocking to come to his classes. After all, this was a school for magic – like Hogwarts but in real life. However, 'real' magic, that is, sleight of hand, tricks and performances, were not what people wanted. They wanted to believe in a fantasy world where you could do real-life miracles with mystical energies controlled by magic wands. Who wanted to do card tricks?

There was a gentle knock on the door, quiet and hardly audible. This was followed, almost immediately, by a stronger, louder knock. Ben called out loud for them to come in, and the door was opened by one of the students, a slim young lady with short brown hair, who ushered in a very shy-looking lanky young man with a light brown shaggy mop of hair almost covering his eyes, which looked at the floor. He shambled into the room slowly and falteringly, encouraged every step of the way by the lithe young woman. Neither of them said anything. The girl looked like she was going to, but was waiting for the lad to start things off. He, in the meantime, was waiting for everyone else.

"Good morning," Ben said to them tentatively, and then he checked his watch. The morning's speeches had seemed to be so long that it might be nearly midnight by now. But no, it was just about still morning. The young lad mumbled something in response, but Ben didn't quite catch it.

"This is Mark," said the young lady, finally deciding she should speak for him. "He wants to join your group."

Ben looked at Mark for a brief moment, wondering why he wanted to be in a group that would be performing, one day perhaps, to the general public. Then he looked up at the young lady, who was definitely, as far as he could see, performance material. She had a kind of stage presence, like a striking beauty which might capture her audience. Her short hair fell into place perfectly; she had a bright smile and big brown eyes that could probably melt steel. Her long limbs might well be described as slim, but were by no means skinny and her movements were graceful, like a dancer.

"And you?" he asked her, almost hopeful. "Are you here to sign on to this class, too?"

"No, I'm upstairs," she said, her sweeping arm indicating above them with a grace and beauty which said 'I'm not just *like* a dancer, I *am* a dancer'. "I just came in to give Mark some support."

"Pity," said Ben, then he turned his attention to the lad, "and you want to be a magician?"

"I love m-magic," he said in a slow, ponderous voice. "I h-have since I was y-young. I want to learn all ab-about it. But you'll throw me off the c-course after the f-first six s-sessions."

"I'll what?" Ben said in the gentlest voice he could and still sound incredulous. He really regretted saying what he had said in the main theatre this morning. The point of what he said was to put off slackers, not to strike fear into the hearts of people who didn't need much effort to strike fear into the hearts of.

"You said. Upstairs," said the lad, whose stutter disappeared when he used particularly short sentences. He still kept his head down, apparently unable to meet Ben's gaze. Ben moved to stand up to match the lad's height, but he stopped himself, deciding he would remain seated to enable the young man to be taller than him. The young dancing girl spoke. (He really mustn't describe her like that, even in the privacy of his own thoughts.)

"Mark has Asperger's," she said. He nodded to acknowledge that he knew what she meant. That explained a lot. Ben was fairly familiar with Asperger's Syndrome, a form of autism. He once had a long conversation with a colleague on the Internet about whether all magicians were autistic in some form or other, because they all focussed their attention on magic, its history, its 'practice', and its personalities as if they were important. So he had looked up autism and discovered Asperger's, an interesting aspect of the autism spectrum, particularly in terms of 'normal' relationships. Asperger's Syndrome was referred to as high-functioning autism. Often, people with Asperger's have very high IQ's. They don't seem to empathise with other people very well, can't read body language and often take everything literally, meaning there are some jokes they would not understand, they don't have a grasp of irony and, in general, lack what the psychologists call 'non-verbal communication skills'. Sometimes, Ben recalled from his research, they can be physically clumsy.

Some went to university, particularly where they were given appropriate support and understanding. Only a small percentage, however, ever held down jobs. Modern social service agencies and disability charities were working to change that. Ben looked at Mark. This young man might achieve greatness, or never achieve in his life, depending on how people like himself treated him. From his stutter and general demeanour, it was possible, Ben realised, that he had already been put down a lot in his life.

"Do you like magic?" he said to Mark.

"Love it. S-since I was little."

Ben stood up and faced him. Or rather, faced his mop of untidy hair, as Mark's head was still bowed and his eyes still scanned the ground.

"Look at me," he said. The girl moved protectively towards the young man, but stopped as Mark raised his head to face his tutor.

"I promise you," said Ben, slowly and carefully, "that I will not throw you off my course. If you love magic, if you do whatever you can to express that love in the lessons, I will do what I can to help you. I don't care what you achieve, or what you fail to achieve. I only care that you love magic, and I will do everything in my power to help you get the most out of that love. I will not throw you off the course."

He wondered if that promise was one he should not have made, but the look on the lad's face was just a joy to see. He glanced at the dancing girl, oops, he meant at the dancer, and saw that she, too, was beaming.

"I've got one class still to sign up to so I can fill my sheet," she said. "Can I join your magicians, too?" She looked around at the empty classroom. "You got room for one more?"

"You'd be welcome," he said with a smile, somehow not offended by her reason for wanting to join the class. "Your name?"

"Shelley Hickman," she said.

"And I'm Mark," said Mark, his voice a little louder as he found his confidence, "Mark T-Tyler."

"Ah," Ben said, "Hickman and Tyler. Not brother and sister, then."

"No," said Shelley with a big smile, "we only met this morning. I'm a boarder and Mark lives in the village. I thought he needed a..."

"Champion?" suggested Ben when she paused.

"Friend."

The two of them signed his sign-in sheet, and Mark looked round the room, as if expecting to find lots of magical paraphernalia scattered about the room. He was obviously disappointed to find nothing. Ben had only moved in a couple of days ago, and while all of his stuff was now tidily stored in the next room, his classroom looked like, well, a classroom. He realised now, late as usual, that he should have given some time to making the place look a bit more like a magician's study, with something in it to welcome the new students. A big prop, like a brightly painted vanishing box or a guillotine in the middle of the room would have made this cellar room a little more inviting. Either that or it would have given them nightmares as they peered through the half-light at a pale blade in its huge wooden frame.

"Got to go," said Shelley breezily, "I want to take a good look at the dance studio. See you." And she was gone. Mark looked at the doorway where she had been a few seconds before, as if he had not noticed she was leaving until it was too late. Ben was aware that people with Asperger's, while they are frequently quite clever, often miss ordinary things like people leaving the room. However, the way Mark looked at the door made Ben turn and look, too. There was another person standing there. A young man, smartly but casually dressed, with very dark, tightly curled hair and a Hispanic complexion.

"Hello," Ben said. "Another one for the class?"

"'Ollo," said the newcomer.

"Are you signing up?"

"I wan' join yo class," said the young man.

"You want to learn about performing magic?" Ben said back to him, realising his English was not so good.

"Magic. Si. Yes."

"Certainly, come in. Your name?"

"Paterro. Miko Paterro," he had to spell it out for Ben.

"And why are you interested in magic?" Ben asked, noticing that Mark was staring at him, and hoping that the young Spanish student did not mind. Or preferably, did not notice.

"I learn good with my hands, but no' with my voice."

"Ah," said Ben, then he cleared his voice. "Well, welcome aboard." Here was another person who, like Shelley, wanted to use the class as a convenience, rather than to express his interest in the art. He tried not to let it make him feel downhearted.

"Aboard?" queried Miko.

"It's a figure of speech," said Mark, proudly displaying that he knew all about them, and without a stutter. "It means…" then he turned to Ben. "What d-does it mean?"

"Welcome to this class. I was referring to this group as if it were a ship."

"Aboard," Mark suddenly got the joke, and started to laugh as if it was funny. Miko missed most of the exchange between them, but smiled politely as if he understood. Then he signed the sheet onto which Ben had optimistically put 25 spaces and left. He was Ben's sixth student.

Mark sat down next to Ben and hunched forward, looking

at the tutor as if he was waiting for something to happen. Ben felt uncomfortable, because he did not want to throw the young lad out, but lessons didn't start until tomorrow.

"Lessons don't start until tomorrow," he said. "Have you settled in?"

"My mum works in the g-gardens here in the s-summer. I c-come up here and j-join her m-most days, so I know the p-place. I d-don't need to settle in. C-can I stay here and talk to you f-for a minute?"

"What about?"

"M-magic," he said, as if it was obvious. Then, after a thought, "Who is your f-favourite magician?"

Ben had to think about that, even though that question would come up for the students later in the term. "I've got lots of favourites. It's different for different things. My favourite for stage mystique is Toby Travis. I love David Copperfield's big television stuff, but I think he's too big for British magic. For comedy, it has to be Tommy Cooper." Mark's face lit up when he said that, so he asked, "What about you? Who's your favourite?"

"Mine is Tommy Cooper too," he said, and he started to recall the different things he had seen him do on television, laughing out long and loud as he tried to describe what he had seen in detail. He forgot his stutter and almost fell off his chair laughing, almost as if he was watching it live that very moment. Ben had to do very little other than listen and struggled to get a word in as Mark detailed Tommy Cooper's career and progress in the Magic Circle and in television, all the way to his death during a stage performance. Mark was of the opinion that the whole clumsy magician thing was not real, but just an act, in spite of some views that suggested that his performances were klutzy because the man himself really was clumsy.

"People laugh at me when I get things wrong," Mark said, "but not in a kind way, like with Tommy Cooper."

Ben looked at his watch, and then jumped up.

"It's twenty past one!" he said. "We've missed the start of lunch!"

"You're like me," said Mark, suddenly turning serious, "I forget meal times, too." And they rushed upstairs together to eat. Mrs Mandover, the head cook, was normally quite hard on people who were late for lunch, but when she saw that Ben was with Mark, she just smiled at them both and gave them an extra large helping of her steak and kidney pie. It seemed that she, too, was from the village, and knew about Mark.

Ben wanted to separate himself from his enthusiastic young student, but Mark let him go first in the queue and then followed him to a table to eat. Ben only half-listened to him continue his examination of Tommy Cooper's life and career as he looked around the room for his other students. There were three who had signed up before the beginning of term who he had not yet met, and he wondered who they were. He looked for groups of boys together. There were a lot of girls among the students, but they would probably rather be singers and dancers than magicians. So far, Shelley was the only female member of his 'elite' bunch.

He noticed the really beautiful singing tutor with the golden brown skin who looked half-African, and wondered if they would meet much. He sincerely hoped so. Since he had arrived a few days ago, he had spent much of his time sorting out his equipment, and had not yet found where the staff room was. He was sure he would find it in due course, and, who knows, maybe that singing tutor would be there?

In the afternoon, Mark Tyler followed Ben back to the 'magic room', where they both started to move some of the chairs out. The groundsman came in to help them and moved a few of the desks out, but Ben couldn't answer when he was asked how many he would like left in.

"I've got six students so far. Maybe a few more will turn up by the end of the day. Why don't we leave ten here and hope for the best?" That would leave some space for some props and a performing table or two. Perhaps he could move all of the desks out and bring in some more comfortable chairs? He knew there were some spares outside the student's lounge, so perhaps he could commandeer them. If his class was going to be this small, it was an opportunity to be comfortable. He would just wait until he knew for sure that his class was not suddenly going to grow to overcrowding.

When he got a few minutes alone, he reviewed his members list. There were the first three that had signed on, who he was yet to meet, named Herron, Drontlin and Berkley. Then there were the ones he had met today - a Spaniard who could hardly speak English, a young man with Asperger's Syndrome, and a girl who was not really interested in magic, just dancing. Ben wondered who else he would get, as there was a bump, rather than a knock, at the door, and Richard Wellington struggled to get in, narrowly avoiding scraping his knuckles on the door frame as he steered his wheelchair into the room.

2.

"There were once two friends," said Ben at the beginning of his first lesson of the term on Tuesday morning, just after 10.30am. He was holding up a long piece of soft rope, which he began to position in one hand. "They were good friends. Inseparable. It was almost as if they were just one person." He moved the rope from one hand to the other, keeping his hands open and his fingers apart as much as possible so that his small audience could see clearly that there was without doubt only one piece of rope and nothing else in his hands. His audience watched carefully, one or two of them looking as if they wanted to catch him out. There were just six teenage boys in front of him – Shelley had not turned up.

Mark had mumbled something about 'Meesh' coming later, so Ben had hoped there would be another student wanting to join their group, but seven, if Shelley had not changed her mind about joining this class, would still be enough. He repositioned the rope so it was held in place by the fingers of one hand. Then he lifted the centre of the rope up so that it was all held in the one hand, and took a pair of scissors with his other hand.

"Then, one day, something terrible happened. They broke friends." He cut the rope, and at that moment there was a knock on the door. It was a light knock, and it wasn't Shelley. The beautiful features of the golden-hued singing teacher appeared around the door. Ben was ashamed that he had, as yet, not found out even what her name was. He really must find that staff room.

"Excuse me, Mr, er, April, isn't it?" she said with a sing-song voice easily as golden as her complexion. "I wonder if you would have room for another student?"

"Yes, certainly," he said, almost stuttering like Mark. "As you can see, there's only a few of us."

"Oh," she said looking around at all the male faces. "Is this a gentlemen-only club?"

"No, we've got one young lady with us."

"Where? You haven't made her disappear already, have you?"

"She's not turned up yet, I'm afraid."

"Might be a clash of classes. I'm sure it'll sort itself out," she said, and ushered in the new student, a young woman, possibly older than the others, dressed in expensive clothes, her brown hair bleached with a single blonde streak, and a confident smile on her face.

"This is Juliette MacIntyre," said the singing tutor. "She's signed up for my singing class, but she needs another group to fill her sheet. Are you okay with that?"

Ben stood, hangman's rope in hand, spellbound by his visitor's beauty, so he said, "Yes, of course, come in Juliette," in a cracked voice, and in a moment, the tutor was gone and three young men, as spellbound by the new student as Ben had been by her tutor, scrambled to offer her their chairs. Ben almost went to call after his colleague to ask what her name was, but thought better of it in view of the fact that he had a class to lead.

He took a second to work out where he had got to. He always told a joke about the two friends who had argued at this point, but the moment was lost. He looked carefully at the two pieces of rope in his hands, in the hope that Xander and Al would stop paying attention to Juliette and start looking at him again. He cleared his throat, which got Xander's attention at least. He had felt from the moment he met 'Big Al', which was about ten minutes ago, that he would never have this young man's interest.

"They hated being apart," he continued his story, hoping that he had not lost the flow. "So they decided to say sorry to each other and make friends again." He tied the two newly-cut ends of the rope together, and held out the knotted piece in open hands for them to see.

The classroom door to his left opened again and Shelley came in. She was dressed in her dancing gear, a tight leotard which displayed her slim figure extremely well. Six youthful mouths opened as all eyes left the rope in Ben's hands and stared at the dancer.

"Sorry I'm late," she said. "The dance lesson ran over."

"That's fine," said Ben, "but I think it would be good if you went and had a shower and got dressed, don't you?"

"I thought you'd be angry if I was any later."

"That's very good of you. But if you are so committed to your dancing that you 'run over', then I'll make allowances. And I would prefer you came into the lesson fully dressed."

She looked down at herself, as if she suddenly became aware of what she looked like.

"Oh, yes, of course," she said, embarrassed. "I'll be as quick as I can."

"Thank you, but there's no need to rush," said Ben, "at least let me finish this trick."

Strangely, Mark, who would not normally, because of his condition, pick up on a subtle remark like this, laughed as if it was the funniest thing anyone had ever said.

Ben looked at the rope in his hands. "This was an attempt at the famous cut-and-restored rope trick," he said, looking at the knot. "But it looks as if the forgiveness between the two friends wasn't complete. It seems that, sometimes, when someone does something wrong, it leaves a knot in your friendship that spoils everything. Wouldn't it be great to be able to forgive so totally, so absolutely that the friendship is completely," and as he pulled the rope tight, the knot flew off leaving the piece of rope entirely whole, "restored."

His audience continued looking at Ben and his rope. There was no applause, partly because they weren't totally sure what happened, as they had not been watching the whole time due to interruptions. There was just an awkward silence. Mark had stopped chortling at the 'let me finish the trick' remark and started to pay attention, but he had missed what had happened. Big Al wasn't bothered what happened, just as long as he was sitting next to Juliette, who was paying serious attention, but had not been in at the beginning of the trick, so she could not really appreciate it.

When Richard Wellington had arrived in his wheelchair to sign on to the course yesterday, Ben began to despair. What he really wanted was a group of eager young magicians ready and willing to benefit from his wisdom and able to perform, and, who knows, one day become stars. What he seemed to be getting was people who were using his class as a convenience. When Richard appeared, however, he began to change his mind. He told Ben how, a couple of years earlier, he had been hit by a drunk driver and how his spine had been permanently damaged as a result. In many failed attempts to walk again over the next few months, he began to lose heart and give up. He would never walk again. However, as time went by, he strengthened up his resolve and decided to be a campaigner for disabled people. He had signed up to this college of the arts in order to learn skills relating to performance and presentation so that he could go out into the world and campaign for the rights of disabled people everywhere. He wanted to encourage people with disabilities and help able-bodied people to understand and help those less fortunate than themselves. Professor Kennington had made some changes to the premises in order to accommodate him, but Ben couldn't help believing that part of the reason Richard had chosen this particular class was that it was the most difficult class to get to in a wheelchair. If he went out of the main entrance and down the slope to the back, it was easy to access this class, as the building was more or less built on a slope, so the back access was lower than the front, but when poorer weather came and the rain started, going outside in order to avoid the stairs was going to give him problems.

Richard was a nice lad, and, although he wanted to be a campaigner, he appeared not to be belligerent or unpleasant about it. He made it clear to Ben that he wanted to help people understand the disabled, not fight against authorities for not doing enough. Nevertheless, Ben did not mention the wet-weather access situation that came to his mind during their chat on the previous day.

Ben had only just met the other lads in the group when they came in to the lesson a few minutes ago. Xander Herron was a tall, good-looking young lad with a clever mouth. He had sharp, intelligent blue eyes and the clothes he wore suggested that he knew about the latest fashions. Ben wondered why he had chosen this college rather than some smart university somewhere, but he immediately berated himself for thinking negative thoughts about this establishment. Xander no doubt had his reasons for being here as a boarder, far away from his home in the city of Oxford. Xander was witty and attentive, although Ben couldn't help noticing that he was more aware of himself than others around him.

Big Al Drontlin was big. That was probably how he got his name. He was by no means fat, more like chunky. He was noticeable wherever he went. Not too tall, but big enough to compensate for that. He obviously wanted to be the centre of attention, and set about making disciples of one or two members of the group. He did not waste too much time on Xander, because he saw immediately that he would have to take second place to the sharp-witted, charismatic young man. He quickly noticed that Miko needed a friend, and incorporated him into the Big Al gang. He didn't need anyone who understood English to be one of his followers – in fact, he probably thought it was better that Miko did not understand him, as long as he had an obedient little toady to follow him.

Big Al already had one follower, Len Berkley, a skinny individual who made up for being taller than Al by hunching his shoulders. Whenever Big Al made a joke, however silly, Len would laugh. He would not sit down until Big Al had first found his seat. Ben wondered if he would be able to think for himself, or if he might have a panic attack if Big Al wasn't there. It wasn't that he was a bad person or anything like that. He had a pleasant enough demeanour, and spoke politely to Ben and the other tutors at the college, when he spoke at all. It was just that, without Big Al, Len seemed to amount to nothing at all.

And then there was the latest addition to the group, Juliette MacIntyre. She was nicely dressed, good-mannered, well-educated, and no trouble at all. She had perfect features, smooth skin and the rebellious blonde streak seemed perfectly placed as if she'd had advisors to tell her where to put it. The obvious high cost of her clothes suggested she would have been able to afford them. She paid attention to her tutor, and ignored the drooling of one or two of the lads who she obviously distracted. But why was she there, in a magic class?

"I suppose it must be said, although I'm not going to make you sign up to anything, but we will be dealing with secrets in this class," Ben continued to the group. "It is respectful to leave the props alone unless I give you permission to touch them, and to keep any secrets we reveal from the rest of your fellow students, and for that matter, the tutors, no matter how much they ask, or bribe you, or whine to know how it is done." He paused.

"The students, I mean, not the tutors." Ben looked at Mark for his response, but he had missed that one. He looked as if he was in the process of making a solemn promise.

"Today we're going to look at the whole of how the tricks are done. There are basically, as far as I can make out, four ways to do a magic trick. None of them involve sorcery, witchcraft or casting spells."

"None of them?" asked Xander, with an element of disappointment in his voice.

"None of them," responded Ben, waiting for the joke.

"Does that mean you won't be teaching us how to turn my mum into a frog?" he asked, and the students gave him a better laugh than they had given Ben up to now.

"I'm afraid not," said Ben, "and I'm certainly not going to show you how to saw her in half." At last he was beginning to build a rapport with some of the group. Big Al didn't laugh at anything that Xander said, so, of course, neither did Len.

"Four ways. The first is sleight of hand, or a 'move'. This is often called the skill of magic. It's frequently shown in card tricks, and it's what I would like you to be spending a lot of time practising. It's the art of doing something clever with your hands to make a trick work."

"Can I do something clever with my hands with you?" Big Al said to Juliette, and Len laughed out loud.

Juliette smiled politely at him and said, "I doubt it."

In the awkward silence that followed, Ben continued. "Then there is the gimmick or gadget, a device that does the trick for you. It might be something with a secret compartment, a magnet or a mirror. Sometimes, it makes magic easy, because the device does the work for you. Sometimes, it makes magic boring because it detracts from your real skill. Some of you will take a great delight in all the gimmicks and gadgets I have here in my collection, and will favour them over really working at your moves, sleights and performance skills. That will not necessarily make you good magicians."

"What about David Copperfield?" asked Richard, noting that Ben had not objected to the others interrupting. "Doesn't he use gadgets and devices? But he is considered to be one of the world's greatest performers."

"And I would agree with the world about that," said Ben. "But David Copperfield is a highly skilled performer who works with a highly skilled team. Without his skills, his knowledge of audiences, even some of the things he does would not look that good.

"Thirdly, there is the self-working trick. You know, think of a number, double, half it, add seven, take away the number you first thought of and the answer is seven. There are some fantastic ways that maths can be used to do all your magic for you. We'll be looking at number magic later in the term.

"And finally, the most used method of all – misdirection. Misdirection is when you're pointing over there," and he pointed to his right with a sweep of his right arm, and half the class looked that way, "and the magic is going on here." His right arm drew their attention back to his left hand, which held a small orange handkerchief.

"For those of you who were looking in the wrong place, I just got this out of my pocket. It wasn't magic, just misdirection. Magicians use misdirection a lot, but here are two examples – a magic wand and a woman." He paused to make them think, if that were possible.

"The magic wand has no power in itself, no phoenix feathers or mystical energy, but it can be used to hide what's really going on. You might want to conceal something in your hand, but if you close your hand people will be suspicious. If you close it around a wand, then they think you're just holding a wand. They won't think for a moment that you are holding something else as well." He turned to pick up a plain polished wooden wand from the table by his seat, and when he showed it to his audience he was no longer holding the orange handkerchief.

"And a woman," he continued. "My beautiful assistant. She's there to move when she should move, and stay still when the audience should be watching the magician instead. She's wearing a beautiful gown that makes all the men in the audience want to look at her, and all the women want a dress like hers." He leaned forward and spoke in a quiet, secretive, conspiratorial voice, "And they are not paying attention to what the magician is doing."

At that point, Shelley provided the perfect illustration of misdirection by turning up for the rest of the lesson, showered and dressed more conservatively. Her short hair was almost dry, and still as perfectly in place as it always was.

There were going to be two magic lessons a week, each one ninety minutes long. The first on Tuesday mornings and the other on Thursday afternoons straight after lunch, with 'unlimited' practice times between 9.30am and 4pm on Fridays, where all the studios and theatres would be opened to any members of staff who were available to supervise them. Professor Kennington had asked for reports from all his tutors as to who turned up to take advantage of this 'free study' time.

Because his timetable meant that he was only teaching for three hours a week, the principal had asked Ben to be around the grounds as much as possible and meet the students, in off-duty times, to be generally a part of the pastoral care of the college. As he was living on the premises, that would put a particular emphasis on the boarders. Many of the students went home most Fridays, leaving about sixteen for the small on-site team to look after at the weekends.

After the first lesson, during which he introduced the group to a basic coin vanish as well as the secret of the cut-and-restored rope trick, he decided it was time for a walk around the grounds. It was the end of the school day, and many of the local students left on the village bus or were picked up by their parents. For the rest, there were a number of activities on the grounds. There was a small putting green, three tennis courts, a volleyball court, badminton and a couple of flat green areas that could be used for football or whatever else the kids wanted to do. Frisbee and volleyball seemed to be the favourites.

Ben sat down on a log seat and looked out over the north-facing grounds in front of the house. None of the facilities were taken yet, but some of the young people were gathering near the football field. There was a row of large old trees which separated the main playing fields of the front of the house from the stream that marked its northern border. On his left the grounds extended some distance, past the tennis courts to the boundary of the college grounds, beyond which was farmland. In his opening speech, no doubt the principal had told the students how important it was not to cross that border and that the farmer who patrolled his side of that piece of land carried a shotgun with him. To his right was the driveway that led to the house, a parking area for visitors' cars and the fence which separated the college land from the land of the other, much nicer and more supportive farmer.

There was someone standing in the bushes that made up part of that east border fence of the college premises. From what Ben could make out, it was a man in a dark suit. The bright autumn sun was behind him, but the shadows were not too long and Ben was certainly not mistaken. He looked around to see if there was another member of staff nearby for a second opinion, but nobody else was out yet. He looked at the man again, just standing there, a few metres off from the guests' car park, just watching the young people gathering. He must have been standing in the farmer's field outside the college grounds.

Perhaps he was a parent, looking for his son or daughter, although that was a funny place to stand. He would probably not have been able to get to there easily from the car park. Most of the young people had gone home, and Ben decided to wait until there were no cars left to take anybody home, and the only people left were the boarders. Then he stood up from his log and started to walk towards the stranger, wondering what he would say to the man when they came face-to-face. The stranger saw him, and moved away into the shelter of the nearby tree that broke the flow of the natural fencing.

When Ben got to the tree, there was nobody there. The man had done a runner, using the tree as cover. He looked around for a while, but it soon became apparent that the watcher had moved on. He decided that he should tell the principal about this as soon as possible. He turned to return to the house, and saw his colleague, the beautiful singing teacher, walking towards him.

"Mr April," she said with that smile, "I've been looking for you."

"Ben," he said, "Please call me Ben. I let the kids call me Ben, so I ought to extend the privilege."

She chuckled a musical laugh. "Ben. We're going to have a little informal staff meeting by way of a first day review."

"It's a little early for that, isn't it?"

"If we waited for another day it wouldn't be a *first* day review," she teased. He didn't catch on to the humour.

"I mean a review."

"I know," she laughed that enchanting laugh again. "Have you found the staff room yet? I haven't seen you in there so far."

"I've seen a man."

"In the staff room?"

"I mean a stalker. Over by the tree over there," he indicated behind him.

"Oh," she said, standing still and carefully looking over towards the college boundary. She saw nobody. "We had better report it straight away."

"Should we leave the kids unattended?"

"Don't worry. Becky and Tony are patrolling." Becky and Tony were two of the carer staff employed to look after the boarders. They lived in, and their duties started at the end of the 'school day' when the tutors' work finished.

"Erm, I think I've been quite rude," Ben said as they walked towards the staff room.

"Rude?"

"Yes. I haven't asked your name yet."

She laughed again. "I'm Emily. Emily Darkchilde."

The staff lounge, as Professor Kennington preferred it to be called, was a lovely large L-shaped room with two pillars blocking a clear view of the whole room. There was tea and coffee making facilities on one side. It was filled with big armchairs and sofas that made you sink in when you sat in them. It was used for staff meetings, but mainly designed to be a place to relax. Ben decided that he had made a mistake by not finding this place earlier, a mistake he would certainly rectify by spending as much of his spare time here as possible.

Professor Kennington, who positioned himself in one of the very few places in the room visible to everyone, sat in a taller, more upright chair, and welcomed Ben and the others in as he sat and waited for the rest of the team. He did not ask anyone how their various lessons and activities had gone until everyone was present. So before everyone had turned up, Ben took the opportunity to inform him of the stranger in the field.

"I approached him, but he vanished."

"One of your magic tricks, Ben?"

"I would joke about it myself, Professor, but you hear some pretty awful things about children being kidnapped. And I know that nearly all our students are technically adults, not children, but we still owe them some sense of safety here."

"Yes, I agree. We'll make sure that the rest of the staff know straight away. Although I am not so sure that the students need be unnecessarily alarmed. What do you think?"

"It's worth warning them to be wary of strangers, possibly to report anything unusual. But not to alarm them," agreed Ben.

"It's possible there may be some innocent explanation," said the professor.

The rest of the staff were soon there. The last one in was Bryn Jones, the head of art. He was wringing his hands as if he had not quite finished drying them.

"There's a bit of a fuss outside," he said in his deep Welsh accent. "Apparently, there's been a stranger watching the students from the fence."

"Is he still there?" asked Ben.

"He was there until about twenty minutes ago. He's gone now. Becky and Tony are on it. The kids all know, they're out there speculating about who he's after."

"Who he's after?" queried Ben.

"They think we have a celebrity among us, secretly, you know, and this man is a stalker."

"It's probably a farmer, curious about what's going on in our little community," suggested the professor, calling everyone to order.

"Well, day one," he said to everyone, when they were finally settled down. "At least, the first full day of lessons, anyway. How do we think it went?"

A number of the staff said it was early days, hard to tell, and things like that. The dance teacher, Carolyn Cleese, was delighted with the enthusiasm of her group, calling them 'wonderful', and Emily Darkchilde also commented favourably on the start of her class, mentioning 'one or two in particular'. All in all, everyone seemed to have a great start to the term. Ben decided to go with the 'early days' school of thought, although all this positivity and optimism made him feel a little depressed at the thought of his class. However, he said nothing about it.

"Good, good," said the professor, taking in the general positivity of the staff, his 'team' as he liked to call it. He seemed to Ben to be the kind of person who would always stand by his staff. He did not lay down the law about how they should teach their various classes, because they were, after all, in a creative industry, so creativity would be encouraged with regard to teaching methods. He could not afford, therefore, to be too prescriptive in his policies.

"Now, with people signing up to their final additional classes over the last couple of days, do we need to reschedule anything? Anybody double-booked?"

Surprisingly, there were no lessons directly double-booked, but there were one or two classes that were too close to each other.

"Shelley Hickman arrived late to my class this morning because the dance class ran over. Is that likely to be a regular problem?"

"We finished on time," Mrs Cleese said, "but then there is tidying up, showering, things like that."

"Yes," the professor mulled it over for a second or two. "Ben's group starts the moment that your lesson finishes, doesn't it? Then, when Ben's group is over, the students have nothing to do for an hour until lunchtime. Perhaps, Ben, you could start at eleven o'clock on Tuesdays instead of ten-thirty?"

"That would be good," said Ben, with a smile to Carolyn, who he hoped he had not upset with his complaints. Ben was amazed at the professor, who seemed to have the ability to remember everyone's timetable without having to use notes. It would not surprise him if he knew the names of all the students by now, as well.

After the short meeting, most of the staff disappeared into the grounds to search for the mysterious stalker, who, by now, seemed to have disappeared. Ben stayed in his chair. He had not really had a difficult day, but teaching his students seemed to take it out of him. The professor also stayed behind.

"You're okay down in the cellar, are you?"

"Yes, it's fine down there."

"Enough space?"

"Plenty. I might move furniture a bit now, though, now that I know the size of my class."

"Good idea," said the professor, and he paused for a moment before leaving the room. Ben wondered if he was going to say something else, but changed his mind.

After quite a while, he walked outside. Students were well into their sports and games, and a pleasant smell was wafting from the kitchens in the house behind him. It would be dinner time soon.

He looked out over the fields beyond the trees. There was nobody out there now. Not a stalker, or a lost parent, or whatever he might have been. The sun was getting weaker and the air cooling after a hot summer. Ben wondered if he would see the prowler again. But not this evening.

3.

"Some syllabuses," started Bryn Jones in the local pub on that Friday evening, "say that you must study the work of this artist, or that artist, and produce a piece of work in the style of whoever."

"Syllabuses?" said Ben. "Is that the plural of syllabus?"

"Isn't it Syllabi?" said Emily Darkchilde.

"No, I'm sure it's syllaboo's."

"And who's Whoever? Is that an artist we haven't come across before?"

"I think he was a friend of Pickax-o."

"Before you carry on making fun," said the Welshman in his glorious musical lilt, "just let me remind you who's buying the next round." Ben and Emily shut up immediately, allowing Bryn to continue his rant.

"I agree that we should study the greats, but why shouldn't we be allowed to paint in the style of Bryn Jones?"

"I hear that Bryn Jones is one of the greats himself," Emily suggested.

"I suspect you only think that," said Bryn, "because you *have* remembered who's buying the next round."

"So what you're saying is that you study the artists, then use your own style," said Ben.

"Precisely," Bryn said the word as if he was a Sherlock Holmes-style of detective coming to a grand conclusion.

"That's what I teach in my magic class."

"You teach your students to paint in their own style?" asked Emily, far too interested in the relaxation process that the pub offered to get involved in talking shop. She was going to scupper this conversation, no matter how serious it got.

"I teach my students to study how a magician does a trick, how he performs, then find their own performance style. What about you?"

"I don't have any magicians in my singing class."

"What about Juliette?"

"She's not a magician. But she is the most glorious singer."

"She'll be a magician before the end of term."

"Practise a lot in your cellar today, did she?" Emily challenged.

"Well, not exactly."

"Well, not at all," said Emily. "She spent the whole day with me."

"Competition, is it?" said Bryn, fascinated by the way Ben and Emily's new friendship was developing. Ben had gone quiet, and Emily stopped being silly. She must have realised that she had upset him. Mark had been the only student who had spent the day in the magic room, although Miko had spent an hour or so there, and Richard stopped by to ask when they were going to learn some more tricks he could do on the new table that he'd had fitted on his wheelchair. They had looked at card tricks during their second lesson on Thursday. This had fascinated Miko, Richard and Xander, but the girls were bored to tears by it all. They were certainly not likely to learn any of the moves Ben had taught them, and even the easy mathematical tricks seemed not to interest them.

Miko also wanted to learn more card tricks, so Ben had promised to give them another session some time during the term. Personally, he did not like card tricks that much, although even now he carried a pack in his pocket nearly everywhere he went. You never know when people would stop you in the supermarket and ask for a card trick (although, nobody ever did). He had done a session on card tricks in his lesson for a number of reasons. Firstly, to get them out of the way. He really was not a fan, but everybody expected it, so you had to do it some time. Secondly, because people expected it of you. Thirdly, card tricks cover a range of skills. Some are so simple a child could pick it up and perform in moments, others teach basic handling skills which take a bit of work to get right, and some sleights take hours of practice and years to perfect. What he did not like about magic with cards was that there was no point to them.

"You know, you've been with us a week, and I haven't seen you do a trick yet," said Bryn into the silence.

"Didn't you notice? I just made half a pint disappear," Ben answered with a smile. He knew many magicians, particularly amateur magicians, who foisted their tricks, particularly card tricks, on people at a moment's notice. He had decided long ago that he would not be like that. Card tricks especially were particularly boring, as some of his class had already attested.

"Come on, I'll see if anyone's got a pack of cards," said Bryn.

The secret of foisting tricks onto people, thought Ben, was to wait until they've asked several times before bringing out your cards. Even better if someone gives you a pack first. And someone did.

Friday night was pub night, and the staff made a point of unwinding at the Tin Whistle in Lockley village, a couple of miles from the college itself. This team bonding, or whatever it was, had been instigated by Bryn when the College of the Arts was just an art college, and had been part of the culture of life at the college ever since. The staff and local friends from the village enjoyed half an hour or so of magic from Ben with a pack of cards and a few coins. He actually started to enjoy himself, too, and the attention he got from his audience.

Ben had qualified as a teacher but had never got as far as teaching. He dreaded the paperwork and the hoops they made you jump through in the teaching profession, and had started to build a bit of a reputation on the magic circuit when he took up performing to earn a bit of money to put himself through college. Halfway through his education, however, some long-lost uncle of his father that nobody in the family could remember died, leaving his family a share in a substantial amount of money, finishing off his ambition to pay his own way and furnishing him with a reasonable sum to squander on magical props. His family had visions of him doing something really useful with his life, and they considered his magical 'career' just a phase he was going through on his way to doing something important.

However, having money to spend on training and props enabled him to start a short but lucrative career in magic shows. When not performing, Ben studied performance skills in his local college near Aldridge, the non-Brummy speaking part of Birmingham, which was where he was when Professor Kennington found him and offered him a more permanent position and a place to live as well.

He wasn't sure he was going to like it here in the wilds of Norfolk, several miles from any major town, but the people were friendly and the big house was pleasant to live in. Sometimes the students were a little noisy at night, but a polite word from him or one of the other live-in staff usually quietened them a bit. It wasn't, after all, as if he'd be staying there forever.

He finished his round of tricks while people were still asking to see another one, and started to make his excuses and head for home. Bryn lived in the village so he could afford to drink a little more and walk home, but Ben wanted to stay below the limit so he could drive back to the college. When he got up to leave, Emily stood up as well.

"Any chance of a lift back?" she asked.

"I didn't know you lived in the school."

"I don't. I live in Newbridge, but that's some way away. I usually stay over on Friday nights. I always join Bryn's traditional pub time on Fridays, and I don't like to drive back, even if I haven't had too much to drink. As I'm doing an extra class for the local primary school children in the morning, I go home at lunchtime."

"Delighted," he said.

They didn't say much for the first couple of minutes of the journey, then Emily had to say something that was on her mind, "I think I owe you an apology. I didn't mean to put you down."

"I didn't realise you had," he answered.

"I put Juliette on you for her convenience. And I had a go at your group in the Whistle just now. And everyone else's class is called a class, but everyone calls yours a group as if it wasn't a legitimate class."

"I was hand-picked by the professor."

"All of us were hand-picked by Mike," she responded. He wondered what kind of apology she was giving him. She realised that she wasn't making much of a good job at settling with him, too.

"I talk too much," she said, "I must stick to orange juice in future."

"You'll have a hangover in the morning."

"You can't get a hangover from orange juice."

"I mean tomorrow morning."

"I don't get hangovers."

Driving home along that final winding country lane heading for the college, Ben noticed a car parked on the side of the road. In it there was a man who looked like he was dressed in a suit. He wasn't sure, in the dark, but he wondered if it was the man he had seen watching the students in the school earlier in the week.

"Did you see that?" he asked Emily.

"Car parked on the side of a country road?" she said. "Somebody stopped for a snog on the way home."

"I thought I saw that man who was watching the school the other day."

They had already passed the vehicle and were close to turning into the main driveway. She looked back at the parked car behind them.

"You can't see a thing in this light," she said.

"You're probably right. I have an overactive imagination."

The following day, Ben got up a little later than usual, refreshed and looking forward to seeing Emily Darkchilde again. Unfortunately, he did little more than catch a glimpse of her at breakfast, because she went home a few minutes after her class for the local village children finished at 11.30. He, in the meantime, walked around the college and its grounds. He walked out of the long driveway and down the road, but he found no sign of any car or anyone watching the college. He wandered back to the main premises. It was a nice day, and many of the students were out. He walked around the back of the school building, past the outbuildings which stood between the main college and the lake at the bottom of the back lawn. By the lake, he saw Miko sitting on his own. He walked up to him, and noticed that he had a pack of cards. He was practising some of the more difficult moves that Ben had taught them all. He asked if he could join the Spanish lad, who nodded.

"How's it going?"

"Okay," said Miko, for whom the word might mean 'great', or 'terrible', it was just an English word that he could say.

"You can practise in the cellar... I mean, in the magic room, if you like."

"No. Alone is good."

"Need help?" Ben asked, finding himself reducing the size of his sentences in response to the Spaniard's way of speaking.

"Please. Okay," came the reply. So Ben pulled out his own pack of cards, and carefully, and with as few words as possible, spent a pleasant hour or so going through some moves with Miko. It was surprising how many subtleties of card-handling could be taught without words. Ben felt that the one-on-one time they had that morning might well be worth several hours in the classroom to his young student.

In the afternoon, Ben spent some more time in the cellar, as it was very quickly becoming known. He adorned the walls with soft cloth sheets in rich colours, got out all of the desks and chairs and replaced them with comfortable seats from upstairs and checked that all the lights worked so the place could be bright, medium or dim. At the end of a tiring but satisfying day, he stood at the door and looked at the room, imagining he was someone who was coming in for the first time. The place looked welcoming, unusual and much more the magician's cellar than an old, half-underground classroom.

Sunday was a lazy day. Clouds cooled the air, and only a handful of students went out to the sports fields. Many hung around the different social areas inside the building. There was a room with a couple of pool tables, air hockey, and a table tennis table, which was full most of the day. Eager dance students who wanted to practice couldn't because there was no dance teacher available and all the classrooms were out of bounds unless a tutor was present.

Ben had a chat with Shelley while both were waiting for a go on the pool table.

"You play?" asked the girl, surprised that somebody as ancient as he was (28) would be able to lift the cue.

"Not with any great skill," he said, picking up a pool ball which had already been excommunicated from the game and making it disappear in his hands.

"I wish you taught us how to do that instead of cards on Thursday," said Shelley.

"I did," he replied. "Not on Thursday, but in the first lesson. When we all had a go at making a coin disappear. It's the same technique."

Shelley remembered her attempts at a coin vanish with a little embarrassment. She had not been very good at it. "But the ball is so much bigger."

"It's all misdirection. I made the biggest gesture with my empty hand. You looked in the wrong place." He put the 'vanished' ball back into the tin with the hand that Shelley had not been watching.

"I don't think I'll be very good at magic," she said.

"Oh, I wouldn't assess yourself just yet. We have to go through the clever moves to start with, to learn a few basic skills. Once you've got past that, it gets exciting."

"I didn't go for the cards much."

"Actually, I'm not much of a fan of card tricks myself. But maybe some of the group will get really good at the discipline, and do nothing else. You don't have to spend a fortune on big props like I have, just a pack of cards."

"Discipline? Is magic a discipline?"

"Oh yes. As much as your dancing is. You'll be studying choreography at some point, won't you?"

"Yes."

"Think of the stage performance of a magician as a dance. Look at the choreography of the performer's routines. Big arm movements to draw the audience's attention, smaller movements to hide the secrets." He thought about what he had said for a moment. "Doesn't work so well with card tricks, though."

There was a shout from one of the students from the other side of the door. It was a girl's voice.

"No, no, no! I will not be treated differently from anybody else!"

"Excuse me," Ben said to Shelley, as he opened the door to see what was going on. It was Juliette, just finishing off an angry telephone call on her mobile. She slammed the small device closed, and looked up to see Ben looking at her in the doorway of the games room. She composed herself instantly, smiled at him with perfect politeness and composure, and turned to walk upstairs to her room. He entertained the thought of following her to ask if she was alright, but the wide wooden staircase led to the girls' rooms, and was as out of bounds to the male tutors as it was to the male students.

He turned back to Shelley, to see if she might be able to help, but someone had nabbed her for a game. He decided he would not wait for a game himself, so he left the queue for a cue and went down to the cellar. When he got there, he found someone was already in the room. It was Professor Kennington, the principal.

"Hello, sir," he said from the doorway.

"You don't need to call me sir. Most of the team call me Mike, although I'm not fond of the abbreviation. I prefer Michael. You've made a good job of this," said the older man, looking around the room.

"Thank you. Is there something I can do for you?"

"A hypothetical question."

"No, really."

"I mean *I* have a hypothetical question for *you*. What if I asked you to tell me your secrets?"

"You want to join my class?" he answered with a grin. But the professor seemed to be struggling with something, as if he had a real, non-hypothetical question on his mind.

"No. I don't want to be a magician. I just want to know how it all works."

"Then I wouldn't tell you. It works because we keep it a secret. If you know all about it, it stops being fun."

"But I am the principal of the college. I could sack you if you didn't do as I ask."

"You wouldn't ask me to break the college rules. And giving away the secrets is a bit like breaking the rules."

"Even if I threatened you with the sack?"

"I would not be working for you in the first place if I thought you were like that. And if you threatened me, I would leave anyway. I'm rather hoping, as we speak, that this is still a *hypothetical* question?"

"It is," said the professor, with a smile. "I am not going to be asking for your secrets. I just wanted to know how strongly you felt about keeping confidences."

"Is there a secret you want me to keep?"

"Mmm," said the professor, the expression on his face displaying the struggle he felt as to whether he should share his secret or not. "Excuse me," he said after some thought, and he squeezed past Ben who was still standing in the doorway, and left the cellar.

4.

Ben April managed to get away for the day on Monday, which was his day off, but he felt guilty going off-site this close to the beginning of term. He wanted to be around for his students, and, in fact, for the whole college. Nevertheless, on Tuesday morning, the whole class were there and on time, including Shelley. He started with a demonstration of cups and balls, which he had set up beforehand on a small table with a silky tablecloth.

"I've seen Paul Daniels do this one," said Mark, eagerly awaiting Ben's performance. Ben's heart sank, because he, too, had seen Paul Daniels do it, and he knew that he was not anywhere near as good as the great TV magician, who had developed the idea of doing this trick at great speed. Nevertheless, in spite of a number of comments and general conversation about who had seen who doing cups and balls before, he did his routine. A small red ball vanished from his hand and appeared underneath the cup, then the cup was emptied and shown to be empty, and the ball was definitely in the hand that was nowhere near the cup, then it wasn't there anymore and it appeared back under the cup. Eventually, Ben made the ball disappear altogether and there was a lemon under the cup.

The students chattered all the way through his performance, but there was still a 'wow' at the end when the lemon appeared. Then he took away the lemon, put the red ball down by the side of the upside-down cup and sat down. Big Al got up and grabbed hold of the cup, lifting it up to see if he could find if the cup was in some way gimmicked, only to discover that there was a tennis ball under it. Everybody laughed. Len only started laughing after Al, too, laughed.

"That's amazing," said Ben to Al, "How did you do that?"

Big Al took a mock bow to his little audience, who all clapped politely.

"Today's lesson," said Ben, "is about being an audience. Please sit down, Al, and we'll have a look at how good it feels when the audience is nice to you, how we should behave when one of our fellow students is performing, whether it's magic, or dancing," he looked at Shelley, "or singing," he indicated Juliette.

"Firstly, we do not need to shout out 'I know that one' every time I get a trick out of my box, and we don't chatter through anybody's performance. Not even mine."

Ben looked at Mark, who was twisting and turning his head to see if he could see past his tutor.

"Mark?"

"You haven't got a box."

"Ah," Ben said as he remembered that people with Asperger's Syndrome often take things literally, and don't understand subtleties and inflections. "Figure of speech."

"Oh, yes," said Mark, happy with the explanation. He sat back and continued to listen. Ben hoped he had caught on to the bit about saying 'I know that one'. He didn't want to dampen the lad's enthusiasm, but he did want to help him fit in to the rest of college life. He was also aware that Big Al and Len were laughing at Mark, so he gave them a stern glance in the hope that it might make any difference.

"Normally, polite applause is good, even if you don't think the performance was that good. If you saw a slip or a mistake, there's no need to point it out straight away – wait until after the performance, when we will have a feedback time to talk about the salient points of the performance. When we comment, we must point out the good things, as well as the bad things, about a performance. We are here to build each other up, not to criticize unhelpfully."

"I thought we were here to learn magic," said Xander.

"So show me something you learned last week," Ben challenged him.

"We learned about Vincent Van Gogh, and his emotional state," said Xander. "He wasn't the only artist in an emotional state when he painted, too." Even Big Al and Len laughed at that one.

"I imagine Mr Jones will be in an emotional state, if he has you in his class," said Ben.

"I thought he appreciated my wit."

"Now, anything you learned in *this* class?"

Xander showed them all a coin that vanished, something that they all did in the first lesson, and Xander did it well. Even if he did not come to the practice time on Friday, he obviously spent some of his own time, like Miko, working on his skills.

"Did you know that it's better to make a two pound coin vanish than a two pence coin?" Ben asked them.

"Why?" Xander asked for the whole group.

"Because it's worth more money. It's psychology. In the eyes of your audience, the higher the value of the money you vanish, the better the trick seems. Which is what we'll be talking about on Thursday. But for now – the audience. It's all very well me telling *you* how you should behave, but your average audience might not feel the same way. How do you control an audience so that they appreciate what you're doing, so that they know when to applaud?"

Ben continued to tell them various techniques for getting the audience to appreciate you. Being really good at what you do was at the top of the list. But little techniques and ideas were shared between them that might be helpful to the dancers and singers as much as to magicians in the group, before Ben finally got round to letting them in on the secret of the cups and balls.

The college prospectus covered a reasonable range of performing and associated arts. Of course, the most popular were singing, dancing and drama classes, but there was also an art class, a separate sculpture group, creative writing, film-making, and, of course, magic. Students had to sign up to at least three of these main courses in order to stay at the college, but that was only about 12-16 hours a week of tutor time, so there was time to add another class or two to the range if anyone wanted to. Mid-term there would be short optional courses on stagecraft and public speaking, and Professor Kennington would also have liked to put in juggling, clowning and something from a stand-up comedian, but had not yet finalised those details.

Shelley approached Ben at lunchtime about one of the other classes she was in.

"I'm in film-making as well as dancing and your group," she said, and he refrained from correcting her use of the word 'group' rather than 'class'.

"Are you finding it interesting?"

"It's okay."

"But you prefer dancing."

She grinned as she nodded. Then she said, "I was wondering if you could do us a favour."

"Us?"

"Some of us who are in the film class. We've got an assignment to make a video to advertise the college and its courses. I wondered if you'd let us video your magic class."

"If you like," he suggested, "but why not video some of the members of the class performing, rather than a tutor teaching his class?"

"Are they, I mean are *we* ready for that?"

"I should imagine that our part of the video would only take up a minute or two. I'm sure we could come up with something in the next few lessons. How long have we got?"

"About three weeks. And it might be less than a minute. We've got to take a couple of hours' footage and cut it down to three and a half minutes. That's the whole advert, every class we film. We're doing about cutting and editing."

"You can film us so that you can cut us from the film?"

"I'm sure you'll be the star of the show," she laughed.

At the beginning of the Thursday afternoon lesson, Ben announced this to the group, and watched their faces. One or two were delighted with the idea. Mark loved it, but was nervous as well. Xander looked pale, as if he was about to faint. The class, in general, agreed it would be a good idea, but they needed to learn a bit more in practice – Ben was giving them a lot of theory, and they wanted to do something, not just hear about it. Except Juliette.

"You can only video us with our permission, can't you?" she said.

"That's right," confirmed Ben.

"I don't want to be video'd."

"Why not?" Xander asked. "You're beautiful. You'd brighten up anyone's video library."

"Smart mouth," said Big Al, and Len snorted out a laugh at him.

"It doesn't matter why," she said, ignoring the compliment. "I don't want to be on a video."

"That's fine," said Ben, "I understand." In fact, he did not understand.

He would have understood if it had been Mark, or possibly Len, but Juliette seemed a self-assured and confident young woman. She would not be the one that he would have guessed would object. "Is it alright if they video in here without you in the frame?"

"That would be fine," she said, "as long as I am not in the frame at all."

There was a little awkwardness for a second or two, which Ben should have dealt with, but he was quiet, trying to work out what was going on with Juliette. She was, after all, a student in a performing arts college, and she hardly had shyness issues. It was Shelley who broke the silence.

"Thanks, Juliette. It'll be me holding the camera, so I'll make sure you're well out of the picture."

"Thank you," said Juliette, the warmth still not fully returned to her smile. "I think I might ask to be excused on the day."

"You were saying last time about our audiences not always doing what we want them to," said Xander, deliberately changing the subject. "Have you ever had a really awful audience, Ben?"

"Have I? I used to do children's parties!"

"I always thought children were the best magic audiences," said Richard.

"Little angels sitting quietly while you perform for them?" suggested Ben with more than a little sarcasm.

"Well, I expect you would probably be so good that they be really attentive."

"Like Al, here?" Ben asked.

"Yeah, like me!" Al said.

"I remember one party," Ben started, doing what he had promised he would never do – reminiscing. A clown friend of his always used to say that nostalgia isn't what it used to be.

"Someone had hired a church hall, and invited all the most evil of the children in the town to their son's party. The parents all brought their kids in, and in spite of my request that at least one adult stayed in the room with me, they couldn't get out of the hall fast enough. As soon as I turned up, it was 'they're all yours now' and they vanished quicker than a rabbit into a top hat. It was just me and them, the little bu – angels. They hijacked my equipment! Half my props were ruined.

They got into my secret compartments and broke my unbreakable wand. They got to my magic frog before I could stop them. Mixed up all the cards, and bounced the frog around the room like a... like a..."

"Frog?" suggested Xander.

"I don't think I'll ever be able to use the frog again. I think it's croaked."

Ben quickly came back to the present and got them working. They practised some new, easy tricks – Ben thought he'd give them a break from learning the difficult sleight of hand that he had shown them over the last couple of sessions. Richard Wellington, with his neat little table on top of his wheelchair, was getting really good with the cups and balls he had shown them on Tuesday. Miko was still well into his cards, and Mark, Shelley and Xander were keen on learning something bigger and more colourful.

"If we're going to be filming," said Shelley, "wouldn't it be great to get something really big and colourful on video?"

"With fire," added Mark. Ben looked at him. He wasn't joking.

Xander suggested the guillotine.

"The guillotine has been at the back of my storeroom since I moved in here," said Ben. "I haven't mentioned it, or got it out to show anyone, although I've thought about it, since the term started. Have you been into my cupboard?"

"No, but I have been reading your website," Xander said with a sparkle in his eye.

"So you're the one," Ben said. "But no, not the guillotine, and I'd be grateful if it didn't get round the campus that we have such a device on the premises."

"What's a campus?" asked Mark.

"It's like a camp, but with us in it," said Big Al, and Len laughed.

"But this isn't a camp," said Mark, and Big Al and Len took the opportunity to have a laugh at him again.

"You weren't ever at a party in Wolverhampton, were you?" Ben asked Al. He let Mark join him looking through the huge storeroom that Professor Kennington had kindly allotted him for his magic equipment, what Xander had begun to call his 'cellar cellar', and they found some big rope and handkerchief tricks which were not only colourful, but would involve a reasonable number of the group in order to perform.

Under Ben's direction, Mark and Shelley wrapped the rope around Xander, feeding it into his jacket and tying it to his wrists with the big coloured handkerchiefs. Then he pulled on the rope, making it look as if it had passed completely through him. Richard, Miko and Juliette stopped what they were doing to watch the big moment. Big Al and Len just pottered around not doing very much, and taking no notice of what was going on.

At the end of the session, Richard asked if he could take the cups and balls up to his room instead of coming down here to practise on Friday. "The forecast is for rain tomorrow, and I can't get down here without going outside."

"Of course," said Ben. He realised he had not yet spoken to the principal about access problems that Richard might have. Richard himself wanted to be a campaigner for disability rights, and this showed that, unless somebody made a fuss, nothing would get done. He made a note to himself to speak with the professor about it that very day.

"Before you go, I must remind you that I will be here tomorrow for anyone who wants to practise. The people who improve the most over the next week or two will be the ones I will choose to do the big trick on video."

"Can I tie Shelley up?" said Big Al to his sidekick audience.

"I will be practising upstairs in the dance hall tomorrow," said Shelley by way of an apology. Richard had already made his excuses, so Ben expected a day with just Mark. And that was exactly what happened.

He gave Mark a couple of books to read about the history of British magic and about showmanship in the magic profession, and taught him one or two tricks that he wasn't going to show the others. Miko popped by during the day to say 'hello', and so did Xander.

Miko stayed for a few minutes to play with some sponge balls that Ben had showed them, then he took his cards out of his pocket.

"I pra'tise upstairs. Okay."

"Okay," said Ben with a grin. Or possibly a grimace.

When Xander turned up, however, it was not to practise. He had a pretty blonde girl on his arm. He was there to show her where he worked, if work was the right term for it. He said 'hello' to Ben, and introduced Lizzie, his partner for the day. He showed off the cellar, and she looked slightly interested.

"Big Al said there was a guillotine down here. Can I see it?" she asked.

"Sorry, it's locked away," explained Ben. "It comes out only when I want to chop people's tongues off. Come to think of it Xander, if you see Al, send him to me, would you?"

On the following Tuesday, Shelley turned up with a huge video camera from the film department, just for a practice run. Some of the lads moved the big sheets of material that adorned a couple of the walls to make the back of the class look like a stage. Juliette joined in like everyone else, but took a step back out of the way when Shelley brought the video camera into play. She *really* did not want to risk being in the frame.

Big Al made faces into the camera when it was pointed in his direction, but other than that, thought Ben, he was about as much use as a hairdryer in a Buddhist monastery. Len stood by his side as usual, and Ben wondered what would happen to Len if Al disappeared. He picked a silver dollar out of the little box that contained his supply of small props and flicked it towards Len. Len, on a reflex, plucked it out of the air with some skill.

"Can you make it disappear?" Ben asked. He looked at Al.

"No, I asked you, not him. I'll no doubt give him something to do in a minute." Len looked at the coin for a second. He shaped his hand the way Ben had taught them, then had second thoughts.

"No," he said, and handed the coin back to Ben.

Xander and Miko moved a small, low table into the right light. On it was a smart-looking felt 'close-up mat'. They set up the camera into a fixed position on the light but sturdy tripod that Mark had brought down for Shelley, and pointed the camera down at the mat. Miko did a few tricks on the mat, and they all saw through the viewfinder the position of Miko's hands as he worked his cards. Even this early in the term, he was really good.

They had to reposition the camera to view Mark as he roped up Xander, sitting in a chair back-to-back with Richard, and filmed him pulling the rope through both of them. Mark had never actually worked out how the trick worked, but as long as he did all the moves right and tied the rope in the right places, it would always work for him anyway.

Juliette encouraged and cheered from out of camera-shot, and was, as much as she could be, supportive, the good audience Ben had taught them to be. He almost wanted to ask if she had changed her mind, seeing the wistful expression on her face, but he was sure she would stay back there out of the way.

It was Xander's turn to get in front of the camera. He stood like a zombie for the first few seconds with a small red handkerchief in his hand, and then started to talk gibberish as he pushed the handkerchief into his fist. He stuttered worse than Mark, and finally gave up on the performance, putting his palm up to the camera, and saying 'sorry' as he walked out of the frame. Ben noticed that his face was wet with sweat. Where was the quick-witted, fun-loving Xander that Ben had nicknamed 'Smart Alex'?

Big Al and Len were even less help than usual. Xander and Mark were eager to help Shelley get the equipment back to the 'film studio', Mark because he was always eager to help, and Xander to get out of the cellar for some fresh air. The others had not commented on Xander's performance, not even Big Al.

Later on that day was the usual Tuesday evening staff meeting. Professor Michael Kennington, who a small number called Mike, presided, but this time he did not ask 'how is it going so far?' as expected. Rather, he started by talking to Ben directly.

"You said in your opening speech that after your first six sessions, you would be throwing some of your students off the course."

Ben was taken aback. He obviously intended to use what he had said to discuss the students with all of the staff. "I said I might be," he replied cautiously, not actually remembering what he had said. Unfortunately, Kennington remembered exactly what he had said.

"You said 'I imagine I'll be throwing some of you off the course'. You also said you would evaluate every student after six lessons. I believe your next lesson is the sixth. I'm not sure whether I altogether approved of you saying what you said at the time, but upon reflection, I don't think it's a bad idea. I'm not into making policy for my staff, but it's certainly a good idea to get rid of the time-wasters now, this early in the term, and give the others a chance to work unhindered. Now, do you have anyone who might not last the course, so to speak?"

"Al Drontlin," said Ben almost without needing to think.

"Oh, yes, 'Big Al'," agreed Bryn Jones. "Waste of space, that one."

"While I like to believe that nobody is a waste of space – I think both Einstein and Tolkien were once referred to as such by their schoolteachers – I agree that young Mr Drontlin is only along for the ride." Professor Kennington looked around at the other tutors in the room. "Anybody else?"

After a spell with no input, Emily Darkchilde suggested, "Perhaps we should look at the good students, give ourselves a few positive thoughts, rather than just talk about the poorer ones."

"I agree," said Jim Hunter, the creative writing teacher, "I've got one or two budding best-sellers in my writing group."

Emily said, "I am particularly impressed with young Juliette MacIntyre. She has a stunning voice, and the discipline to make good use of it."

"My dancing group are all just wonderful," said Carolyn Cleese, who worked on the floor immediately above Ben's cellar. "They are all so enthusiastic, and they are coming together as a team so well. I wouldn't want to lose any of them."

"There's that young Spanish lad, Mickey," said Bryn.

"Miko," Ben corrected him.

"Yes, him. Now he's a good lad. Gets his head down and gets on with his work, even if he doesn't understand a word I am saying."

"Nobody understands a word you say," said Emily with her usual musical laugh, and because it was she who said it, he did not take offence.

"Mark Tyler's good," said Ben. "Loves his magic."

"Mark Tyler?" said Bryn. "Are you kidding? Isn't he that backwards kid from the village?"

"I'm not sure that he is backwards," said Ben, glancing towards the principal for support, "in fact, I expect his IQ is even higher than yours." Bryn gave Ben a harsh look, which made him realise that he wasn't going to be able to get away with the things that Emily got away with. He obviously wasn't pretty enough. "In spite of how high that obviously is," he added.

"I take it, Ben, that you would not regard him as a slacker?" the professor asked.

"No, definitely not."

"Then he will be welcome to stay as long as we are useful to him. I would love it if we didn't have to turn anyone away. Not even young Al Drontlin."

"We are only into our third week," Ben said. "Perhaps a warning would suffice, and we keep an eye on young Mr Drontlin?"

"I would appreciate you doing that, Ben, but please let me know if he really should go."

Ben just worked out what was happening. Professor Kennington had put the responsibility onto him. Which was fair enough, he supposed, because he had said in his opening speech about throwing him off the course if he didn't put the work in.

The following day was Wednesday, and Ben spent some time walking around the grounds. From the front of the house he could hear the dancers to his left, in their room above his cellar, and at the back of the house he heard the singers. He was not sure whether he was hearing Juliette singing or whether it was one of the others, but there was some beautiful vocal music being made in the singing lessons.

As he walked at the back of the house, he wandered by the entrance Richard Wellington would have used to get in to his lesson. He realised that, in spite of his promise made to himself last week that he would act on Richard's access problem, he had done nothing. He started to run immediately towards the principal's office (back around towards the front), when he noticed Big Al and Len kicking a ball around on the playing fields.

He approached them.

"Al, Len. No classes then?"

"No. My next class isn't until 11.30," Al explained.

"Nor mine," said Len.

"Glad to catch you, then. Can I have a word?"

"Sure."

"Just you, Al. Len, can you give us a moment?" Len nodded shyly, then wandered off a little, but not too far.

"How do you think you are doing here?"

"Okay, I suppose," Al replied, idly.

"Alright, let me put it another way. What do you think you are doing here?"

"What?"

"That's what I asked."

"I dunno what you mean."

"What do you do on Fridays?"

"Fridays is open study day."

"I know what it is. I want to know what you do."

"Open study?"

"Where? With whom?"

"With Len."

"In what class?" Ben had decided to say the words loud and slowly, in case Al somehow really did not understand what he was getting at.

"I dunno," he said.

"Well, look, Al," said Ben, struggling to say the things he ought to be saying, "the term is well underway now. All the students have settled in and are starting to get down to some serious work. Except you. I wonder how we can change that?"

"Are you tryin' to get rid of us?"

"Us? Who us?"

"Me and Len."

"I'm not talking about Len. I have no idea how he would answer me, given that he hasn't spoken a single word without your permission since you arrived. I'm talking to you. How are we going to help you get the most out of the college?"

"I've had enough. You can't teach me anything," he said, and he called over to Len and the two of them left Ben standing in the middle of the football field with a football at his feet, while they made their way indoors.

Ben took a good kick at the ball, aiming at the nearby goalposts. He missed.

5.

"Al Drontlin has decided to leave us," Professor Kennington told Ben on the following morning. Ben was preparing his dungeon room for the afternoon's class, so the principal had decided to come and visit him rather than have him sent to his office.

"I'm sorry to hear that," said Ben, who was really sorry, although not surprised. "Did he give a reason why?"

"He did not," said the principal. "His mother telephoned me last night and asked if she could pick him up this morning. She said he wasn't happy here and it would be better if she took him somewhere else. She sounded, I don't know, a little exasperated, I think. I am not very good at reading people's emotions, especially over the telephone, but I think she knows what her son is like. She's not blaming anyone here."

Ben, who *was* quite good at picking up emotions, could detect the sadness in the professor's voice, and, in fact, in his general demeanour. In spite of the fact that he would already have worked out that this would happen, and that he had given the job of talking with Al to Ben, he still took the responsibility upon himself. It was natural for a college to lose some after the first few weeks, but that did not make it any better for this relaunch of the old art college that Professor Kennington had worked so hard to create.

"What did you say to him on the field yesterday?"

"You know we were on the field?"

"My office overlooks the front of the house. I was watching the two of them in the field. I was about to go down and have a talk with them myself, when I saw you down there. It was a short conversation you had, wasn't it?"

"Yes, it was. I did the 'how can we help you get the most out of the

44

school' bit. Or at least, I tried to. I think he caught on to where the conversation would take us from the start. He wasn't interested, and took off."

"Yes, I saw that bit. As I said, I am not that good at judging people's emotions, but your body language was easy enough to read. Not much of a footballer, are you?"

"Not yesterday, anyway."

"I'm not in any way blaming you, Ben. This was going to happen. I don't think any of us could have stopped it. I expect Bryn will be pleased when I tell him."

"I expect he's sorry he didn't have the job of kicking Al out himself."

"Bryn is a good teacher," Kennington said, not prepared to give Ben cause for the slightest criticism of another member of his staff. "And he knows his subject. He is very devoted to the school. He's been here longer than me, even. It's just that, er" and he switched to an excellent impersonation of Bryn's Welsh accent, "he doesn't tolerate slackers, that's all."

Ben and the principal shared a little chuckle, and quietened down. The morning light which crept in through the high windows faded, and the black clouds outside darkened the room. Ben had only turned the overhead lights on, not the main beams, and the dullness seemed to support the mood of its two occupants.

"What about Len Berkley?"

"I telephoned Len's mother as soon as I had finished talking to Mrs Drontlin. Now there's an understanding lady. She said she had sent Len to us to give him a bit of independence. He's been at home all his life, and doesn't get out much. She thinks we can do him some good, and she wants him to stay here."

"Life with Big Al is hardly independence," Ben suggested.

"But at least it was away from home."

"He'll be lost without Al to tell him what to do."

"He'll probably find a new person to follow."

"Alexander Herron, more than likely," thought Ben. "At least Xander is a good influence."

"And, I believe, so are you, Ben. With such a small class, and a bit of spare time on your hands, perhaps you can spend a little, er, 'quality time' with Len."

"I wasn't so successful with Al."

"Len isn't Al, no matter what it might have looked like."

Big spots of rain fell against the slim panes of glass in the high windows. The rain that had been forecast since the beginning of the week was finally here. And it was due to be heavy. Finally, another priority pushed itself back into Ben's mind.

"Oh, no!" said Ben. "I forgot all about Richard Wellington!"

"What about Richard Wellington?"

"He's the lad in the wheelchair. He has an access problem to my class. It's okay in the summer, or when it's dry, but it's October, and he has to leave the shelter of the house to get to this cellar. I said I would see what I could do about it last week, but I forgot. Then, with this business with Al Drontlin, it went out of my mind again."

"Ah, yes," said the professor, "I have been working on something, too. We can't put in lifts, or stair lifts, because that last flight of stairs down to here is too narrow, and this is a listed building. What we can do, however, is put up a shelter from the students' common room to the back entrance. I've had someone do me a quote, and I have planning permission. I just need to get it done, now."

"But not by this afternoon, I'm afraid."

"No, of course not. And that's when he next has to come down here, isn't it?"

"Unless we go up to him. Most of the rooms on the ground floor have easy access, don't they?"

"All of them, I think."

"Can we borrow the ground floor theatre this afternoon?"

"I think that can be arranged. We've tried to work it so that the two theatres aren't normally used at the same time, so if there is anyone in it, I don't think they would mind moving upstairs for young Mr Wellington."

It did not take much arranging. The drama class had booked the downstairs theatre, but were happy to move upstairs, which was free, especially when they knew it was for Richard. Ben got round everybody at lunchtime (not too difficult to do with a class of seven), and told them of the new venue just for this Thursday afternoon. Mark volunteered to help move anything he wanted from the cellar.

"That's a thought," said Ben. "I wanted to do big stage illusions today, so that we could be ready for filming next week. We'll need to get a few people to help us."

"Will we be using the guillotine?" Mark asked eagerly.

"Ah, well, I suppose, seeing as Big Al spoiled the surprise, we might as well. But no tricks with fire. Not yet."

Miko, Xander and Shelley helped Mark and Ben immediately after lunch, and the props were in place in the tiny cubby-hole called 'backstage' in good time for the start of the afternoon's session.

Ben sat down at the back of the theatre, looking onto the stage. He had made it his habit, whenever doing stage shows, to look at the theatre in advance, usually from the front, back and both sides. This was to see if any of the tricks he was performing would be inadvertently revealed by a bad angle. He remembered on one occasion being a member of the audience in the Magic Circle's own theatre, which had been specially created for magicians. It was a lovely place, big enough for a spectacular and atmospheric show, and small enough to feel cosy and friendly. However, on one occasion, when he was sitting right at the side, against the wall about six rows back, he could clearly see behind one of the performer's props. That was when he decided he would check out any big venues before performing.

As he sat there, he reviewed his dreadful attitude towards Richard Wellington. Richard was a pleasant young man, and when he was around, Ben wanted to do anything he could to help his mobility problems, particularly as his cellar was in the most inaccessible place in the college. However, when he was not there, Ben didn't think about Richard or his problems at all. He just let any old thought get in the way, whether it was Big Al's lack of motivation, Emily Darkchilde's stunning good looks, or whatever secret Professor Kennington had that he had almost, but not quite, decided to share with him. Richard himself was not completely without fault. He said he wanted to be a campaigner for the rights of disabled people, but he actually stayed in the background as much as possible. He did not misbehave, but neither did he shine. He certainly did not push himself into the limelight, and he seemed to make himself invisible as much as possible. (Not a bad trick in that great wheelchair of his.)

Ben scanned the stage, which was really little more than a slightly raised platform with curtains on either side. Suddenly, he realised that, once again, he had overlooked something. There was no way for Richard to get onto the stage.

Miko was the first to come back from the cellar with the last few props – a couple of smaller items. Ben had supervised the transport of the big props, but the silk handkerchiefs and rope and stuff like that were no problem for the students to do on their own.

"Miko," said Ben, "can you go and find someone to get one of the ramps from outside?"

"Ramps?" repeated Miko, saying a word he had never heard of before.

"Yes. From outside. But they're not outside, are they? They are in the caretaker's storeroom."

"Outside," said Miko, grabbing hold of a word that he thought he recognised.

"Yes. No. In the caretaker's storeroom."

"Yes. No." Miko must have thought he was getting an impromptu English lesson.

"Ramps. For wheelchairs?" said Ben, miming rolling the wheels of a wheelchair with his hands. "For Richard."

"Ah," said Miko with a beaming smile, "for Richard. I go for Richard. Get outside ramps from inside."

"Do you know where they are?" Ben asked, then he asked the question again in shorthand. "Where?"

"Where? No. I don' know where. But I ask. Ramps. For Richard." And he, too, mimed the wheelchair action. Luckily, Xander and Mark arrived with the ropes and a few bits and pieces just at that moment, and Xander took over the task of helping Miko find a ramp. The rest of the class were assembled and ready to start before they returned with one of the lightweight wooden ramps which the caretaker had made just before the start of this new term.

Before they began, Mark gave back the two books that Ben had lent him last week.

"You've read them?" he asked.

"I read a lot," said Mark.

"Both of them?"

"Yes, they were great. D-do you have any m-more?"

"Even 'Magic and Showmanship'? It's not exactly the easiest book in the world to read."

"Well, I skimmed past the actual illusions a bit, you know, the bit about making your own vanishing cabinets and all that, but that's not what the main part of the book is about, is it?" That was a long sentence for Mark, Ben thought, and he had delivered it without a stutter.

The class for the day looked at stage performances, in contrast to the close-up magic that had dominated their studies so far. They were all to have a go at getting on stage and performing a trick they had learned in a full stage setting.

Shelley wheeled Richard onto the stage, and, although his cups and balls routine would really have better suited a slightly smaller, closer setting, Ben acknowledged that he was getting quite good at it. Ben noticed again, however, that he did not have a great stage presence – he was not really noticeable, even on the raised platform. He mulled over what could be done to remedy that. Was it lighting, the focus of props, elevating him to a position where his head would be where a standing person would be? Or was Richard simply one of those people who was not easy to notice, the kind that Ian Fleming wrote about in his spy books? Unfortunately, his chosen subject was not spycraft.

Miko was next. Before he went up, he asked, "I do cards?"

"That's good. But remember we are a distance from you," Ben replied, emphasising his words with his arms. In fact, after thinking about it for a moment, he leaped up on the stage and pulled his own cards from his pockets. He fanned them out.

"Normally you would show the cards to someone like this," he said, standing by Miko on the stage and showing his cards as if it was just the two of them. His voice, however, was raised so that the rest of the class could also hear him give his lesson. "But the audience is out there, so you need to show them the cards like this." He changed his body position so that he was displaying his card moves to the whole audience. Miko copied his moves to great effect.

"Point your right foot to the back of that side of the theatre, and your left foot to the front of the other side. Your body is positioned in a way that draws in most of the audience," Ben emphasised all his words with exaggerated actions, pointing at Miko's feet and the back and front of the theatre where appropriate. He may not have completely understood all of his words, but he was certainly a quick learner when the words combined with actions. He positioned himself well on the stage, and Ben stepped down to let him continue.

"That was in 'M-magic and Showmanship'," said Mark, "but it was for assistants. And the a-assistant's f-feet should have been p-pointed towards the magician."

"That's right," said Ben, "but we aren't using assistants today, so we have to adapt."

"I do show," interrupted Miko, "but English. I'ss difficul' for me."

"Do your best," Ben encouraged him. "We're all on your side."

Miko's performance was good. His cards skills were fine, his stage presence and position were good. He obviously learned quickly. However, his poor use of English gave some comical moments, as he pointed at his choice of helper and said, "You! Here!" a couple of times during the act. Ben thought about teaching the whole team how to treat their helpers when they got someone from the audience. Nevertheless, the group had obviously taken his comments on being a good audience to heart, as they gave him a great, supportive round of applause as he returned, beaming, to his seat.

When Shelley stepped up onto the stage, her presence captured the whole theatre. She walked up the two steps onto the raised platform slowly, back to the audience, and she turned and walked with the grace of the dancer in her to the centre of the stage, where she faced the audience and bowed. All eyes were on her, and she seriously commanded the attention of everyone in the audience. Although she was only dressed in her casual clothes, she looked as if she was designed to be the centre of attention. She got out her rope and scissors, and proceeded to make a pig's ear of the 'cut-and-restored-rope' trick.

She held the rope incorrectly, she hacked at it with her scissors when they would not cut cleanly, and dropped the small piece that would have made the knot if she had got that far. Still, she got polite and supportive applause from the team as she returned to the audience, casting an apologetic glance to her tutor on the way.

Len was worse. He had not actually learned any tricks over the first two and a half weeks that they had been there, and, although he seemed okay as he got on the stage, he did not actually do anything to entertain his waiting audience. He mumbled some thanks and said some polite things about his tutor, but otherwise, just bowed and left the stage. Mark applauded him enthusiastically, but everybody else did nothing.

Juliette was the next person, and she mounted the stage with confidence, and performed with style and wit.

"Good evening everyone," she said.

"But it's," Mark started to say, but Ben whispered, "She's pretending," and he shut up quickly and enjoyed the show.

"I wonder if we fully understand the power of the mind?" she continued. "We can imagine ourselves to be anywhere in the world. We can even imagine worlds we have never seen. We can think of the impossible, and make it happen in our minds. Xander even imagines that I could fall in love with him."

Everybody laughed. Xander called back, "You never know, you might get lucky!"

"But can we really transfer our thoughts? Is it possible that I could predict the outcome of your actions before today? I have here an envelope, and in it is my prediction of the outcome of the next few minutes of our combined mental exercise. I wonder if I could ask someone to look after it for me?"

Mark volunteered enthusiastically.

"You see?" she said. "I knew it would be you." And everyone laughed again, but only for a moment. Even with the interruption of humour, Juliette had control of the theatre, and was weaving her spell of mystique among the assembled group. Ben was spellbound. He was sure that he had not taught them any of this.

"I want you to imagine you are holding a pack of cards. Hold your hands out like this – no, not you Mark, you're looking after my prediction. It would seem like I was cheating if I included you, and that would never do." There was another barely perceptible chuckle. She was being amusing, but she had captured the audience with her words and was not ready to let them go just yet. Ben watched in total amazement.

"You too, Mr April. If you have your hands like that, you'll drop your imaginary cards." He obediently held his empty hand open in front of him. She had not yet called him Ben, and it seemed right to let her continue to call him Mr April.

"Separate your cards into red and black in front of you. Pick a colour... Miko." She turned suddenly to the Spanish lad, who became flustered.

"Er..."

"Red or black, Miko?"

"Black."

"Please give the red cards to someone else then." She demonstrated with her own hands, so Miko passed the imaginary cards to Len.

"Len, you have the red cards, hearts and diamonds. Hold out both your hands. Imagine the hearts in one hand, and the diamonds in the other. Your choice. Left or right hand?"

"Left."

"And which cards do you have in them? Hearts or diamonds?"

"Hearts."

"I did not influence your choice?"

"No."

"Pass them on to Shelley. Shelley, pictures and numbers, one set in each hand." Shelley took the imaginary cards, and held out her hands.

"Pictures or numbers," Juliette said again. "Your choice, without my influence."

"Pictures."

"You have three cards then, all hearts. Pass them on to Mr April. No. If he chooses you will think I have arranged this with him. Pass them to Xander." Xander took the cards.

"Fan them out, Xander, and let Richard choose one card from the group of three." Xander mimed fanning the imaginary cards out, and Richard mimed taking one of them. All the time, Juliette's voice was clear and musical, gentle and, well, almost spooky.

"What card do you have, Jack, Queen or King?"

"Queen."

"You have the Queen of Hearts. Mark, it's your turn now. Open the envelope and tell me what is inside."

"It's a card," he said after ripping the sealed envelope open rather messily. "It's a playing card."

"Which card is it?"

"It... it's the Queen of Hearts!"

The applause was incredible, coming from such a small group. Juliette bowed politely, and left the stage to join the rest of them. They shook her hand, patted her on the back, and congratulated her heartily.

"As well as singing, your other class wouldn't be drama would it?" Ben asked her. She smiled affirmation to him.

"That was a brilliant combination of the different disciplines."

They took a break to chat for a few minutes, but Ben was aware of the time ticking away. He called them back to order and introduced Mark, who eagerly got up onto the stage and pulled the guillotine and some other bits and pieces onto the stage from the side. Mark had his head down to start with, but when everything was in position, he looked up at his audience, his eyes clear and full of excitement. When there was nobody in the cellar but the two of them, last Friday, Ben had introduced him to this piece of equipment.

"Ladies and gentlemen, may I have a helper from the audience," and without waiting for volunteers, "Shelley."

Shelley was surprised at being called up – this was not something that they had rehearsed. Nevertheless, she got out of her seat and came to the front. Mark had felt comfortable with her, although he was not normally at ease with girls, since she had been his champion at the beginning of the term. She gave a slight curtsey to the audience, but did not overdo it because this was Mark's big moment.

Mark got a chair for her.

"You look tired, sit here," he said, and put the seat behind the guillotine so that, if she sat in it, she would not be seen. So when she did sit in it, he said, "Where have you gone? Oh, there you are!" and he lifted the blade up to the top of its frame so that she was visible to the audience again. All the time, he was fumbling about as if he did not know what he was doing, but Ben noticed that there was no stuttering – he was doing everything exactly right. He was just pacing it a little too fast.

"You still look tired," Mark continued. "Why don't you rest your head here?" and he pointed to the hollow made in the guillotine's lower head-piece.

"I'm not sure I should," she said in mock fear.

"It'll be fine. I think I know exactly what I'm doing." He put special emphasis on the word 'think'.

"If I go to sleep, will I wake up again?" she asked, going along with him and slowing him down a bit.

"Nobody sleeps through *my* show!" he ad-libbed, and the audience's amusement turned into serious laughter. She obediently put her head into place, and took her time about it to increase the humour. He stood up, 'accidentally' knocking the upper part of the hollow into place, trapping her in.

"Oh, clumsy!" he said. Then he took a bucket and put it in front of the guillotine. "Just in case." By this time, tears were rolling down the cheeks of the audience. Len was nearly falling off his chair. Ben was trying to assess his performance, but the others' laughter was beginning to get hold of him, too.

Then, Mark 'slipped', and let the blade go with perfect timing. It seemed to pass through Shelley's head and to the bottom of the frame. He quickly unfastened the blocks, and helped Shelley to her feet and held her hand for the final bow. The audience were still laughing as they clapped and cheered him. When their applause finally subsided, one man at the back continued clapping. The principal, Professor Kennington, had come down to see how they were getting on, and had seen Mark's act.

"That was brilliant," he said with genuine enthusiasm. "Best magic I've ever seen."

"Oh, thanks," said Ben sarcastically. The professor congratulated the glowing Mark, and left to visit other classes. Ben acknowledged Shelley for the way she had helped him, and she smiled one of her shining smiles back at him.

"Xander," said Ben, when the excitement had calmed down a bit and they were ready to continue. "Your turn."

"Can I sit this one out?" Xander asked from his seat, his humour gone, the normal confidence he expressed was miles from him now.

"Well, everyone else has had a go," said Ben.

"I don't think I'm ready for this just yet," he said, then continued with a grin, "what Juliette said about not falling in love with me cut me to the quick. I'm heartbroken. I might never play the piano again."

"Okay," said Ben with some understanding, recognising that he was covering his real feelings. "But why don't you just get up on the stage for a few minutes. To see what it's like." He hoped that if Xander stood there, he would find his strength. But it did not work like that. Xander stood up and climbed onto the stage, standing close to its centre and looking out at his small audience. He opened his mouth to say something, but not a word came out. Sweat beaded on his face and forehead. Ben thought he could actually see his legs shaking.

"Right, my turn," he said, leaping onto the stage and ushering Xander off quickly in an attempt to save his embarrassment. "Although, after Juliette and Mark, I'm going to be a bit of an anticlimax."

He did a couple of tricks which his audience seemed to appreciate, but after the reception that the class had given Juliette and Mark, he really didn't feel he was as good as them. But time was up, and he got them to help pack things away and put them back in the cellar. The class was buzzing, and although he had felt for Len, Richard, Shelley and Xander, he was delighted with how the others had got on.

At the end of the 'school day', as he called it, he did his usual walk of the grounds. He saw the day students leave, looked around for stalkers, of which he saw none, and wandered about the premises. He saw Len, sitting alone on a log bench by the football field, looking lonely.

"Mind if I join you?" Len shrugged, so Ben took that as a 'yes' and sat down next to the lad.

"Lost without Al?"

"'Course not," said Len.

"What then?"

"What do you mean?"

"You look a little lost."

"I don't like it here. I want to go home."

"You were okay up until yesterday."

"That was before you got rid of Big Al."

"I didn't get rid of him. He chose to leave. But one of us would have eventually had to ask him to go. He wasn't putting any effort in. I was trying to help him work. He was no good for you, Len, dragging you down with him."

"He was alright."

"What about you? What are you going to do, now that he's gone?"

"No idea. I think I might learn that guillotine trick, if you'll let me."

"Let's let Mark have that one. We'll find a trick that's just for you. Nobody else. We won't even tell the others how it works, if you like."

"How did Juliette do that prediction thing?"

"Equivoque," he said by way of an explanation. In the past, he had done a version of the same trick himself in his act, but his was a comedy version. Her spooky approach was better.

"What?"

"We'll no doubt explain it in due course. But like your special trick, let's ask her permission before revealing the secret."

"Yeah," he said, with the beginnings of a sense of purpose in his eyes.

On Friday, more people than usual, including Juliette and Len, joined the free practice time in the cellar. Mark, as usual, stayed all day, and the others spent a reasonable length of time down there before going on to whatever else they had planned to do. The use of the big stage had seemed to envision the young people, and they were eager for more. Xander, however, did not turn up to the cellar to practise at all that day.

6.

On Saturday morning, there was some weak sunshine after the rain. The lawn at the front of the mansion was not too boggy to go out and play games, so some of the small number of students that were around that weekend were outside, although most of them opted for volleyball on the hard court. Ben and Professor Kennington took a walk around the grounds. The professor used a walking stick that Ben could not remember seeing him use before. Perhaps it was because, as they made their way around the whole of the grounds' perimeter, there was uneven and muddy ground, and he would need assistance for some of the walk. He also noticed that the professor was wearing decent walking shoes. He looked down at his own feet. He was wearing trainers.

The perimeter was only a little more than a mile, but they walked slowly, starting at the visitors' car park and walking towards the stream at the northern boundary, then they would walk along the stream behind the big trees and bushes which frequently stopped balls from the playing fields leaving the premises, and down towards the western boundary.

"I got another phone call," said the professor. "From Len's mother this time. She says he contacted her, and wants to go home."

"Oh, dear," said Ben. "It seems I have that effect on people."

"You?"

"I had a word with him on Thursday, trying to encourage him."

"Don't feel bad about it. Len's mother asked us to try and keep him here a bit longer. She's sure it's just because Al Drontlin has gone, and Len's finding his feet again. She has spoken to him, and suggested he gives it a week or two more. After that, he can decide for himself whether he should leave."

"A week or two. That's not very long."

"I think it can be a very long time indeed, if you are unhappy and want to sort yourself out. I can certainly remember times when an hour or two seemed like forever."

The stream was running fast this morning, and the sound of it made Ben feel relaxed, in spite of his concern for Len, and his puzzlement over Xander's unreasoning terror of being on the stage.

"I've been thinking about extending the school day for our day students," Professor Kennington said, starting a new thread of conversation. "Not for any extra lessons or anything, but to give our young people more time together. It's just that one or two of the tutors have said that the boarders are, in general, bonding well, but the day students just turn up, do their lessons, and go home. There have been one or two arguments between the two, er, parties."

"I wouldn't make it compulsory."

"Compulsory arguments?"

"Compulsory extra hours."

"No, that's true," the professor said, thoughtfully.

"I've got boarders and day students in my group, er, class," said Ben, "I don't think they have any problems. In fact, I'm not always sure which are which."

"Mark Tyler is your only day student, the rest are boarders," the professor said, once again displaying his amazing memory and knowledge of his school without notes.

"You're hoping that this first year of the new college will get you a reputation and the classes will grow in size over the next couple of years. I bet you won't be able to do that then."

"Do what?" inquired the professor, standing still for a moment and looking out over the western farmer's fields.

"Know everything about everyone's classes."

"It's a shame I'm not a betting man," he answered. "Otherwise I might take you up on it. We have room for nearly 100 boarders and getting on for 200 students altogether. If we achieved that then the school could pay its way."

"What about an outing?" Ben got back to the original subject of student group dynamics, not wanting to go near the fact that the new college was *not* paying its way yet.

"That's an excellent idea. Colchester Zoo, perhaps, or that museum down in..."

"Not a museum," suggested Ben, interrupting. "I don't think it would suit everyone." He thought of Xander or Miko in a museum. They would get bored in a matter of minutes. Then he thought about Mark in the Magic Circle's museum of magic. They would never be able to get him out.

"We could check out the zoo, or see if there's any good theme parks around here."

"I am not really a fan of theme parks," said the professor.

"Ah, but we are not doing it for you, are we sir?"

"Michael," said the professor, "please call me Michael. And you are right of course. We must do something that the students would like, whether we enjoy that kind of thing or not."

'We?' thought Ben, who loved theme parks.

They walked on towards the back of the school, and down to the lake. It was a little muddy around there, so the usual pockets of students were not there this morning. The lake was owned by the man who lived in the cottage to the south, and provided a border between his land and the college grounds. The man was some big landowner or businessman from London, and he was kindly disposed toward the college and the village of Lockley down the road. He spent a great deal of his time in London or jet-setting around the world, and was not out and about in Lockley very much, but had, in the past, been very supportive of the college, turning up when he could to their various special events during the year. Ben and the professor stood and looked out over the still waters.

"Mark was good on Thursday," said the professor.

"Yes. He loves his magic."

"I took him on as a favour to his mother. She's done a lot for this house over the years. For this college. Asked nothing in return. His father left them a few years ago. She loves her son to bits of course, but he can be a bit of a burden sometimes."

"He has Asperger's."

"Yes, I know," said the professor. "So do I."

"What?"

"I think, when you are talking to your principal, the correct expletive is 'I beg your pardon'."

"What?" he said again, without apology.

"I said I have Asperger's Syndrome. Of course, back when I was a lad, nobody had heard of it, so I was considered just a bit eccentric. I had a lot of support from my parents, well, from my grandfather in particular, and went to all the right places of higher education to get me here. When I say a lot of support, I do mean a lot. It wasn't an easy road. That's why..." he stopped.

"That's why what?" asked Ben. "I mean, that's why I beg your pardon?"

The professor thought long and hard before saying what he said next. "That's why I employed you. I know about young Mark's particular obsession. His focus, rather. Aspergers people often tend to have a focus, an enthusiasm for a particular subject. His is magic. Don't tell anyone else, but he is the only student here who only attends one class. Yours."

Ben was not offended for a moment. Then, after the moment was over, he began to feel just a little offended. When he thought about it, it seemed like this; the professor had invented an artificial class in his college to help a friend. All the others in his class were just additional extras.

"I'm here for Mark, and nobody else?"

"Oh, no, Ben you're here to add to the rich range of subjects that this new and forward-thinking college has to offer the students. Mark was the person who inspired me to include magic in its performing arts section, but I don't mean I employed you to look after him, as if you were no more than an expensive babysitter. But he is the reason that I thought of employing someone like you. That's what I meant."

Aspergers sufferers, if 'sufferers' was the right word, are frequently known for their absolute honesty, according to what Ben had read. That may have been the reason that he believed the professor and did not quit on the spot. Actually, when he thought about it later, he knew he would not have quit anyway. He was growing to love the dysfunctional band of misfi... of students that made up his group, even if they couldn't make more than two proper performers between the lot of them.

"And your focus, your obsession?"

"Is to create and run an unusual college, which covers arts, performance and some very different and diverse subjects which will attract different and diverse people."

"Oh, I think you have achieved that," Ben said with a laugh, and they began to walk up the slight incline to the school. When they entered by the back entrance, the principal went upstairs and Ben went to his cellar for a while to check on things before going up himself. He sat down on one of the comfortable chairs, wondering if this was the secret that the professor had indicated he wanted to share with Ben, that he had Asperger's Syndrome. He had originally thought that the principal had some confidential information about one of the students, but had not told the staff yet. If there was something they needed to know about someone in their care, surely he would say?

Having spent nearly no time at all pottering about setting up his equipment, he thought of home for a few minutes. He was not the homesick type, but somehow the conversation he had just had with the professor made him think about things in his life which he would like to have done differently. He would have liked to have made his mother proud, for example. She would, of course, have told him she was proud anyway, and she always supported him every step of the way, but she was not impressed with magic as a career choice. Perhaps she felt differently now that he had resumed teaching. Nevertheless, it was *magic* he was teaching.

Then, there was Mary. Everyone (except Mary and himself) had always thought they would get married. They had been childhood friends, but when she had gone off to be an aid worker in Africa, they had somehow fallen out. It was as if everyone thought she was some kind of saint, while he had just dropped out of teaching. It had left something like a gap in Ben's integrity, and now, miles from home and even further from his ex-best-friend, he started to wish that there was some way to mend the wound.

After a few minutes he got up and went upstairs himself. At the top of the narrow stairs, through the heavy fire door and along the corridor towards the main entranceway, he heard the most beautiful sound coming from the 'singing room'. The children from the village had gone, so only Emily Darkchilde was left. Her voice was simply incredible. Ben stood still for a moment listening to her singing 'Love Changes Everything'. He decided he must immediately go and listen to her some more, or propose to her, or something. He may well have been the magician, but it was she who cast her spell on him.

As he walked towards her classroom, he noticed Xander sitting on his own on one of the benches in the main entrance foyer. He was not, for a change, surrounded by young ladies.

"Oh, hello," said Ben. "How are you, Xander?"

"Hello, Mr Ben," said Xander, accidentally using the name by which the magic man was known to the students out of his earshot. His tone, however, was not as sparkly as it normally sounded.

"Mr Ben," repeated Ben, "'as if by magic.' Very funny."

Xander perked up a bit and grinned, "Sorry."

"You okay?"

Xander opened his mouth to answer, but was not too sure of what to say.

"You get stage fright. It's not unusual, and we can deal with it."

"I could drop out of your class."

"I'd rather you didn't."

"And then there were six."

"As I said, I'd rather you didn't. But it's not because of the numbers. It's because of you. You're a live wire, you bring your own peculiar – or is that particular – brand of humour into the lesson. It's a positive energy, not a ridiculing one. You never made fun of Miko's lack of English, or of Mark, or... well, you did have a go at Big Al, but he deserved it. You're clever, you're literate and you're a credit to the class."

"Until I have to get onto the stage. Then I fall to pieces."

"There should be nobody in the theatre right now. Do you want to have another go?"

In the quiet that followed while Xander was thinking, Emily's stunning voice sang, "Nothing in the world will ever be the same" from her classroom. It seemed to Ben that he was going to miss her again.

"Yeah, okay," Xander said, and they made their way past Emily's classroom to the theatre. There was nobody in there, so Ben gestured to Xander to take the stage. He walked up the two steps, and turned to face the invisible audience. He looked at Ben.

"I'm terrified," he said. He spoke in an even voice, although he looked pale. Ben laughed.

"No, really," said Xander. "I'm terrified. My legs feel weak and I'm all cold and clammy. When I looked out, I imagine a real audience there. I hate it."

"Come on down," said Ben. "You know, a lot of magicians never get on a stage. They do close-up. Lots of magicians do nothing but close-up." Xander stepped down from the stage and the colour began to return to his face.

"So you won't ask me to leave your group?"

"Of course not."

"Not even if I refuse to go up on a stage ever again?"

"I would never ask you to do what you don't want to do. Unless you don't want to study and practise, then it's tough luck, I'm afraid. Mind if I ask what your other lessons are?"

"Art and creative writing."

"And how do you feel about displaying a painting up for everyone to see?"

"Mr Jones intends to do a show of all our work at the end of term. I'm looking forward to it."

"Are you any good?"

"I don't think I'm the one to ask. I enjoy it, but am I any good? Next time you see Mr Jones, ask him."

"How does he get to be Mr Jones and I am Mr Ben?"

"I'm sure Mr Ben is a mark of respect, sir," Xander said with his customary cheek. Obviously his confidence was seeping back now that he was no longer standing on the stage.

When Ben got to Emily's classroom, she was gone. He wasn't sure whether to laugh or cry. Perhaps at the end of the term, when they organised a show, or display, or whatever it was they did for Christmas (he assumed it wouldn't be a Nativity play), they could get some of the staff to perform. Then he could stare at the beauty of Emily's face and listen to her stunning voice while she was on stage without risking a slap round the face.

He wandered out into the sunlight again. A car was pulling away from the house. It was probably Emily driving home. He shielded his eyes with his hands to see if he could identify her car, but it was too far away. From the trees beyond the little road at the end of the driveway, Ben thought he caught sight of a flash of light, possibly a reflection from the sun, like someone using binoculars. He looked more carefully, but could see nothing. He watched for a few minutes, but then he gave it up as a figment of his imagination.

The next lesson was on Tuesday morning, and Shelley had brought her work-partner, Andy Goldman, to help with the videoing of the class. Ben overheard some of the students talk about Andy and some other members of the film-making class joking about their names.

"Meesh, Goldman and May. The three of you could start a company. You could use your initials," joked Xander as they were setting up. Juliette had got permission from the principal to miss this session, and Xander spent most of his time close to the camera operators to stay out of shot.

"When you're filming magic," Ben said to Shelley and Andy, "you've got to respect the secrets the magicians have. That doesn't mean you won't know how the tricks are done, you'll probably see that, but you mustn't show it to anyone else. If you accidentally film something you shouldn't, you must cut it from your production. Also, you should only film people with their permission, but I expect you've already covered that in your own classes. Other than that, you can film whatever you want!"

Shelley was superb with a camera, Ben observed – much better than she was in his class, which, he reminded himself, she had only joined to fill her required subjects. She was not like Al had been, wasting time and putting in no effort, it was just that magic was not really her subject. With the camera, she knew where people should be, and what they should be doing to construct a good image. She looked like she was in her element. She also seemed pleased that she was not doing any magic today.

Len had a go at some of the card tricks that Mark and Miko showed him. Miko's dexterity with clever moves was beyond him, but Mark showed him some simple moves and counting tricks which looked good and produced a decent result. Ben hoped that when the final video was prepared, the shots of students helping each other would not be cut out.

After a little less than an hour, Andy took the camera and Shelley took the rest of the bits and pieces back to the 'film studio', which was another of Xander's names for their classroom. Shelley came back within ten minutes, by which time the class had settled. Ben beckoned her in. They all sat in a three-quarters circle in their comfortable chairs.

"Well, we've had a session in the theatre, we've been filmed for a promotional DVD. What now?" said Ben to them all with a smile. "I'll tell you. This tops the lot. We're going to spend a lesson or two studying past masters."

There were groans, of course, from the group. Mark was delighted, although Ben thought he could probably teach the class rather than learn from it. Shelley, also, did not groan, but smiled. Perhaps this was her kind of thing.

7.

Len's two weeks' 'trial period' was soon over, and, although he was not completely settled, he was persuaded to stay on at the college. Ben had found that, without Al Drontlin's influence, he was listening more, and was beginning to become a bit of an individual, rather than anybody else's follower. He had started to enjoy his magic, and was seriously looking for a trick or two to make his own. He liked to handle the props, so something hand-held other than the normal cards, coins or sponges would be the thing to look for.

During that two weeks of weather that included bright sunshine, high winds and short bursts of heavy rain, the builders came in to do some work at the back of the house. They built a small low wall by the back wall of the great house, connecting the students' common room to the lower entrance which led to Ben's cellar. The wall was about half a metre high, and one and a half metres from the existing rear wall. Then they built in poles to hold a slanted corrugated Perspex roof, which they fixed to the house and waterproofed. This was to be the sheltered walk-way (or, in Richard's case, wheel-way) to provide access to the cellar area. It was meant for Richard or any future wheelchair-using students, but was useful for anybody else who wanted to use it during bad weather. It was inexpensive, quick to assemble and would shelter its users from all but the worst of weather.

"Today," said Ben on a day which was both sunny and windy, "we're going to have a short look at 'associated arts'. If you look at your syllabus, this course says magic and associated arts. It's actually about magic, but I thought we could take a look at some of the disciplines which are often connected with magicians. They are balloon modelling, puppetry, ventriloquism, escapology and juggling."

"Balloon modelling?" said Xander.

"Yes, and puppetry, ventriloquism, escapology..."

"Are you going to teach us to make balloon models?"

"If you want. I must say, I'm surprised at your enthusiasm. I expected you to go for escapology. Look, I brought my stuff." He showed them long lengths of chain and a couple of sets of police handcuffs. He had pulled out all his equipment that was not 'pure' magic. He had balloons, of course, and a variety of juggling items, but no puppets. He was not into puppets or ventriloquism at all, and was glad that they had not jumped onto that as a subject.

"Can I chain up Shelley?" Xander asked.

"Do you want to know what chain tastes like?" said Shelley with a cold smile. Nevertheless, it was balloon modelling that got the vote for today. Ben agreed as long as they would allow him to do escapology next week. During their studies on past masters, Shelley had taken a great interest in Harry Houdini, and had studied well, so perhaps that was going to be an area where she would excel.

She wasn't actually too bad at balloon modelling, once she had got past her fear of the balloons bursting. Once they had popped once or twice, you got used to it. However, that didn't stop her making a face when she was doing a big twist. It took only a few minutes to teach them the two basic twists, and they were making odd-shaped dogs in no time.

"You can make a long-necked dog or a short-necked giraffe, which is it to be?" Ben said as he handed out the balloons. He noticed that Juliette took part, although she looked as if she was beyond this sort of children's activity. The others were having a great time, helping each other to get the proportions right and giving each other advice on how to make the shapes look like what they were supposed to be.

Len had a go for a while, and then he put the balloons aside and examined some of the juggling equipment. Apart from the balls and clubs, there were sticks, diabolo and spinning plates.

"Would you like a go?" Ben asked, and Len said yes. Ben picked up a set of flower sticks and handed them to his student.

"These are flower sticks. You might have heard of them as devil sticks, but these have 'flowers' on the end of them." He showed Len the rubber rags that were attached to the ends of the colourful sticks. "It helps slow the movement, making them easier to use." In a short while, Ben showed him how to throw them from one control stick to the other, the rubber that sheathed the sticks making it easy to catch the flying rod without it rolling out of control.

"Can you do tricks with them?" Len asked.

"Oh, yes, but not until you're comfortable with the basic moves," said Ben.

"Can I borrow these to practise?"

"Certainly," and he showed him a thick book about juggling, entitled 'The Complete Juggler', and said, "I learned from this book."

Ben learned later from other members of staff that, over the next few days, Len was hardly seen without his flower sticks and juggling book. Every spare minute of the lonely lad's day was spent working on his juggling. When he entered a class, he put them down carefully at the back of the room, and picked them up again when he left. He practised a lot at the back of the house by the lake when the weather allowed, and in any room with a high enough roof when it was raining. As the flower sticks were not the best known of juggling items, this was fast becoming the thing that Len could make his own.

"He's getting good," Mark said on the Friday when they were preparing for the day's practice sessions. "Meesh is very impressed."

"Meesh?" said Ben. He had heard the name before, but had never met her. Or him.

"Yes," said Mark. "She said he's getting along well. Although he doesn't often practise in front of us."

Len popped his head around the door a couple of times during the day, but he seemed not to want to practise when the others were around, so he did not stay. It was not, for most of the day, the best weather for practising outside, but he put his coat on and went out anyway. Ben was not sure whether it was good for such a lonely young lad to have taken up something which was so isolating, but at least he was taking an interest in something.

The college did not have a half-term holiday, but instead, the last week in October, the week leading up to when the clocks were to change to Greenwich Mean Time, was given over to Halloween preparation. The college held a Halloween party on the Friday closest to the 31st October, and made it quite a special occasion, because it was the first opportunity in the year to make a display of their newly-learned skills.

Any parents who were available were invited to the event, which took the form of a light tea followed by a small show with a number of pieces from students of the various different performing arts on the syllabus. Mostly, the visitors were parents from the local villages and towns, who sent their children here as day students.

Bryn Jones' art class decorated the whole of the downstairs corridors and reception halls, along with the theatre, with spooky designs and spider-webs, and decked the walls with their dark and moody Halloween paintings. There were plots among the students of late-night after-show parties in the boarders' rooms, but the tutors got wind of them and made sure that there were no rule-breaking mixed bedrooms, and so they arranged for a more legitimate location for an after hours party in the cellar. Ben thought that this might have spoiled some of the fun because it was approved by the staff.

The show itself was full of interesting oddities. There were two or three songs and dances suitable for Halloween night. Mark did an improved version of his guillotine routine, fairly early on in the evening, once again accompanied by Shelley. It was even funnier than the first time, as Mark had learned something about comic timing, and was constantly practising in front of Ben, polishing up his performance until Ben was fed up with seeing it. Nevertheless, his work had paid off and he received a resounding round of applause. Once again, his stutter disappeared in his performance mode.

One of the students from the creative writing class read out a short story he had written, standing at a small wooden lectern. Short as it was, it still provided a spooky, scary mood for the rest of the evening.

The last performance was a piece led by Juliette. She entered at the doorway to the theatre, which was at the back of the auditorium. She had been fitted with a microphone and started speaking before the audience realised where she was. As she talked, she wandered through the audience, looking at each student and guest as if she was searching for someone in particular. The tone of her voice and the demeanour of her body as she searched the room made each member of the audience feel that they did not want to be the one she was looking for.

"There is a story," she said, "about a witch. She was young, and ignorant of the power she wielded, a supernatural power which the local people feared. She was beautiful and wicked. The young men of the town loved her and feared her, and wanted her and hated her."

She tapped one of the lads on the shoulder, not one that Ben had seen before, and he stood up from his seat and walked to the front of the auditorium. He walked up onto the stage, which was dimly lit, so only his silhouette could be seen.

"They plotted to kill her," she said, "so they asked a locksmith to make a tomb for her, and chains and padlocks to hold her in place so that they could bury her alive."

The lights on the stage came up slowly, so that it was clear that the young man there was now holding heavy-looking chains, and standing by a large wooden box, looking like a cross between a treasure chest and a coffin, large enough to hold a person in it. At the base of the box there was a swathe of red material, something like a curtain.

"She knew they were plotting," Juliette continued, "so, as the magic awoke inside her, she made her own plans against them. Then, one day…"

Another young man from the audience, Miko, stood up and grabbed her roughly by the arms. She screamed a scream that was so sudden and piercing that Ben jumped in his seat, even though he had prepared this one with them. Miko roughly pulled her to the stage. She struggled to be free, her acting ability making up for Miko's lack of it. Miko and the other lad from the drama class chained her up, and forced her, struggling, into the box. Then they wrapped chains lengthways around the box, and fixed padlocks onto the clasps at the front. Then, the other lad stood to the side of the stage, and watched.

Juliette's voice sounded from inside her apparent coffin. It echoed, and was dark and angry. "They thought they had won! They thought she would die. But she would get her revenge." The clinking of her chains as she struggled, invisible inside the box, was picked up by the microphone.

Miko stood on the box's heavy lid, and lifted the curtain up to his chest, covering the box and most of himself. Then, suddenly, he threw the bar on which the curtain was hung up into the air so that even he could not be seen. He let go of it for only a moment, then other hands caught it and lowered it slowly to the ground. It was not Miko, but Juliette who stood on the box now.

The audience delayed a few seconds before clapping, many of them taking a moment or two to take in what they had seen. Before the

70

applause completely subsided, Juliette said her final words, "The man who had caught her and tried to bury her alive was never seen again."

She bowed low, and then helped the young man from the drama class to unfasten the chains and padlocks from the box, and open its lid. They both helped the chained-up Miko out of the box, and then all three of the performers turned to the audience.

"Sleep well," said Juliette after a pause, and they took their final bows. After that, they found the keys to the padlocks that held Miko in place, and freed him in front of the audience. The other lad then returned to his seat, and would later tell all his friends that the box, the padlocks and the chains were all for real, because he was not in on the performance beyond what he had done.

The equipment was being tidied away and the people got ready to go home or back to their rooms in the college, when Ben was approached by a middle-aged woman with a mop of brown hair and a face that looked familiar. She was obviously Mark's mother – the likeness was remarkable.

"Mr April?" she said.

"Mrs Tyler?"

"That's right. How did you know?"

"I'm a magician."

"Well, I wanted to thank you for what you have been doing for my son," she said, accepting his explanation without question. "I wasn't sure at first whether it was wise to feed his obsession. Sometimes it's better to steer them away, you know?"

"I suppose so," said Ben, "but I am very glad you did let him come here."

"Michael, Professor Kennington, said it would be good for him. He seems to know something about Asperger's Syndrome. How is he getting along with the other students?"

"Professor Kennington?"

"No, Mark."

"They are really good with him. I thought at first there might be some teasing, but they are fine. Especially since he developed that routine with the guillotine."

"He developed it?" said Mrs Tyler. "Himself? Without any help?"

"Yes, himself, but not without any help. When any of us, me

included, develop a routine or an idea, the rest of us put their own ideas into the mix in the hope that we come up with something good. One of the other students, Shelley, helped him develop the timing and some of the comedy on that one."

"Shelley? I don't think he's mentioned her at home. He talks a lot about you and some of the students."

"Shelley was his assistant on stage."

"Oh, that's good. He doesn't normally get on well with girls."

"She has been a generally helpful and supportive young lady for a lot of us. It's good to have her around." The conversation seemed to die down at that point, but Ben noticed that Mrs Tyler looked as if she wanted to say something else. Her eyes were focussed on something from her imagination, and her lower lip began to move as if she was about to speak, but she had not worked out what she was going to say, yet.

"Do you want to sit down for a minute, Mrs Tyler?" Ben suggested, looking around for the nearest chairs. All the seats were normally left in the auditorium, but some had been cleared to the back of the room to enable the cleaners to get in tomorrow. She nodded and they sat down on two chairs that had not been cleared away yet.

"He has not always been treated as well as you and your students seem to treat him," said Mrs Tyler, marshalling her thoughts. "He doesn't relate well to people. Sometimes his stutter and his manner in general seem to bring out the worst in people."

"I'm afraid the world is not always understanding or giving, is it?"

"That's the kind of thing Michael would say. Professor Kennington. That Mark's disability is society's problem, not his own."

"Mark has to cope with it himself, but the rest of us could help."

"I worry for him when he leaves home. He forgets things. He has no idea how to look after himself. He doesn't know how to fill in forms, or communicate his needs to someone else. When he has to go to the doctor or something, I have to be there with him. He's nearly twenty, and I can't be there forever." She was holding back her tears.

"But right now, he is where he should be, being looked after properly, living at home with a family who loves him."

"For one year."

"What?"

"Your course is one year long. He's taking a holiday from his normal, hard life. What happens when the year is over?"

Ben had not thought of that. He had not thought of what he was going to do after the course was over, let alone what his students would do. He would give them an unofficial diploma of some sort then they would all go on to whatever they were doing next. Perhaps their training would count for something in their future, but he couldn't really see how. Most of them, like Shelley and Juliette and probably Len, were only on the course to fill the gaps in their timetables. What university or workplace would accept three hours a week of learning magic tricks as a step towards any kind of qualification?

Ben had thought that perhaps the magic and other minor performing arts would become legitimate subjects, and that maybe he would be teaching this subject for a few years to come. He was happy with the salary, and, until he wanted to get married or move on, he had somewhere to sleep. His savings, because he did not spend much of what he was being paid, were building up nicely to accommodate whatever future he might decide on for himself. However, the professor had already implied that the college was not paying its way. If he had to axe a course from the syllabus, it was obvious which one it should be, particularly as it had only been created for Mark in the first place.

"I think we should be happy that Mark is somewhere right now, doing something he loves doing. Who knows, he might even end up earning some decent money performing."

"Oh, I hope not," said Mrs Tyler.

"You hope not?"

"The world of show business is so horrible and cut-throat. People have been horrible enough to him up to now, you and the professor excepted. If he got into the business, I think it would destroy him."

"There are a lot of people, especially children's entertainers, who work alone and don't feel exploited. Organisations like Equity can be very supportive. Don't write off the industry just yet. There might still be a place for him." As Ben said all that, he realised he wasn't really believing it himself. Mrs Tyler had a point. Mark was never going to make it out there on his own.

"I'm sorry," said Mrs Tyler after a pause. "I have kept you from your work. I expect, the last thing you need after a busy week preparing for this show is a worried mother unloading onto you." She got up to leave.

No, thought Ben after she had left the building, she was exactly what he had needed. He had, of course, had his concerns for the various students in his group, but he had not taken any of them seriously enough. He had been playing with his favourite toys, all of that magical equipment of his. He had shared his games with them, the students at this college who had nothing better to do than to join his little club. He had simply not been taking them seriously enough.

He went up to his room to change out of his smart 'meet-the-parents' clothes and into something more casual for the late night celebrations. Some of the students, by then, were already changed and making their way down to the cellar, his classroom, for the party. He realised that he was tired after this week, and particularly after the conversation with Mark's mother, which had challenged his own thinking. Teaching Mark a few tricks was hardly going to help him in his life, was it?

He sat down on his bed, and remembered some words from a book he had read. He did not have the book right now, because he had lent it to Len Berkley, but he remembered them because they had helped him in the past. Dave Finnegan, the writer of the book 'The Complete Juggler', refers to himself as 'Professor Confidence', and says that one thing that learning to juggle can do is to build up your confidence. Perhaps Ben was doing something similar here at the college. Possibly, Professor Kennington knew that when he had hired him.

Back in Birmingham, his childhood friend Mary had told him that he should do something useful with his life. She had studied to be a nurse, and he to be a teacher. At the end of his studies, he had decided to drop out of teaching, although he was fully qualified now, and continue with the magic which he had used to earn money while he studied. Mary had been angry with him for turning away from doing good for others in order to 'have a bit of fun himself'. Now he was teaching again, and he wondered if he was still not doing anyone any real good.

He finally made his way down to the cellar where a crowd of people were filling the room, making it seem much smaller than it was when he was teaching the small group in there normally. All of his magical equipment was locked away in his storeroom except for the guillotine and the wooden crate which had been used in the ground floor theatre today, and were currently stored in the tiny area behind the theatre area known as 'backstage'. Of the 63 students currently at the college, only the boarders were there, along with a few of their tutors whose duty it was to make sure things did not get out of hand, or as Bryn Jones put it, "to make sure they don't enjoy themselves too much". Mark was not there, as he had gone home with his mother, and Ben was pleased about that. As much as the young man deserved congratulations for his efforts today, he would not have coped well with the party.

Ben sat down in one of the few chairs in the room. It was tucked away in the far corner, more or less unlit. Actually, most of the room was more or less unlit, but at least he felt inconspicuous.

"Hello," said a musical voice. Obviously, he was not as inconspicuous as he felt, because Emily Darkchilde had found him. Oh, well, he thought, if he was to talk to anyone at all, she was the best person.

"Hi," he said.

"You're looking tired. Long day? Long week?"

"Long last few minutes," he replied, and her laugh began to heal everything.

"What happens at the end of the year?" he asked.

"We have a holiday, then the next year starts," she replied.

"I mean here at the college. In June. What kind of qualification does the professor expect to hand out to my magic students?"

"When a college or university gives out its certificates, different people treat them in different ways. Some people might think that a qualification earned in Oxford or Cambridge might be worth more than one achieved at Sheffield. I'm sure Sheffield University students don't think that. A certificate from Lockley College of the Arts is valid. It means something. And Michael Kennington wants it to mean even more as our reputation grows."

"So he does intend for the college to continue. This isn't just one man's dream?"

"No, I think it *is* just one man's dream," said Emily. "But that's not necessarily such a bad thing. He has the backing and support of a good many people out there. There's money from big London businesses behind his dream. And there's the man himself. I believe he has the ability to make his own dream come true."

She paused in her idealistic spiel for a moment, and looked at him. "Is it the professor you are doubting, or yourself?"

"It's me, without a doubt. Sorry. *With* a doubt."

"Why?"

"Because learning a magic trick hardly counts as a college subject."

"What about learning performance? I don't know for sure, but I would guess that those two tricks your students did on stage tonight are not the most difficult tricks in the world to do. But *performing* them the way they did – that's what made them work so well. And we're only a few weeks into the first term. It seems to me you've achieved something already."

"Am I setting Mark Tyler up for a fall when he leaves here? Magic is all he lives for."

"He's disabled, isn't he?" said Emily. She did not come across him much in her life at the school, mostly because he wasn't in her dance class, but from what little her teacher's eye saw, she could tell there was something wrong.

"Asperger's," he confirmed.

"Ah, yes," she said. She seemed to go a little cold for a moment. "I had a student with Asperger's a couple of years ago, when I taught in a primary school. He was very violent. He was one of the reasons I took up this job."

"Really?"

"Yes. He was eight years old, and he beat me up. I spent a couple of nights in hospital. The school weren't allowed to expel him, because he was disabled and 'didn't know any better'. So I expelled myself instead. I couldn't handle facing him again. Then I came here. But I don't think, after that, I could deal with Mark if he was in my class."

"Mark's not like that. He's as gentle as a... as something that's gentle. And he's not had an easy life."

"You've done him some good, I think. I haven't got your patience or understanding."

"*I* haven't got my patience or understanding. It's Mark's love of magic that has done the work."

"Modesty. I love it," she smiled. But Ben still wondered what he could achieve in one year, not just with Mark, but with any of them.

8.

"When choosing a member of the audience to be your helper," Ben told the class, "the last person you want is the one who is too eager. Neither, for that matter, do you want someone who does not want to be chosen. If you are choosing from a small audience, you shouldn't choose the person you think is the most beautiful woman in the room."

"That narrows it down a bit," said Xander, somehow managing to nod towards Shelley and Juliette at the same time. "So who should you choose?"

"Choose the person who looks interested, but not too enthusiastic."

"Why not any of the others?" asked Len, who found himself able to interrupt and ask questions like Xander, Shelley and the others. Ben had encouraged interruptions because it was important that he knew he was communicating well to his group, and their questions told him that they were paying attention.

"Because you are the star of the show, Len, and you don't want anyone to upstage you. An over-enthusiastic person might wish to be up there just to be the star of the moment, and might mess up your magic trick. A shy person might not want to be picked, and ruin your performance. I have a friend who is a first class and experienced performer, but has chosen the wrong person to help him. She was nervous, and was nearly sick in one of his performances."

"And the most beautiful woman?" said Xander. "Why not her?"

"Because everyone else will be jealous of her. Pick the oldest woman on the table instead, and butter her up a bit, because that will put everyone on your side. Obviously, if you are entertaining at a birthday party, make sure you choose the birthday person at least once during the show.

"And treat your chosen helper with respect. I have seen a lot of magicians insult their targets. One of my favourite magicians does that, even though he knows how to choose the right people. I love to watch him, but I wouldn't want to be chosen by him. Part of the job of entertaining people, I think, is to leave them feeling good about themselves if they have volunteered to help you.

"Then, of course there's the boy – it's usually a boy – who says 'I know how that one works' every time you start to show a trick. You might feel like putting him down, but the reason he wants attention might be because he hasn't got a lot of confidence and wants to look good in front of the crowd. The last thing he needs is to be put down."

"So what would you do?" asked Shelley.

"I would treat him as if he really did know how to do the trick," replied Ben. "I would remind him that real magicians like him and me would be quiet and keep the secret. If that works, I'd let him help me with a trick later in the show."

"And if it didn't?"

"I'd give him a slap."

Everybody laughed except Mark, so Ben explained that he was joking, and went on to give a couple of good-natured ways of keeping control. He continued to talk about how to handle your helper, about not being too physical, talking politely and making sure you remember to use their name during the performance. The group joined in with the conversations, thinking of examples of where they could go wrong, even role-playing an unhelpful assistant, much to the hilarity of them all. Ben had started a few sessions on performance etiquette and style, referring back to the time they had spent studying particular magicians. Over the two weeks following the Halloween party, he had put a lot more into serious study of performance, including some written work, and spent less time on teaching them actual tricks, although they learned at least one new trick each session. On Fridays, however, it was time to play with what they had learned.

With twenty minutes to go until the end of the session, the group had milked all discussion possibilities about choosing a helper from the audience. Ben thought it would be good to show them a new trick. He looked around at his students, singling out in his mind Shelley, whose magic ability was so poor, and Richard, who wanted to make an impact but seemed to lack the ability. Then he looked at Xander and Miko, and knew what he wanted to do. He excused himself while he went into his storeroom to get the right equipment, and came out a few minutes later with a CD player, heavy black cloth and a silver ball and stand.

He plugged in the CD player and put in a CD for background music. The track he played was a familiar, haunting melody, the theme tune of the Harry Potter films. As the opening tinkle of music began, he put down the stand for the silver ball, a small round base that was just big enough to stop the ball from rolling across the table. On the stand he carefully placed the light, silver ball. Then he lifted the heavy black cloth and covered the ball. All of this was done to the music.

He stepped away from the covered ball, as if he had done what he wanted to do, but, as the music built up and led into the orchestral bit, he turned to look strangely at the ball. It was as if he thought it had done something it should not have done. He looked carefully at it. Had it moved? He went to hold two ends of the cloth, and as he did, the ball beneath it started to move, as if trying to escape its cover.

The cover, apparently led by the ball, leapt into the air. It seemed that Ben was struggling to keep control of it as it pulled the cloth, and therefore Ben himself, around the room, dancing to the music. At one point the ball left the cloth and tried to dance around him, sliding up his arm and behind his back, then sliding back under its cloth again and, as the music quietened back down to its finish, it settled back on its cradle. When the music had finished, Ben removed the cloth, and then threw the ball out to Xander, who caught it and examined it.

Ben bowed for his applause, and then showed them all how it worked. It was simple to learn, but difficult to do well, and as one or two were taking their turns at trying to make the ball float, the others were talking about performance quality and how best to help the audience appreciate it. Mark loved it, but was happy not to give it a go. It was a spooky item rather than a comedy one, and he did not see how he could make it funny, so he felt this was easily one for the others to develop.

"This is one for you, Juliette," said Xander, but she was preoccupied. Ben had heard one of them say that she'd had news from home, but Ben did not feel that his relationship with her was such that he could ask for details. He just asked if everything was alright, and she, polite and well-spoken as ever, said yes.

Miko loved the ball because it involved no words, Len liked it because it was a bit like juggling, and Richard did not like it because you had to be more mobile than he was to do it well. Shelley disagreed with him, and the two of them discussed how good it would look if you had one of those things, a 'zombie ball', flying around your wheelchair. Then, their time was up. Juliette was quick to leave, and the others gradually departed, leaving the place quite tidy. Mark, of course, was the last to leave.

Friday saw more of them spending time in the cellar, although not all of them stayed for the whole time as they had other subjects to learn. Juliette and Shelley stopped by briefly to say 'hello', but they put most of their practice time into singing and dancing respectively. As a result, Shelley's magical skills did not improve much, and Juliette's performances were more about the drama of magic and less about the skills of sleight of hand or handling complex gadgetry.

When only a few of them were in there, Ben occasionally taught them a particular trick he thought would suit them. Mark spent the whole day there every Friday, so he learned everything his huge mental capacity for magic could soak up. Sometimes Ben had to let him know that it was someone else's turn to develop a trick for themselves, but Mark was always giving and supportive. He was completely gentle, almost docile, and nothing like the violent child that Emily had described. Ben had looked up a little more information on Asperger's Syndrome since speaking with Mark's mother, and had discovered how diverse the effects of this condition were. Mark was possibly luckier than he had imagined having his temperament, not to mention the support that he received, both from home and here at the college.

At lunchtime, Mark once again sat with Ben at the dining table. Ben was getting used to it, and now that he knew more about Asperger's Syndrome, he understood how hard it would be for Mark to mix with the others for lunch. He would have to link up with just one person each mealtime to make it easy for himself.

"Excuse me," said Emily Darkchilde as she came to the table with her lunch tray in hand, "may I join you?"

"Certainly," said Ben.

"I was asking Mark," said Emily. Mark looked up, then down again, obviously embarrassed.

"Of... of c-course," he said, "p-please." She sat next to him, not looking completely comfortable herself. Ben wondered why she had decided to take this opportunity to get to know Mark better. He was also, secretly, hoping that the real reason for her asking was to spend time with him, but he realised that what she had said at the Halloween party about her experience of people with Asperger's had something to do with it.

"I don't see you around much, Mark. How are you getting on?"

"F-fine, thanks," he answered, spitting some food out of his mouth as he answered. He kept his head down and his mop of untidy hair covered his embarrassment to a certain extent.

"I loved your show the other week," she continued, struggling to maintain the conversation. "You were very clever with the guillotine. I'm surprised that Ben let you use such a dangerous device so early in the term."

"It's n-not d-dangerous," said Mark, leaping to Ben's defence, missing the humour in Emily's comment entirely. "It's s-safer than it l-looks."

"I think Miss Darkchilde is teasing you," Ben said, sensing his distress. Then he realised that the only teasing he had ever received before was malicious and unkind and had hurt him. "Having a joke with you," he corrected himself.

"Sorry," she said, looking as if she really meant it. She really wanted to come to terms with her unease about Asperger's, but she was not making a good job of it. "I didn't mean to make you uncomfortable. Should I go somewhere else?"

"No," said Ben and Mark quickly, at the same time. Ben continued for both of them, "Please stay. It's just that having the company of such a beautiful woman is making both of us tongue-tied."

"Th-that's just what I was g-going to s-say," Mark laughed. Miko also joined them at the four-seated table, mostly because he, Mark and Ben all found eating in relative quiet together was easy to do. Emily, however, did not find the silence quite so comfortable. Ben wanted to talk it through with her, tell her that he recognised her discomfort and appreciated her efforts to deal with somebody else who had Asperger's, but he obviously could not say anything in the presence of the two students. Emily finished her food quickly and excused herself. Ben felt that sometimes he could get on really well with her, when they met as adults without students around or when they were at the pub together on one of Bryn's Friday nights, but things at the school seemed to be a barrier to their friendship.

Ben and Mark also finished their meals a short while later, and returned to the cellar for the last couple of hours or so of the college week.

Len spent a little time in the cellar with them later in the afternoon, looking at some of the other forms of juggling that Ben had to show him. Ben asked to see what he could do with the flower sticks so far.

"I don't think I'm ready yet," the lad replied.

"Are you getting on alright?"

"Yeah, I love it. But I want to build up a proper performance before I show anyone. Like you said yesterday."

"Good idea. But sometimes it's good to have just one or two people to see you perform, to help you be the best. What about me and Mark?"

"What if someone comes in on us while I'm practising?"

"Well, you've practised in various different places in the college, including outside in the field. Other people have seen you."

"They've just seen bits."

"And have they said anything to you?"

"Meesh said I was good."

"That's encouraging. Come on, there's just me and Mark here now. Show us what you've got."

"He's got a set of flower sticks," said Mark, wondering why Ben needed to see them, as it was he who lent them to Len in the first place.

"Figure of speech," said Ben again, and Mark grinned sheepishly. Len got his flower stick and the control sticks ready and flicked the flower stick in the air, kicking it as it fell toward the ground so that it went up again, where he caught it with his control stick and sent it all around him. He bounced it off of his elbow, spun it round one stick, then the other, threw it (not too high in the confines of the cellar) and caught it again, and generally showed amazing control of the device, a product of hours of determined practice.

"That's fantastic," said Ben as he and Mark gave Len a round of applause.

"I want to try something new," said Len, "with different equipment."

Ben showed him juggling scarves, of which he managed to master the basics quite quickly, but they moved too slowly for him so he went on to something else. Mark also tried to learn the scarves, following carefully as Ben described the moves, but he didn't have the hand-eye co-ordination to do it properly. Mark had the ability to really appreciate what Len could do and he couldn't, so Len was greatly encouraged by Mark's honest support.

There was a polite knock on the door, and Len stopped juggling immediately. Juliette put her head around the door.

"I just came by to say goodbye," she said.

"Goodbye?" said Ben. "You're leaving us?"

"Just for a week," she said. "I'm going to visit family. I'll be back on Monday week, so I'll only miss a couple of lessons."

"Problems?"

"No, one of those rare family holidays."

"Okay," said Ben. "Have a good time. See you when you get back."

She departed, and Ben noticed it was time to pack up. After they had put things away and Len had left with his book, his flower sticks and a new diabolo to add to his collection, Ben went upstairs to say goodbye to Mark when he went home for the weekend. He had developed the habit of seeing the students off when they went home, in spite of the fact that only one of the day students was actually in his class.

He saw Juliette with a small suitcase heading for the car park. Xander quickly came to her assistance, offering to carry her bag for her, and they walked together to the car park where a number of parents waited for their sons and daughters.

As Ben watched, he felt the blood draining from his body. There was a man in a smart suit standing by a car he thought he might have seen before, in the car park, as if that was where his car belonged. He shook hands with Juliette, and took the suitcase from Xander with a polite nod as Juliette got into his car. It was the man he had seen standing by the tree at the beginning of term! Ben was about to run from where he was at the front of the house to the car park to stop the man from taking Juliette from them, when he was stopped by a shout from the front door. It was Professor Kennington, who was with Emily, beckoning him over.

"Ben!" he shouted. "Just the person I have been looking for. There's something I think you need to know."

Ben took a step or two towards them, but he kept his eyes on the car park. From what he observed, he concluded that Juliette knew the person who had picked her up. She gave him a smile, polite but not entirely friendly, and they shook hands in a formal greeting. That could have meant nothing, of course, as that was the way she often greeted people – polite, but bordering on aloof. She didn't seem to feel that he was a threat to her, although his attitude toward Xander was almost rude, as he ushered him away as if to protect his young passenger.

"It's alright," said Emily as she approached Ben. "Juliette's fine. The professor will explain everything. But not out here."

Emily and the principal took Ben into the staff room. It was empty, as the rest of the staff would be tidying up, going home or in their rooms getting ready for Bryn's end-of-week celebrations in the village. The professor took them to a corner and sat them both down.

"I'm sorry to keep this a secret from you both," he started, "but I was sworn to secrecy myself. I have never liked keeping secrets, and I must say there have been times when I wished I could have told you all about Juliette's situation. Especially when you reported a stalker at the gates, Ben."

"And the stalker is?" asked Ben.

"A bodyguard," explained the professor. "Juliette particularly asked not to have a bodyguard on the premises. They have been staying at the Tin Whistle in the village."

"They? More than one?"

"I think there are three of them. They take turns at watching over us. Our own little guardian angels."

"Why?" asked Emily. "Why does she need bodyguards, and why must it be kept a secret?"

"She is the daughter of the British ambassador to a country in the Middle East, with which our current political relationship is strained, to say the least. They haven't told me which country it is. All I know is that this ambassador is currently engaged in some very difficult negotiations, and activists from this unnamed country may be trying to track down young Juliette in order to kidnap her and hold her as a threat against her father's actions. I'm afraid I know very little more than that, and I have been sworn to secrecy. I have told you simply because you have been suspicious of the people who were watching this college and, of course, you, Emily, have had most to do with young Juliette. You needed to know."

"And this was the secret you were considering telling me earlier this term?"

"Yes. I'm sorry. I did not want to keep it from you both."

"It explains why she didn't want her photograph taken," said Ben.

"Who else knows?" asked Emily.

"Nobody," confirmed the professor. "And it must stay that way. If people were to find out who Juliette really is, then her life, and, for that matter, the lives of her fellow students here at the college, might be in danger. If she told her friends, they might text or email their friends, and word would get out. She has, so far, resisted having a bodyguard with her here on campus, wanting to be treated like a 'normal' student, but it will not be long until there has to be someone here for her, and then we will have to make up some kind of cover story to help her out."

"I overheard her on the phone," said Ben.

"I beg your pardon?" said the professor.

"A few weeks ago she was on the telephone to someone saying that she wanted to be treated like the other students."

"Yes, she has been a good, well-behaved young lady, but she feels the stress of it all, no matter what she shows on the outside."

"Will you let her know that we know?" asked Ben.

"Yes, I think that would be helpful for her. What do you think?"

"I agree," said Ben. Emily nodded, but she had something else on her mind.

"Emily?" said Ben. The professor had not noticed her distraction.

"I was just thinking," she said. "She's a really good singer. She combines what she learns in Drama with her fabulous singing voice to create a sensational presentation. From the look of her performance at the Halloween show, I'd say she does the same in her magic. But she can't use her skills, can she?"

"What do you mean?" asked Ben.

"If she can't be known, can't be seen on stage or photographed, why is she choosing all the subjects that will lead to the spotlight being on her?"

9.

When Professor Kennington announced that there would be an outing rather than just a Christmas party, the whole of the college got involved in its planning. This was to be part of the bonding that the principal wanted to instigate, particularly between the boarders and the day students, which was why it was held mid-week rather than on the weekend. The date of the event, however, was arranged for late November, which was not that close to Christmas because of how busy the college would get with its Christmas shows and first term assessments. This would probably mean that there would be lots of 'unofficial' Christmas parties, too, organised by the students or even the tutors for their own classes.

After a bit of looking around on the Internet, the staff and students, between them, decided on an outing to a (fairly) local leisure complex. Situated not too far from Norwich, the centre contained everything you might expect from a normal leisure centre, with a few extra activities as well. There were several sports pitches, bowling, ice skating, indoor fitness activities, various bars and, of course, a swimming pool. On that particular week, there was a funfair, too, which had parked itself in the extensive grounds of the complex. This added attraction made for a huge and varied day out for staff and students alike.

Because of the relatively small size of the college, the staff (including kitchen and domestic staff) and students only took up two coaches. As they both entered the car park, Shelley laid down a challenge for Ben.

"You're still young," she said, "I bet you can do everything in the complex."

"Not in one day," he replied with a smile, deciding not to remark on the 'still young' comment.

"Oh, I don't know," said Emily, who had overheard the challenge.

"You're 'still young', after all." She had obviously *not* decided to overlook Shelley's age comment. Ben rose to the challenge.

"Everything we have time to do. What about you, Emily Darkness?" Ben said, drawing her into the challenge, too. "Is there still a childe in you?" It sounded better in his head than it did when he said it out loud.

"Done," she said.

"You will be," said Xander, who had been listening in from two seats behind them. They looked out of the window as their coach began to park. A north wind was blowing and the rain was spotting lightly over the centre. That was going to limit the outdoor activities a little, perhaps, but there was still plenty to do indoors.

Shelley's first challenge for Ben was ice skating. The ice rink itself was quite a large place, with tiered rows of seats for when they put on shows, and a bar and cafeteria area near to the skate hire. The 'gang', at least, the ones that wanted to skate, all gathered outside the entrance to the rink until they were all there, so that they could all go in as a group.

Shelley was one of the first of her group to be ready and she was soon at the ice. With all the skill and grace of a dancer, she sailed onto the ice. Ben followed her, taking just a little less time, and, for that matter, a little less care and attention, doing up his laces. He paused before leaving the safety of the non-slip rubber matting. He had only been skating once or twice before, and he was certainly not a dancer, so he was not as confident as Shelley. Still, he was still on his feet. Actually, he was still on the rubber matting. He shuffled about in preparation to leave the safety of the entrance to the ice. Xander and Miko passed him and started skating with some ease and proficiency.

Come on, he told himself, the best way to deal with the ice is to step boldly and confidently out. Don't dawdle, he thought to himself, don't be nervous, just go! And he went.

Thump!

While Ben sat on the ice for a second, trying to work out what went wrong, Emily came by and looked down at him from above.

"You're taller than I remember," she remarked from her vantage point towering above him.

"Ha-flippin'-ha," he said, and she helped him up.

Mark Tyler, back at the skate hire section, was still putting on his boots. This was his first time at the rink – he had tried to look up ice skating in his computer at home for some help, but although he found plenty of information, facts, figures and dates, he was unable to research anything that actually helped him skate. He had heard somewhere, probably from some of the students who had skated regularly, that it was wise to wear an extra thick pair of socks, so he did. As a result, unfortunately, his skates were too tight, so he'd had to go back to the desk and change them for the next size up. Also, doing them up was a nightmare, as once they were tied, they didn't feel as though they were tight enough. Ben watched Mark's progress from the rink, and decided to go and help him.

"Chicken!" shouted Shelley as she sailed by them for the fourth time and watched Ben leave the rink. Emily, who was not a proficient skater, but was still strong on her feet, decided to go off and see if she could keep up with the bubbly dancer.

Eventually, with some help and advice from Ben, Mark was in his skating boots, laces tied up really tight all the way up to support his ankles, and heading for the ice. Even that was not as easy as other people were making it look. Mark stumbled once or twice on the safety matting, his feet wobbling unsteadily, but he made it eventually, almost on his hands and knees.

Then, he was on the ice. He slid, not entirely in control of his direction, a metre or two out from the side, out of reach of where he would have been able to support himself. Then he stopped. With some effort, he managed to stand up straight, but he couldn't move. If he tried to separate his legs, which seemed to be joined at the knees, he would have collapsed onto the ice. So he remained exactly where he was, legs stiffly straining to keep him upright. Ben struggled to go out and join him. Although, once he finally made it there, he was not sure what he could do to help.

Just then, two small girls, around seven years old, shot past them with tremendous style and confidence as they raced each other around the rink. Ben wondered, with some annoyance, why they weren't at school. Behind them, Shelley and Emily slowed down to admire Ben's and Mark's efforts so far.

"Oh, look, there's Ben," said Emily to Shelley.

"And not clinging to the sides like you might expect," said Shelley.

"He seems to be doing alright, doesn't he?"

"Help," said Ben in a feeble voice. The girls finally took pity on them and offered their hands to help. Shelley looked after Mark, and Emily took on Ben. They enjoyed themselves attempting to move around the rink. Ben particularly enjoyed himself when Emily leaned in close to offer her body, rather than just her hand, for support.

After a while, however, Ben felt he was improving. The two little racing girls had passed them at least twice in the last few moments, and there seemed to be a four-year-old boy teaching his mother how to skate. This is ridiculous, he thought, unfastening his hand from Emily's. If they can do it, so can I. So he stepped out with confidence...

...and fell over again with a bump!

Emily was much nicer to him this time. She didn't laugh at all; she just reached out to help him up. Unfortunately, that was not the wisest thing to do. As they struggled on the slippery surface to reach out to each other, Emily fell, taking an innocent by-skater with her. This third skater was a rather large man, who was already out of control before he collided with the both of them, and ultimately all three spun across the ice in different directions.

Some stewards quickly came to their rescue. They helped Emily to her feet first (they always seemed to pick up the girls first), then attended to the others. It took two of them to lift the big man up and cart him off the ice to recover. After the stewards finally got round to helping him, Ben decided it was time for a break, while Emily skated on. He made it to the side on his own – somehow the falls had seemed to increase his skills, he thought, hopefully.

Ben sighed with relief as his feet were feeling warm and comfortable, recovering from the strains of being on the ice. He had unfastened his skates' laces to air his aching feet a little. He wondered how the professionals did it. Of course, they didn't use skate-hire skates. After quite a short while, Mark joined him at the table in the café.

"That's better," he grinned at Ben as he sipped his drink.

"Enjoying it so far?" Ben asked.

"I d-don't think it's for m-me," he said. "It's the c-co-ord-ination."

"It could be," agreed Ben. "Me, I'm just no good at it."

They soon returned to the ice to skate some more. They helped each other a lot, and their skills improved a little. At least, Ben could see Mark's skills improve. He, in the meantime, just spent most of his time trying to stop his bottom from making a more intimate acquaintance with the ice.

When they'd had enough, which was only a short while later, they went in and struggled to remove their boots. Ben discovered that his socks were completely shredded, and his skin was rubbed raw in two or three places. Mark had not suffered the same fate, as his 'extra pair of socks' theory had paid off.

Although Ben calculated that he had spent more time sitting down than actually skating (either on a seat or on the ice), he really wanted a break before going on to bowling, which was the next challenge.

"Perhaps we could just tell Emily and Shelley that we did something," he suggested to Mark.

"We couldn't do that," said Mark, then he took a good look at Ben. "You *are* joking, aren't you?" Ben remembered that people with Asperger's quite often have an acute sense of honesty, and that the idea of deception might seriously distress Mark.

"Of course we couldn't. It was not so much a joke, more like wishful thinking." Mark laughed, relieved. They walked to the bowling alley.

Richard Wellington and some friends from his creative writing class had just got in to the bowling alley themselves, and were in place, choosing bowling balls while one of the stewards was preparing a large frame which was used to help disabled bowlers. The object was to aim by positioning the frame and then roll the ball down it to target the pins. It sounded good in theory, but it didn't seem to be working for Richard.

Ben and Mark, joined by a couple of the lads from the drama group, took the lane next to Richard as he attempted his first roll. The ball rolled down the chute and hit the lane with a thump, which took away its momentum. It moved quite slowly along the lane, arcing slightly but staying on target. Just before it struck the balls, an electronic eye picked up its passage and started the mechanism for counting the fallen pins and replacing the others. Firstly, a barrier came down in front of the pins. The problem was that the ball had not travelled far enough, and hit the barrier, stopping it from hitting any of the pins at all.

"What?" bellowed Richard in a loud and booming voice that Ben had not heard from him before. The disabled lad angrily shoved the frame aside. One of his two friends caught it before it toppled over. Richard wheeled to pick up another ball, but having weighed it in his hands, realised he should go for a lighter one, so changed it. He then rolled his wheelchair up to the lane, angling it slightly to allow his arm to swing, and bowled the ball himself, scoring a respectable seven pins.

"Well done," said Ben, who was watching while Mark, who was quite proficient with computer machinery, was entering their names into his lane's scoring panel.

"It was rubbish. That frame that was supposed to help me took away my chance to score a strike," said Richard, far more angry than he should be for what was, after all, only a game.

"Why don't you ask them over to reset it for you?" Ben suggested.

"I'm sure they are busy enough without being at my beck and call."

"Am I right that you wanted to campaign for the rights of disabled people everywhere?" said Ben. "Well, this is part of it. Tell them that their attempts to help you aren't working, and that they need to reset the machinery."

"You know, I think I will," said Richard, and he went off to find someone to help while the others played their turns.

Ben played rather poorly for a game or two. He had opted to leave the side bars down, while Mark had them up to stop all his shots going into the channels at the sides of the lane. Mark threw the ball with a clumsiness you could only dream of, but by bouncing it several times off of the side bars, he managed to build up a decent score. He was the first on their lane to score a strike, something that eluded Ben completely until their third game, when he finally scored over 100. When it was time to move on to the next activity, he had won one game, but his best score of 138 had been beaten by a triumphant and very satisfied Richard with 143 (without mechanical aids), his personal best.

Emily and Shelley came in a short while after they had started bowling, but they could not join the others halfway through their game, so they took a lane with some of their colleagues from Emily's class and Xander. Xander was mouthy and showy with his style of bowling, offering advice to everyone from the college who was playing within three lanes of him, and to one or two players who weren't from the college at all.

Ben and Mark separated from the others to eat, then were joined by Shelley and Richard for the next part of the challenge. The sun had broken through the clouds, and there was a respite from the rain, although the wintry atmosphere did not allow the sunshine to warm the day to any great extent. Nevertheless, it was decided that the fairground should be their next port of call.

"I think I might sit this one out," said Shelley, looking up at the big roller coaster ride.

"You're still young," Ben reminded her, "and it was you who challenged me. And then you called me chicken when I left the ice rink to help Mark. I am not sure I can let you sit this one out."

"I would let you," she argued.

"Would you?"

"Well, no," she admitted.

"I'll hold your hand," said Emily.

"I'm *really* scared," said Ben. "I think you should hold *my* hand."

Unfortunately, that ploy did not work, although it did get a laugh from the students and started a rumour that lasted until at least Christmas, but Ben ended up looking after Richard and his wheelchair, and Emily and Shelley went off to wait in the queue. Looking after Richard actually had its advantages, as the funfair had a disabled-friendly system that allowed Richard and any carer that was with him to jump the queue. This was particularly good, as Richard was a thrill-ride fan. They did the roller coaster twice, the waltzer, a peculiar spinning gadget whose name Ben forgot and the pirate ship before the ladies had finished queuing for their second ride. Ben loved it at first, but after the second go on the pirate ship he was beginning to wish he had skipped lunch. Luckily, there were a number of students who were happy to take on the role of queue-jumper with Richard and give him a rest.

Mark, meanwhile, did give the rides a miss, as he was not a fan of the fairground. He did not like the noise and the bustle of it all. It made him feel insecure. He watched the others, and, to a certain extent, enjoyed their enjoyment, but he stood alone and stayed out of things. When Ben joined him again, he suggested they do something a little tamer like the hall of mirrors or a boat ride.

The calmer activities did him good, and he found he was enjoying Mark's company. Mark was strange. It wasn't very nice to call him that, and Ben would never say so out loud. In fact, even in the privacy of his thoughts he rarely used the word to describe him. Nevertheless, he *was* strange. He saw the world differently, he misunderstood things most people would have no difficulty understanding, and he had great depths of understanding of the world that other people would not grasp at all. He spent ages watching the ducks on the lake, sometimes commenting in his faltering use of the English language about how they moved or interacted with each other. Sometimes he was quiet, but with Ben, it had become a comfortable quietness. It was actually pleasant to be quiet together. Ben was finally catching on that, as well as being a tutor and dispensing learning, so to speak, you could learn from your students.

"My dad couldn't c-cope with my condition," Mark said suddenly as they sat by the lake.

"What happened to him?"

"He left," said Mark. "Because he c-couldn't cope. That's what M-mum says. She says it's not my f-fault. But it is, isn't it?"

"No, I don't think so," said Ben, nervous at getting this deep into someone's life.

"If I was normal, he'd still be with us."

"Not necessarily," suggested Ben. "He's your father. He should cope, as you put it, with whoever you are. Condition or not, you are you. There's good things about you, and bad things, same as everyone else. Your dad would probably have found some reason to leave if he wasn't strong enough or good enough to stay. The fault is his, not yours."

"He's not a bad man."

"No, probably not. You never know what's going on in someone's head, why they do what they do. But his problem is still his, not yours."

They were quiet for a while, and then Ben asked, "Do you ever see him?"

"No."

Emily and Shelley soon found them (slacking, as Shelley put it), and they suggested going for an ice cream. Ben agreed, on condition there were to be no fast rides immediately afterwards. They acquiesced, and then decided it was time to go swimming. They had stored their swimming gear in the coach, but it was agreed that the driver would open it around three o'clock in the afternoon for people, so they were just about on time. Ben was feeling a bit weary and wondering why the day was not over yet, but he had, after all, accepted the challenge.

"Ben," said Mark in an urgent whisper on the way in to the pool.

"Yes?"

"I can't swim."

"Have you got your kit?" he said, aware that Mark didn't want the others to know.

"Yes."

"Then I wouldn't worry about it. It's not so much a swimming pool as a play pool. It'll be mostly shallow, and you can enjoy whatever you want to. Nobody will ask you to go out of your depth."

Mark was happy with that, and it turned out when they got to the pool itself that Ben was right. A large part of the pool was given over to a shallow play area with fountains, seats, warm water areas and, best of all, a jacuzzi. Ben dutifully looked out over the area, watching out for any of the college's students that he recognised. This was quite difficult as, apart from his own class, he recognised most of the students by the clothes they preferred to wear. Xander and Miko were floating in a deeper part of the water, having discovered a mutual interest that crossed the language barrier – they shared a love of watching the girls. Ben, following their line of sight, also noticed Emily in a fabulous bikini that enhanced her beauty even more than usual, and was almost tempted to join her and Shelley as they played in the water, but his body was just beginning to feel the signs of his ice-skating-bowling-funfair exercise, so he quickly found his way back to the jacuzzi with Mark.

Len joined them a few minutes later.

"Having a good day?" Ben asked.

"Yeah," said Len with a little more than his customary enthusiasm (or lack of it). "I was with Xander and Miko, but all they want to do is look at girls."

Ben craned his neck around to see if he could see them without leaving the comfort of the jacuzzi. He found himself feeling a little protective of Emily when he saw them watching her. Having said that, it was no surprise that half of the male eyes in the pool were fixed on her.

The others got out for a while, got back in, and, later, got out again. He stayed put, feeling his muscles relax. When Emily finally joined him in the warm jacuzzi, there was suddenly a queue of boys wanting to get in as well. He decided it was time to move on to the next activity.

The main coffee lounge had a bar. This was the meeting place that the staff agreed would be the best place for anyone to get to if they needed anything. Bryn Jones had volunteered to be the contact in case of emergency. He had a first-aid certificate, and he had no time for "all this funfair nonsense", so he was the ideal person for the job. He had commented that being paid to spend the day in the bar was a task he could put up with. The students and staff were all given his mobile number, and he was left alone to carry the burden of not having anyone bother him all day.

Then, with less than an hour to go, Emily and Ben joined him. Shelley, realising what they were doing (having some 'staff only' time), took Mark away to find some of the others.

"Had a good day, then, have you?" he asked in that wonderful, rich Welsh lilt.

"It's been okay, yes," said Ben, putting on the voice of a long-suffering tutor who has made sacrifices for his students.

"It's been brilliant," said Emily. "We've ruined our feet ice skating, pulled our muscles bowling and had our bones shaken on the rides."

"Rather you than me," said Bryn. "I think the next drink should be my treat."

"Have you been drinking all day?" asked Ben.

"Are you out of your mind?" Bryn bellowed with a smile. "I've been on duty. Lemonades and coffees, alternately, that's me, followed by trips to the toilet. But now, we're due back at the coach soon, so we can loosen up a bit."

They ordered their drinks. Bryn looked at Ben for a moment.

"How has young Mark been?" he asked.

"Fine. I think he's enjoyed himself."

"I noticed you a couple of times, going from one place to another. He stuck to you all day, didn't he?"

"Yes, he did. But it's okay. He's no bother."

"You want to be careful, though."

"Why?"

"Do you not think he might be using you as a surrogate father figure?"

Ben did not answer. He thought it through. Mark was always around him, that was true. Professor Kennington had told him that Mark's only subject here was magic, so it was no surprise that he had not connected with anybody else. When the lad had followed him to the meal table, it had not crossed his mind that the reason was anything other than the fact that he felt it difficult to make relationships with other people. However, after what Mark had said earlier today about his father, Ben was beginning to have doubts.

"He does hang around you a lot," said Emily.

"Perhaps it would be good for him to be separated from me sometimes," thought Ben.

"What other class is he in?" asked Emily. Ben could not answer straight away, because the professor had asked him not to tell anybody. Bryn's detective skills, however, were going to solve his confidentiality problems for him.

"I don't see him unless you're around," he said, "and I see you without him on Mondays, and, I think Wednesdays, when you don't have a class. You're not his actual father, are you?"

"No, I'm not."

"But he doesn't come to the college except on the days you open your little dungeon class, and Fridays, of course, when he spends the whole day with you."

"He has only signed up for one class," Emily concluded from Bryn's deductions.

"Yes," admitted Ben, "and the only reason my class exists is so that Professor Kennington can accommodate Mark."

There was silence for a moment.

"The professor asked me not to tell you. Anyone. So if you could keep it confidential…"

"Of course," said Bryn. "He's the boss. And what he does for the people of the village is important. That's partly how he can keep the place open without making any money."

"What?" said Ben.

"He gets help," explained Emily. "There are some people in the village who have a bit of money. It's not the college, it's the house. It's part of the village's heritage. While it's being used by somebody who respects it, the people with money are happy. So they keep subsidising it."

"So don't feel so bad about your class, Ben lad," said Bryn. "It's not here just for Mark Tyler. It's not even just here for the rest of your students, or acolytes, or whatever you magicians want to call them. It's there for the future of the whole college."

Ben did feel a little better for knowing that, wishing that the professor had told him this before, but understanding why he didn't. Nevertheless, he still felt that helping Mark make relationships with the others rather than hanging around him all day was sure to be a good thing, so he arranged to sit next to Emily on the way home.

The motion of the bus on the journey, coupled with the energy he had expended during the day soon had him dozing on the way home. Somebody's photograph of him asleep, his head resting on Emily's shoulder, would ensure that the rumour started today would last well into the New Year.

10.

Juliette MacIntyre's holiday extended to nearly three weeks, thanks to some quality time she could spend with her parents, but they had to return to work in the Middle East at the beginning of December, so she came back to the college. Everyone there was delighted to see her, of course, but she had returned with a problem.

The day before she came back, Professor Kennington called Emily and Ben into his office. Ben was puzzled, as he almost never used his office. That is, nobody had ever been sent or called to his office. He dealt with everything 'out in the world', as he called it. He met with staff in their rooms, studios or cellars, or used the staff lounge. The office itself was a small room upstairs overlooking the front lawn. The professor popped in every now and then to sign letters, or to watch the students relaxing outside. Two days a week a lady from the village came and did some paperwork for him, and she was the only one that seemed to use the office for any length of time.

The professor led them in to the small room. It was bare, with no decoration on the wall, and consisted of two chairs, a desk with computer and printer, and a filing cabinet. The secretary from the village was not working that day. The professor stood, and did not expect the other two to sit down.

"Juliette is coming back tomorrow," he told them, having closed the door behind them. He spoke in a quiet, secretive voice, although nobody would be able to hear them here anyway.

"That's great," said Emily, but she stopped herself from saying any more, obviously because she noticed the troubled look on his face. Ben noticed it too.

"Bodyguards?" he guessed.

"Just one, this time," confirmed the professor. "But, in spite of

Juliette's objections, not to mention my own, Mr MacIntyre insists that she is guarded *on the premises*."

"The best way to keep her safe would be to keep her secret," said Ben. "If everyone knows she's a VIP's daughter, they'll tell their friends, send photos and emails. It won't be long before everyone knows she's here."

"So what shall we do with this bodyguard to keep her presence here a secret?" Professor Kennington asked.

"He can sleep in a spare staff room," suggested Ben, "but we need to work a cover story for him."

"Her," said the professor. "Juliette has a lady bodyguard. Her name is Helen Bywater."

"Not Helen Highwater?" said Ben.

"No," said the professor, not getting the joke. "Bywater."

"We could say she was a new tutor," suggested Emily. "We're starting a new class. Self defence, or something."

"Arm wrestling," suggested Ben.

"How to kill an annoying magician without making a mess?"

"People would want to sign up for her class," said Ben. "Especially if it was the magician-killing one. She could be a new housekeeper. The house workers are all more or less invisible to the students most of the time. They go about their business when the students are busy doing their work or out of the way. Another person would just be accepted without fuss."

"As long as she didn't spend too much time too close to Juliette," said Emily.

"Yes, well, a number of the students chat to the house staff," said the professor, "so I don't expect there to be much trouble adding one. Except that the house staff would complain that she was not working hard enough."

"Perhaps we could tell them that she is a tutor, or learning assistant, or something," suggested Ben.

The professor sighed. "I do hate dishonesty. Most of my career I have managed to avoid lying. But now, I have to deal with this."

"It is a special case, Professor," said Emily. "It's for the protection of someone entrusted to your care."

"Yes, I know. But I must tell you I have lost a little sleep over it.

All this cloak-and-dagger stuff is a real nuisance. Not to my liking at all." The professor's understatement was not lost on the two tutors. He paced the tiny floor space for a few minutes as if his great mind was trying to find an alternative to making up cover stories, but eventually he conceded that this was, unfortunately, the best option, so they agreed.

The following day, Mrs Helen Bywater turned up for work, escorting Juliette. She strode onto the premises with no attempt to conceal that she was with the young student, which was hardly cloak-and-dagger stuff at all. Emily managed to separate them as soon as they arrived in order to keep the connection between them as inconspicuous as possible, and Helen was taken to Professor Kennington's office for a briefing of their respective roles in the protection of Juliette and, in particular, discussion on how her situation could be kept as confidential as possible.

Helen Bywater herself was not the person Ben had expected her to be. Far from the muscle-bound mud-wrestler of his imagination, she was a slim, well-groomed woman in her mid-thirties. She dressed in trousers and clothes that generally enabled her to move freely, and had short hair and a very feminine shape to her face and figure. She might even be considered attractive if only she would smile. Her eyes, though, were hard; steely blue and sharp. Ben met her only briefly, and took a disliking to her straight away, although he did not know why. Perhaps it was just the circumstances of their relationship.

He welcomed Juliette back with a great deal of warmth when there was no bodyguard in sight.

"Welcome back. We missed you."

"I'd like to say I missed you, too, sir," she said in her customary polite manner, "but I have thoroughly enjoyed some quality time with my family."

"Ben," said Ben.

"Sorry. Everybody in my family is formal about everything."

"You don't call your father 'sir', do you?" Ben joked.

"We're very close, but, yes, I do. At least in company. We go to formal parties with dress codes and no opportunity to relax."

"Not like a real party. Hopefully, you can loosen up a bit here."

"With Mrs Bywater standing over me?" said Juliette, still keeping a civil and controlled tone. "I shouldn't think so, but thank you for the offer."

"I'm afraid you've got a bit of catching up to do," said Emily.

"That'll be alright. I'm here throughout the Christmas holidays with nothing to do. I've had my Christmas early, I'm afraid."

The weeks approaching Christmas in any school would be an exciting and hectic time. Christmas in a college which focuses on performing arts was even more so. Ben and his team made some small contribution to the show, but as they had dominated the Halloween show, they were encouraged by the principal not to hog the limelight this time. Of course, as usual, he put it in a pleasant way. Ben was relieved, because they had been doing a lot of theory and stagecraft, and had not learned many new tricks in the past month. Mark's success with the guillotine trick had made him want to perform it at every opportunity, however, so Ben determined to increase their repertoire, starting in the middle of December, even if they did not need to have something ready for the show.

With the end of the first term, came end-of-term reviews. Each tutor had to give at least a verbal report to the principal on how they were getting on with their groups, and how each member of their class was doing. Ben decided that he would have a chat with each of the students, so that their own assessment of their progress was included in his report. He did not, however, include Mark in this process, as they spent large chunks of time together and talked about all sorts of things all the time. Ben had been worried by Bryn's comment about Mark needing a father-figure, especially as Mark occasionally brought up in conversation some pretty personal father-son types of comment.

On a Monday morning, when Mark wasn't around, he managed to get a few minutes with Miko at lunchtime.

"How are you getting along in the group?" he asked.

"Fine. Is good group. We have lo'ss of fun together. I am learning new perf... ways of doing magic. I love cart tricks."

"Performance."

"Yes, that."

"And it's card trick."

"I not said that?"

"Card, not cart."

"Cart."

"Yes. No. Card. D."

"Yes, no," said Miko. Ben wondered how he could ever have been acceptable as a magic tutor, when he couldn't even make Miko understand his English.

"Can you understand us, when we talk to you normally?" asked Ben. He realised how isolating it must be to be in a country where you couldn't easily understand people.

"Most times. Sometimes, I not listen to people, i'ss too hard. Professor knows. He start helping me with lesson. Teach me English, starting New Year."

It seemed the professor had the same concerns that Ben had about poor Miko's problems with the language. Rather than putting up with it, or giving him magic tricks he could learn without needing the language, it was better to help him understand the language better.

"Do you get on well with people here?"

"Oh, yes," said Miko. "If they not understand me so well, I show them cart trick."

Richard Wellington was watching the table tennis when Ben found him. Some of the students had encouraged him to play, and to make things fair they put a seat down at the end opposite him and sat down to play against him. This actually gave him an advantage over them, as he was used to doing most things sitting down. When Ben found him, however, it was not his turn.

"Got a moment?"

"Certainly," said Richard, and Ben wheeled him away from the crowd into the wide corridor by the stairs.

"Lots of people playing lately," Ben observed.

"It's for the winter tournaments," explained Richard. "Apparently, every Winter-Spring term, when the weather's at its worst so people don't go outside much, all the students and tutors take part in a huge indoor games tournament. It goes on from January to the Easter break. There are all sorts of games – Scrabble, chess, draughts, Yu-Gi-Oh, Othello, table tennis, pool, Warhammer – I think someone said there are more than twenty tournaments you can join."

"So which ones are you going to go for?"

"I'm not sure. Chess is my kind of game. I played it a lot in hospital after the accident. I think there is some talk of banning all magic students from the poker tournament. They think we'll cheat."

"They could ask me to judge it. I could spot a false shuffle or a top change."

"I might have a go at pool. What about you?"

"Me?" said Ben. "This is the first I've heard of a winter tournament. I think it's a good idea, though. I used to play backgammon. I suppose that's on the list."

"I would think so."

"Anyway, I'll work on that after Christmas. It's time for the pre-Christmas student review. It's your turn, Mr Wellington."

"Great," Richard said with a resigned grin. "Did I ever tell you I'm related to the Wellington that beat Napoleon at Waterloo?"

"No," said Ben, "that's fascinating." Then he paused and thought about it. "Except that Wellington wasn't his name. The Duke of Wellington was a title. His name was, let me see, Wellesley, I think."

"Oh, well, it was worth a try," said Richard.

"So let's get on to the subject you are trying to avoid. Review. I thought I'd let you give your views on your progress in the class, rather than me telling you all about yourself."

Richard sat still with his head down in a thoughtful pose. He did not raise his eyes to meet Ben's when he finally spoke.

"I don't know how to put this, exactly. I have been thinking of giving up your class," said Richard.

"Won't you be one class short?"

"No, I signed up for four classes, so I could drop out of one if I needed to."

"And do you need to?" asked Ben.

"I'm not sure it's for me."

"I suppose I shouldn't stop you if you think that's the right thing to do, but I must say I would rather you stayed on the course. Unless it's interfering with your other studies?"

"No, I'm coping fine."

"Then how do you need to give up the magic class?"

"I don't know. It just, I mean, I don't know if it's helping me fulfil my aims."

"So let's have a look at your aims again, shall we, Richard. What is the main reason you're in my class?"

"I suppose it's to learn some performance skills."

"And what is the main reason you are in this college?" Ben asked.

"I wanted to rebuild my life after the accident. I wanted to learn to present my case to the world. I wanted to learn to write, create and perform so that I could stand for disabled people."

"And what is the weakest area of your studies in my class?"

"I don't know."

"May I give you my opinion?"

"Please."

"Performance skills. The thing you most want to do is the thing you are least proficient at. And I think that if you stayed with the class, you would get better. In my opinion, rather than give it up because it's not working for you, you should keep at it because it's not working for you."

"How can that work?"

"Because you're right. You need to get up there and be a hero for your cause. It's right to think you can fight through and make a difference in the world. I sincerely hope you succeed in your aims. But you need those presentation skills, and giving up now could stop you from getting where you want to go."

Richard was quiet after Ben said his piece. Ben wanted to preach a whole sermon, but the decision was really for Richard to make.

"I should not really try to influence your decision, but I would love it if you didn't give up my class," Ben spoke into the silence.

"Because it's small enough and one less person makes you look bad."

Ben laughed. "No, because you are a valuable person and it's good to have you in my group."

"There are times when you don't notice I'm there."

"Are not."

"Are too."

"Are not."

"Are too," laughed Richard, then he stopped laughing. "Seriously, sometimes you almost walk into me; you so don't notice me there."

"I'm just clumsy. Did you know I once nearly knocked a child off the stage when I turned round to pick up a prop? And it was me who put him there. And another time, I nearly fell into my own secret compartment."

"I'm serious," said Richard.

"Sometimes, when I concentrate on helping one of you with a trick, I ignore all the others. So, yes, I do ignore you sometimes, but not because you are disabled."

"Sometimes I feel invisible."

"In my class? Because that would be a good trick."

"No, in my life. And I think I might have felt that way before my accident. I suppose I've always been nondescript."

"Well, in that case, I would say it's really important that you stay in my class, and learn how to be descript."

"Descript? Is there such a word?"

"Don't ask me. You're the one in the creative writing class."

But Richard had a point. He wasn't the most noticeable person in the world. Even when he was the centre of attention, when he was the one up on stage with the spotlights on him, he didn't look all that special. Ben wondered what could be done to change that, how he could help Richard become the person he wanted to be.

Shelley was the next person on Ben's list. She was a little harder to pin down, as she was always out and about, helping someone, doing a project somewhere, running an errand, practising her dancing for the Christmas performance. She did spend a few minutes in the cellar every now and then on Fridays, but Ben wanted to speak with her when Mark was not around, and that was harder to arrange.

The only thing to do was to make an appointment, officially, during one of the Thursday afternoon lessons, to see her later on that day, after Mark had gone home.

"Are you doing anything this evening?" he asked her as they were tidying up at the end of the session.

"Are you asking me on a date?" she said, much to the amusement of Len and Xander in particular. "What will Emily think?"

"Emily?" said Ben, who was just about the only person in the college who was not party to the theories about the two tutors.

"Sorry," said Shelley, cutting short the conversation before she said something she shouldn't. "Yes, I can be free later." And they arranged to have a chat at evening coffee.

Ben liked Shelley. In fact, everybody liked her. At mealtimes, there seemed to be a rush amongst the students to sit at the same table as her.

She helped people who might be disadvantaged, like Mark or Richard, she was a listening ear to the problems of her fellow students, and she was a star on stage. She probably didn't need the stagecraft lessons that Ben was including in his syllabus, because she always shone when she was up there. It was a shame that he could not cut a bit of her stage presence out of her and graft it into Richard. She was just as good as a supporter, too, not drawing too much attention to herself as she helped Mark improve his guillotine routine. Her only problem was that she was no good at the actual magic.

"You never really wanted to do magic, did you?" Ben asked as they sat down to drink their hot chocolate at the end of the day.

"Are you throwing me out of your class?" said Shelley, obviously concerned.

"No, you are far too valuable to me," replied Ben in an even voice. "The support you give to the others is incredible. You have a sensitivity towards people like Mark, Miko and Richard that puts me to shame. You learn the theory and the stagecraft really well. If this class is helping you in any way, I want you to continue. But the magic itself…"

"…bores the pants off me," she finished.

"Then why are you still with us?"

"Like you said. The rest. Helping people. Being support for someone else. Stagecraft. Some of your ideas for presentation are fantastic, like how to angle your feet on stage when you're standing still. I could find them really useful in my future career. But not as a magician."

"Is there anything magical that interests you?"

"Yes, of course. When I say it bores me I don't mean it like that. I love watching you work. I think Miko's card tricks are fantastic. I enjoy taking part in Mark's performances. I just don't feel I am using my time wisely when I spend it practising how to make a coin disappear. I think… well, what's the point? Will I ever use that skill?"

"Actually," Ben chuckled, "I think that myself sometimes. No. I mean, when you are dancing, do you ever think to yourself, 'this move is pointless'?"

"No."

"I don't mean dancing in general; I mean one little bit of it. One single dance, or style, or just one move."

"No. Not at all."

"Then I've lost the point I was trying to make."

"Sorry about that. So is it okay if I stay in your class, but not to do magic, just to learn everything else?"

"Not really," said Ben. "It's a magic class. But if you just try to take an interest in some aspect of the industry then I would be grateful. You know, like Len has taken to juggling. You could try puppetry or ventriloquism. In fact, I've just had an idea."

"Go on," said Shelley when he paused.

"No. I'll have to do a bit of research first. But I've got an idea for an illusion that is just up your street."

"I'm intrigued."

"I'm afraid I have to make some arrangements first. I need to see a few puppetry people first, to see if I can get some kit made up for you. I know it's not normally appropriate for a member of staff to ask this sort of thing, but can I have your measurements?"

"Is this something I should tell Emily?" she said with a grin.

"I really don't get this 'telling Emily' business."

"No, you don't, do you?"

Len was a little easier to track down and with the term getting closer to its end, Ben realised he had wasted a lot of time tracking down Shelley when he could easily have found time to have a chat with Len. He was not sure about what to say to the young lad, however, as, while he could have a frank and open chat with the likes of Shelley or Richard, Len was a shy person who did not easily talk about his progress. In fact, he seemed not to be able to talk easily about anything.

They sat in awkward silence on a bench in the large entrance hallway of the big house.

"Juggling going well?" said Ben.

"Yeah. Fine," came the answer.

"Let me see, you've done flower sticks, diabolo, scarves, plate-spinning. How about balls? Have you given that a go?"

"Yeah. It's okay. But everybody does balls. I wanted to do something unusual."

"Are you ready to do a performance at the Christmas show?"

"No, not yet. I'm taking on a lot of different stuff. I need to be better at all of them before I'm ready."

"What about other magic stuff? How are you getting on with that?"

"I dunno. It's okay, I suppose."

"Have you got an area you would like to explore?"

"More juggling?"

"I mean apart from juggling. Is there a discipline that interests you?"

"No, not really."

"Escapology?"

"Like what Juliette did with the trunk?" said Len. "That was cool."

"I went to an escapology lecture once. I didn't want to go. I just couldn't get out of it," Ben joked, but it did not seem to help Len's nerves.

"I wouldn't want to do escapology," Len said, "I don't think I could talk to all the people I would need to chain me up and all that. Something you said in class, about being in control of your helpers. I don't think I could do that."

"You need to work on your skills, that's all."

"I dunno." Al Drontlin may have left the college many weeks ago, but his influence still seemed to be there, unless that was how Len normally talked. It was difficult to get Len to commit to anything in particular. Perhaps juggling was enough, especially as he was so good at it, but Ben couldn't help fearing that it was increasing his solitude rather than helping him. He was still a shy, lonely lad, who needed a friend.

Xander was the opposite in personality – a happy, confident young man who was always surrounded by friends, usually girls. As such, he, too, was hard to pin down. He was also active around the site, so Ben did not know where he was most of the time. Once again, he felt he had to make an appointment during his lesson.

The class was playing with rope, exploring the different knots that magicians used. It was the last Thursday that the college was open before the Christmas break. On the following Monday evening there would be the big Christmas show, and the next day everyone would pack up and go home. There was not the right atmosphere for learning anything serious, so Ben thought playing would be the best idea. There was a little problem with a trick he had shown them all, where a length of rope would be coiled around his neck and then tied in a knot, apparently passing through his neck rather than strangling him. Everyone was eager to learn the moves required to do this trick, but some were better at performing it than others. He watched them all carefully, asking each of them to check the others for fear of one of them getting the knot wrong and strangling himself, or herself, for real. They did get the moves wrong, and they did look out for each other, and so kept safe. However, he was concerned that they would try it on their own and get into real trouble. He made them promise not to, and they said they would only practise in pairs.

"Can I see you for a few minutes at the end of this session, Xander?" Ben asked in the closing minutes of the day.

"Yes, fine," he said in his usual amiable way. When the lesson did finish, Mark stayed around as usual to help tidy up.

"It's okay, Mark, you don't have to stay," Ben told him.

"No, I'm okay, honest," said Mark. "I don't mind staying."

Xander, who understood that Ben wanted Mark to leave them alone but didn't want to upset him, watched on with amusement.

"But you don't have to stay. Not today."

"I really don't mind. I like helping."

"What Ben's trying to say," said Xander, "is that it's my turn. He noticed that I'm a little envious of you getting all the best jobs, so he wants to let me have a go."

"Oh," said Mark, with just a little understanding. "That's alright. We can do it together." Ben chuckled, realising that from now on Mark would volunteer Xander to help at every opportunity. Anyway, it did not take long to tidy things away, and Mark was soon on his way to meet with his mother, who would be waiting in the car park so as not to embarrass him.

"So how's it going?" Ben asked Xander, realising that this was how he started most of his 'assessment conversations'.

"Quite well, I think."

"You're good in the lessons. You pick things up quickly."

"Thanks."

"There is just that thing about stage fright."

"Yeah. But I'm fine as long as I am not up there on the stage."

"Wouldn't it be a good idea if you had a go at dealing with it? I mean, you are always happy-go-lucky and confident. This is the one area where you have a problem."

"Keeps me humble, I suppose."

"What?"

"Something my mother used to say. We need our little problems to keep us humble."

"I see," said Ben. "And *are* you humble?"

Xander laughed. "No, not really."

"Shall we have another go at the theatre? Just the two of us, with nobody else around."

"I don't see the point," said Xander. "I didn't work before. Why should I suddenly be alright? I'm learning a lot about being backstage. I should think magicians often need backstage support."

"I find it hard to believe that someone of your temperament would be satisfied with backstage."

"And then there's close-up. You said we would do close-up next term, didn't you? Going round tables in a restaurant, that would be my sort of thing."

"Yes, but surely you want to have a range of skills."

"Aren't there some magicians who more-or-less only do restaurants?"

"Yes," admitted Ben, thinking about some friends who did just that, and made some good money on it. But Xander had a problem, and Ben wanted to help him through it. Xander seemed to want to avoid it.

"Meesh is good on stage," Xander continued. "Maybe I could do the magic she can't do, and she could do the performance that I can't."

Xander chatted about things he had learned, and what he enjoyed about the class, and how he was doing really well at the college in general, but would not let Ben take the issue of his stage fright any further. Ben wondered if this Meesh girl was his girlfriend, or at least one of them. And was she interested in magic? Perhaps she should join his class.

The last person to talk to was Juliette. Ben did not worry about finding time to talk to her, because she was staying over Christmas. On the Tuesday afternoon, when all of the boarders had gone home except the two or three that were being picked up on the Wednesday, Juliette meandered around the playing field, flanked at a short distance by her bodyguard. Ben approached her, and Helen looked daggers at him.

"Have you got a moment?" he asked her.

"I've got a lot more than that," she said, just about keeping the cool in her voice.

"Yes, I'm sorry," he said. Then he turned to Helen, who stood nearby looking menacing. "Excuse me," he said to her. The bodyguard ignored him. He took a step nearer Juliette, and Helen took a step, a threatening step, towards him.

"What?" he said. "Do you think I am going to kidnap her? You must have a file on me or something. I've been teaching her since the beginning of term."

Helen still said nothing, but glared at Ben, still threatening.

"Go away," said Juliette.

"Pardon?" said Ben.

"Not you, Mr April," Juliette explained, finally beginning to snap. "I was talking to the Wicked Witch of the West here. Ben's right, Bywater, there's nobody here. I'm not in any danger. In spite of your interference, nobody knows who I am. So go and polish your guns or something."

Ben was shocked at this outburst. Helen Bywater acknowledged her employer's orders and left, still keeping an eye on Ben as she warily made her way back to the house.

"She has guns?" he asked.

"No idea," Juliette replied. "Probably."

"I've never seen you other than cool and polite," said Ben, "except with her. Is she a problem?"

"She stays out of my lessons. But, yes, she is a problem. I always argued that secrecy was my best protection. How much longer are people not going to work out that she is my bodyguard? When any of my friends here find out, then the whole world will know."

"She's only doing her job."

Juliette smiled, and relaxed a little. "I think I am quite an observant person, Mr April, Ben. I think you hate her being here as much as I do."

"You're probably right," said Ben. "I hate her having to be here. But I don't hate *her*. She's just doing what your father pays her to do. Which brings me on to why I wanted to see you. How are you going to perform anywhere if who you are must remain a secret?"

Juliette's almost perfect posture slumped a little.
"I don't know," she said.

11.

As well as all of the end of term students' evaluations, the Christmas break also gave Ben reason to evaluate himself. Mark had invited him for Christmas lunch, and he found himself feeling a little insecure about the close ties that were forming between this tutor and student. Was it right for him to encourage, or even allow Mark to build him up as a sort of surrogate father? Anyway, he had planned to spend the holiday in Birmingham with his family, so he decided to turn down the invitation. Later, he discovered that Professor Kennington had also been invited, and had, in fact, accepted. It seemed that it was a general invitation from Mark's mother, and not a further attempt to nurture Ben as a father figure, after all.

During the break Ben did an after-Christmas show for his local scout group in the north of Birmingham, with which he had been involved since he was a scout himself. They always had their party on the first weekend of the New Year in order to avoid all the Christmas parties in December, and Ben always did the entertainment. The young lads in the group were well-behaved with a good sense of fun, unlike some of the children's parties he had done. He really enjoyed himself, and realised he had not actually done a 'proper' show since he had taken on the tutor job at Lockley College of the Arts. Contrarily, he also missed being at the college and couldn't wait to get back.

Of course, nobody in Norfolk knew him, so nobody was booking him for shows. Perhaps it was time to get some adverts out and to make new contacts in the area around the college – he had plenty of spare time, after all, and it would be good to practise what he was teaching. He got back to the college a few days before the new term started, and went about contacting clubs and places where he might perform. He revamped his advertising literature with a change of contact address and some new details about his position in the college, and sent them out to what he considered might be likely customers. So soon after Christmas, however, business was slack and, in spite of decent references from some of the places he had performed in the Birmingham area, there did not seem to be much going in sleepy Norfolk. Still, he decided he would keep contacting people, just in case something came up in due course.

The college and grounds were cold and quiet, and he wandered around to relax and get his mind in gear, ready for the new term. He noticed Juliette around the house every now and then, looking a little despondent having spent Christmas here more or less alone. She was never too far from Helen Bywater, who strutted around a few metres away from her charge, looking as if she owned the place. She did her best not only to be conspicuous, but also to be no kind of moral support to the sad young VIP at all. Perhaps she did not like the secrecy of term-time, when she had to be as out-of-the-way as possible, skulking about but still guarding her young charge, or 'primary', or whatever it was she called her. Perhaps, now that the holidays were here, Helen Bywater could flex her slim but doubtless well-toned muscles and actually be a real bodyguard. Ben obviously felt there was nothing to protect Juliette from, but still, without the rest of the students here, the bodyguard could shadow the young ambassador's daughter with annoying proximity.

Juliette herself had no trouble catching up with her missed studies, and was not too depressed at being at the college over Christmas. The only time, in fact, that she appeared in any way sad or upset was when the bodyguard was about.

Ben watched the two of them, noting Bywater's insensitivity and Juliette's distress, and decided it was time to do something about it. He had noticed that Helen would never eat at the same table as Juliette, but watched over her from the next room. When she did eat was a bit of a mystery to him, but she did disappear occasionally to who knows where, probably to eat or sleep, or to get into a regeneration chamber or coffin, or shape-shift into her true, horrible form. So Ben decided he would ask if he could join Juliette for their meal. After all, there were, including housekeeping staff and Helen, only about six people in the house before the mad rush that constituted the new term, so it was pointless using more than one table. He sat exactly between Juliette and the watching bodyguard.

"How good is Helen's hearing?" he asked quietly, bending over to her so that he could talk quietly.

"Not good enough to hear you now," Juliette replied, looking behind Ben. "She's just gone off to have a bite to eat."

He resisted the urge to look over his shoulder to check.

"She eats?" he said. "I thought she plugged herself into the mains for half an hour, once every fortnight." His humour did not have the effect on her that he wanted it to have. She so needed to laugh.

"It's not for me to complain," said Juliette coldly. "She is, after all, only there to help. Nevertheless, she does make things difficult."

"But nobody is supposed to know who she is. When the rest of the staff and students come back, what will she do?"

"She should be a little less obvious then," said Juliette. "Like she was before the holidays started."

"How's it been for you?" Ben asked, his voice softening as he realised what an awful time she must have had over Christmas here at the college more or less on her own.

"I've caught up with my work. I joined Professor Kennington at Mark's house for Christmas Day, which was great. We stayed until late into the night. Mark's mum is a fantastic cook. It was great to be with ordinary people joining in their ordinary lives, instead of meeting VIPs and their butlers and bodyguards in big posh houses and having to follow etiquette. Laughing together. Being allowed to belch in public. I think Mrs Bywater sat outside in the car all day. And Miss Darkchilde came over a couple of times to keep me company. Mrs Bywater disappears when the staff are around. She obviously believes I am in good hands with you."

"Mrs Bywater."

"Helen," said Juliette by way of explanation.

"Oh, yes, I know who you mean. It's just hard to imagine anyone wanting to marry her." Juliette nearly spilled her drink laughing. At last, thought Ben.

"She's not unattractive," Juliette informed him in case he had not noticed. "She's probably alright when she's off duty. If she's ever off duty."

"And belching in public? You didn't, did you?"

"No, I didn't. But nobody would have minded if I had."

"Anyway, while she's not here, there's an idea I wanted to put to you."

Ben outlined his plan, and Juliette cheered up a lot. Ben's job, now he had the young student's agreement, would take up rather a lot of the next two days before everyone would return to the college, because it would need everyone in the house to take part – everyone except Helen Bywater, that is. As he went about recruiting the help of everyone who was currently at the college, including, of course, the principal, he felt a little sad that the performance which he was preparing would be appreciated by such a small audience. He was not even sure that 'appreciate' was the right choice of word, either.

Helen Bywater walked the grounds at 3.30 in the afternoon, as the sky was getting dark. It was cold, but clear. A small low wall which hemmed in a garden lawn frequently used in the summer was decorated by balloons, although Helen did not see who had put them there (because he had made sure she was somewhere else when it happened, and was now watching her from inside the house). Each balloon was about a metre distant from the others. As she walked past each one, it burst. At the first pop, she seemed to start, and her muscles tightened ready for action, then she noticed it was just a balloon, and relaxed a little and carried on walking. She hardly flinched when the second one burst, then the third, at exactly the moment she passed by. She stopped at the fourth balloon, and the next one along did not burst. Then she carried on walking, and, as soon as she reached the fifth balloon, it burst. After seven of the eight, she looked around her, into the nearby trees, back at the house, out over the fields at the front of the house, to see if she could find out who was responsible, but she saw nobody (because he was hiding below the window of the dance studio with the lights off).

Later that evening, she would return to her room to find a single red flower on a green stalk, made from balloons, tied to her door. Again, Ben imagined, she would look around to see if anyone was watching her. Ben had decided that he would not risk doing that, because she was no doubt really good at her job, and he didn't want to get caught at this early stage of the game. She had probably worked out it was him, anyway.

At the evening meal, Ben and Juliette shared a candlelit dinner, watched at her usual distance by the bodyguard. Every few seconds, the candles spat and popped with loud explosive sounds. More explosions happened behind Helen and again, she tensed up for action. Ben had to give her credit that, while she was ready to act if she needed to, she was not rattled by the spooky happenings.

Once more, when she returned to her room, she would find something on her door. This time, it was an inflatable black plastic novelty ball with the word 'bomb' written on it.

The following afternoon, on the last day of the holiday, Ben organised a little show on the front lawn. On the flat grass field at the front of the house, he laid out four metal stands and four bars about two metres high. On the ground around the bars there were four huge red curtains. The weather was, again, cold, but it had not rained for several days, so the ground was hard, which was just right for this little exercise. The sky was clear and almost cloudless. As the darkness once again captured the daylight, spotlights made eerie patterns across the front of the house which Ben had made into a stage.

Ben would not normally give away the secrets of his magic, but for this he had to recruit the whole of the staff, the real staff, not Helen, and explain to them what they had to do. As he chatted to the housekeeper and cook, he found out that they had been told part of the truth about Helen Bywater. They believed that she was here because of the rumours of someone watching the school, that she was in security and her presence there was just for safety, but that the students weren't to know so that things ran smoothly and that they were not unduly worried by the situation. It was a good story, because of the truth in it. With her there, there would be no need for anyone else to watch the school.

As the early evening began to descend, Juliette walked upstairs towards her room, followed at the usual respectable distance by her bodyguard. She then passed her room and walked up to the staff quarters by the main staircase, where she waited until she was sure Helen was following, then walked down the back staircase to the boys' corridor, then back towards her own room, and down the main stairs, back towards the back of the house and down to the cellar. She had begun to walk slowly, as if in a trance. Past the cellar and out the back entrance, she continued the walk, zombie-like, around the side of the house and up the slope toward the front garden. Helen was puzzled, no doubt, but must have suspected, after the balloon incident and the exploding candles, that this was another prank, and she was no doubt on the lookout for Ben, whose involvement she must have suspected by now.

At the front of the house were a number of people, dressed in dark robes like druids in some bizarre pagan rite. The bodyguard's brief included not interfering with anything that the staff at the college were doing, so she could hardly call proceedings to a halt to find out what was going on. She had to go along with this little prank and watch while everyone took it to its conclusion. Ben had no idea what was going through her mind as the drama unfolded.

The robed figures walked in peculiar patterns around the framework that Ben had set up. He, in the meantime, stood in the centre of his construction. The others walked around him, sometimes zigzagging through the structure, sometimes walking around it, constantly changing direction in an absence of any recognisable pattern. After a few minutes they stopped and picked up the red curtain. The apparently entranced Juliette walked into the centre of the area marked by the frame. Ben walked back out and supervised the constantly-moving acolytes as they covered Juliette and the frame with the curtains. Then, everyone stopped. All of the dark-robed people were still and silent for several seconds.

Suddenly, Ben yanked at the curtain and it fell away from the now empty frame. Juliette was gone. Ben thanked his helpers with a slight nod of his head, and they walked back to the main entrance of the house.

Ben stood around until all of them were gone, and then he packed the curtains into a small plastic box. After that, he proceeded to dismantle the metal framework. Helen approached him.

"Where is she?"

"Ah, Mrs Highwater," he said. "Have you got a moment? I need to get all of this stuff back into the house."

Helen Bywater poked about at the plastic carton which held the curtains as if, somehow, Juliette could be hidden amongst the tightly packed material.

"What have you done with her?"

"She's gone," said Ben in his most serious and enigmatic voice, mustering as much will power as possible to stop himself laughing. "She has a great sense of drama, don't you think? If you take the box, I'll take the poles."

His respect for her deepened when she went ahead and picked up the box. That is to say, his respect for her started at that point, as, up to then, he had had very little respect for her anyway. But she did not fall into the trap. She just carried his box, and stayed as alert as she always seemed to be, her eyes darting around the front area of the big house for clues to the whereabouts of her missing primary.

They walked in to the front entrance, and, at the top of the stairs stood Juliette, looking down at her, smiling. Ben noticed how much brighter she looked now that they had had a little fun at the bodyguard's expense.

"Hello," Juliette said to Helen. "Miss me?"

The bodyguard said nothing, but put the box down in the middle of the entranceway and walked up the stairs past Juliette to her room. Ben and Juliette looked at each other and smiled. It was not quite over yet. When Helen got to her room, she would discover that an envelope had been pushed under her door – an envelope with an invitation in it.

At the meal that evening, Juliette and Ben, along with Professor Kennington, sat at the same table. There were four places set, and, soon enough, Helen Bywater came to join them.

"Mrs Bywater," said the professor. "Have you come to join us?"

"If it is alright with you," she said politely, and waved the envelope in the air. "I seem to have been invited." She gave no indication that she was annoyed or amused by all of the goings-on.

They pulled up a chair for her to sit opposite Ben, and the staff served them with a wonderful roast chicken meal.

"It was the robed people, wasn't it?" she said to Ben as they ate. "They kept moving, until they were masked by the curtain, so I couldn't tell just how many there were. Then, when they returned to the house, I imagine there was one more person than there was at the beginning."

Juliette nearly choked on her food. Ben remained calm. Sometimes, particularly observant people do see through a trick, and this one was always going to be risky.

"You're very good," he said to the bodyguard. "We have no doubt that Juliette is in good hands."

"But why?" Helen asked. "Why did you want to play silly tricks on me? To humiliate me?"

"No," said Ben. "It wasn't about you. It was about Juliette, and the fact that she didn't get a proper Christmas. I wanted to cheer her up."

"She hasn't been all that happy these past few days," said Helen as if she had only just noticed.

"I've been unhappy because of you," Juliette blurted out with an uncharacteristic show of emotion. "You don't leave me alone. You're always there, lurking in the background, and you never say a word."

"It's protocol."

"Stuff protocol," said Juliette sharply, momentarily losing her aristocratic poise. "I'm here in England, when everyone I know and love is in the Middle East, possibly looking down the barrel of a gun. I'm all on my own, and my only companion doesn't speak to me because of protocol. Do you know what it's like being here on my own while the people I love could be in danger, and we can't be in touch in case it puts me in the spotlight?"

"Yes," said Helen, flatly, after a pause to think of what she should say next. "My husband is currently working undercover somewhere else in the world. I can't tell you where, because they haven't told me. I don't know when I'm going to see him again. I don't even know *if* I'm going to see him again."

That killed the conversation. Ben and Juliette stopped eating and looked at the ground. Well, they looked at the table, but they would have looked at the ground if the table hadn't been in the way. The professor, not completely picking up the atmosphere that Juliette's and Helen's mutual outbursts had created, carried on chewing his food.

"It's interesting, isn't it," said Ben after a long silence, "that you two have so much in common, and you are even forced to occupy the same space, and yet you don't talk to each other. You know, I have noticed a lot of what might be considered inappropriate friendships between kitchen staff and students. Well, maybe they aren't exactly inappropriate, just possibly against protocol. They get on like they were all ordinary adults. Oh, wait a minute. Most, if not all of our students are over 18, aren't they? They *are* all ordinary adults."

"I didn't know," said Juliette in a quieter tone. "About your husband, I mean."

"We both knew what we were getting into. You just put your head down and get on with whatever job they give you. I got the easier job, this time."

"Do you have to do it with your head down?" asked Ben.

"I beg your pardon?" said Helen, not sure whether this was another of Ben's silly jokes.

"Mix a bit. You don't have to act aloof. You can have a conversation with Juliette every now and then – act like two friends, rather than a worker and her job."

"I've got a bottle of wine my parents left me for Christmas," said Juliette to Helen. "I haven't started it yet. Would you join me for a drink later?"

"I'm on duty."

"24 hours a day?"

"More or less."

"Then you need a break. One glass."

"One *small* glass," Helen acquiesced.

"Done."

"Where?" asked Helen.

"In the cellar, I think," said Ben. "At ten o'clock this evening. With the professor's permission?"

"Certainly," said the professor. "I think we can bend the rules, go against protocol, just this once."

Which was a big thing for someone with Asperger's Syndrome to say.

12

"But I had b-better cards than you," said Mark, studying Paul Harris's winning poker hand.

"And you folded," said Paul with a smirk. "Loser!"

"It's n-not right," said Mark. "I sh-should have won."

"Idiot," said Paul, picking up his poker chips. "That's three out of three. I wish we were playing for money. I would be a millionaire."

"N-no, you wouldn't."

"Really? How come?"

"B-because you c-could only win m-m-y m-money f-from me. And I'm n-not a m-millionaire, so you w-wouldn't b-be."

"Idiot," Paul said again. "M-m-y m-m-money!"

Ben was walking along the corridor by the room when he caught this fragment of conversation. He might have ignored it, but he was aware of how much more acute than usual Mark's stutter was. He was about to enter the room where a number of poker games were being played and intervene when he heard Shelley's voice coming to Mark's defence.

"Don't be so superior," she was saying. "You're so hot at poker, but didn't I hear you back out of a game of Yu-Gi-Oh yesterday? Chicken, are you?"

"Yu-Gi-Oh?" he said. "It's a kid's game. I want to play a serious game. But not against retards."

"I challenge you," said Shelley.

"To what? Snakes and ladders?"

"I d-don't think s-s-snakes and ladders is in the t-tournament," Ben heard Mark struggle to say. Although the textbooks said that people with Asperger's did not always understand when they were being made fun of, he was sure that Mark felt got at by the way he struggled to get full sentences out. And he must have understood what Paul had meant by 'retard'. Ben wanted to go in and fight for his student, but he was not sure if his interference might make things worse. Anyway, he reminded himself, Shelley was there, and defending the weak as was her wont.

"Chess," Shelley said.

"So, you play chess, do you?" Paul said.

"No," said Shelley, smiling as if she knew something that Paul didn't, "never played it before in my life. I'll have to get some help."

"You'll need it," said Paul. "I *have* played before. In fact I was chess champion at my school last year."

"I p-p-play ch-chess," said Mark. Ben cringed at what he realised was happening, or, more to the point, what was about to happen.

"As well as you play poker?" said Paul with what sounded like a sneer.

"I had a b-better hand than you," Mark insisted again.

"I accept your challenge," said Paul, but it seemed from Ben's listening post that it was Mark he was accepting, not Shelley. It was time for him to intervene.

"Ah, Ben," said Emily's voice from behind him. "Listening in to the students' conversations? Isn't that against the rules?"

"Is it?"

"I don't know," she admitted. "I just made that up. But I'm glad I've found you. Somebody told me that you had a bit of fun with Juliette's new minder during the holidays. And you didn't even wait for me."

"I had to take advantage of the moment," Ben explained with a smile.

"Please tell me about it. Every last detail." Emily felt for Juliette's situation as much as Ben, and was delighted that he had taken action to cheer her up.

"So who told you? Not Professor Kennington, surely?"

"No, Juliette," said Emily, her tone a little more serious. "I was worried for her. I came and visited her a couple of times during the holidays, took her shopping once to the January sales in Stevenbridge, but she was so unhappy. I couldn't do anything to cheer her up. And then I come back for the New Year, and she's as happy as a puppy. She's told me you set Helen Bywater up, but she didn't give me any details. Except that you called her 'Highwater' to her face."

"She said that?" Ben tried to sound innocent, failing badly.

"Don't put me off. Tell."

"Before I do, I must just sort this out in here," he said, indicating the room where the poker players had been. Emily nodded, and they went into the poker room, where a number of games were still going on. Mark, Paul and Shelley, however, had departed through the other exit. The two tutors decided to go and sit down in the currently-deserted staff room and have a cup of coffee and a chat. What Emily really wanted to know was how he had cheered up Juliette during the Christmas holidays.

They laughed together at the prank he had played on her cold-fish bodyguard, and found themselves in one of those rare moments where they could talk freely and comfortably together. They laughed about the 'disappearing Juliette' trick, shared their concerns about her, told each other stories about home and the holidays, and generally let time rush past as they enjoyed each other's company.

The college had extended for a couple of hours beyond the normal finishing time so that day students like Mark could stay on and join in the Lockley Winter Tournaments, entering whatever games they wanted. Tutors were also invited to join in any of the contests, which was probably why there was nobody in the staff room right now. Ben had intended to join in, but he had been banned from playing any card games at all because he was a magician. That did not stop the students inviting him to watch the games, and, when they had finished, asking him to show them a few of his tricks. Once again, he found that the cards he professed to hate so much gave him and his audience some enjoyment.

He was quite surprised at the variety of indoor games that the students, and, indeed, some of the staff, played. There were 2-metre-long green boards filled with model soldiers and scenery that looked as if it might have been borrowed from a train set, there were huge varieties of card games and board games as well as traditional games. Two of the most popular games were Uno and Fluxx, where players would be able to change direction of play, penalise their opponents or even bring in new rules to affect the game. Ben wondered if he might not sign up for the tournament after all, as he felt sometimes as if he was witnessing a different culture from the one he was used to.

He had managed to get a booking to do a small local show in a nearby town for an old people's home. It wasn't much, but it was a start. He also applied to join a local magic club, but it was an hour's drive away on a Monday night, so he was not sure he would be able to attend that often. He felt that magic clubs were good places for magicians to share ideas and support each other. He had belonged to two in Birmingham when he was busy as a working performer. It was a shame that there wasn't a closer club here in Norfolk.

As the term started, Ben had noticed that Len was still a bit of a loner, but he seemed happier during the lessons, especially since Mark had begun to take him under his wing and was starting to be a great help to him. Juliette was the same as ever, gentle and polite, and did not seem to talk to the others about her Christmas experiences, although he noticed that she occasionally shared a word of greeting with her bodyguard, who had become inconspicuous again.

Xander and Richard had teamed up, which was quite interesting, as Xander was loud and confident (except, of course, when he was on stage), and Richard was quiet and unassuming. They both put a bit of time into practising their magic, with Xander in particular learning a lot of card tricks from Miko. Ben was pleased at the way the class members talked to each other, taught what they had learned and discussed how best to present a trick to turn it into a proper performance.

After the first couple of weeks or so into the new term, however, there was a lot of talk about the big contest coming up, the first big match of the winter tournaments. It was the chess match between Mark and Paul, and Ben was worried about his student being made to look an even bigger fool by his chess-champion opponent. On the next Tuesday evening staff meeting, he said as much.

"Oh, yes," said Bryn, "young Paul Harris is in my art class. Average-sized talent, enormous head."

"And eager to have a go at Mark at every opportunity," said Ben. "With the winter tournaments, Mark's mother has encouraged him to spend a bit more time at the school to try and relate to his peers more. I'm not entirely sure it was that wise a thing to do."

"It's part of growing up," said Bryn. "You've got to take a few knocks sometimes, you know."

"Mark has been taking knocks all his life," said Ben. "I hardly think he needs to learn how to take a few more."

"Fair enough," said Bryn, "but it's a chess match, nothing more. It's only a game, isn't it?"

"No, I'm afraid it isn't only a game. It's Paul's way of making Mark look like a fool again. And Mark is falling for it. And Shelley has encouraged it."

"Perhaps Shelley knows something that you don't," said Emily.

After the meeting was over, Emily took Ben to her music room, which, after school, was used as a games room. Today, it was filled with young people playing board games. They watched Juliette win a game of backgammon.

When she had finished, showing polite good grace to her opponent, she looked up at Emily and Ben with a smile.

"Hello," she said, and noted that the two of them were together. "I'm sorry I missed the outing to that leisure centre. I was told it was really good."

Emily smiled. "Tell Ben what you told me about Mark and his computers. About chess in particular. He thinks Mark is going to look like an idiot playing against Paul Harris."

"Oh, no," said Juliette, still smiling. "Mark is going to have more supporters, to start with."

"Don't tease," said Emily, interrupting before Ben could say anything. "Ben's really concerned about Mark. I think he deserves to know the big secret."

"Big secret?" asked Ben.

"When I went to Mark's house for Christmas dinner, he showed me his computer," said Juliette. "He is really into computers. In fact, I think he's the biggest computer geek I've ever met. He thinks he might even be able to build one himself – from scratch, I mean, not from a kit. He looks up the news, watches TV programmes, and researches magicians, all on his computer. And he plays chess on it. A lot. I think he has played against some of the world's greatest players, and won. He seems to have this ability to see patterns in the game, he says. He can see where the game is going, and predict, or read, what players are planning. But only a few of us know that, and we don't intend to tell Paul. The match is tomorrow at four. Will you be there?"

"Without a doubt," said Ben, wondering if the whole college was in on this. It certainly seemed that way the following day at 4 pm, when the principal announced that the game would be played in the main theatre. It seemed that the whole of the college had been talking about it, partly because Paul had been mouthing off about it to his group of friends, and partly because Shelley had been recruiting support for Mark. This game was never going to be just a bit of fun.

The stage had been filled with chairs to look down on the game played at the front of the auditorium, and a video camera borrowed from the film studio had been set up to film the game and show it on a big screen at the back of the room. There were at least forty people in the room for the start of the game, including most of the staff, particularly Professor Kennington, who had reserved himself a seat right next to the table. Ben also noticed that Richard, Miko, Xander, Len, Shelley and Juliette were there, and not only just present, but active in working up support for their friend.

Paul Harris came into the room first, surprised at the number of people who had turned up to support him for this contest. They all gave him a polite round of applause as he took his place.

When Mark came in only a few moments later, however, the room erupted with whoops and cheers and shouts of support, led by Shelley and Xander, who were good at leading the audience in this sort of thing. Mark stood at the door, gobsmacked, a huge smile on his face, and was soon guided to his seat by Juliette.

The room quietened for the start of the game, and, except for occasional encouraging shouts of support when either of them made a good move, stayed politely quiet for the whole of the twenty minutes or so they were there. The opening moves were nothing special, and then Paul made some quick and clever moves to take the lead. Then everything slowed down, as Mark countered the moves, stopping everything that Paul was planning. Paul started to take longer to make his moves, and Mark took no time at all to take control of the game with every move he made.

With Paul's slowness, the watching students began to jeer him, and with every clever move Mark made, he was starting to get a round of applause, even from Paul's side. Before twenty minutes was up, Paul was in an impossible position, and he gave up the game, toppling his own king in surrender.

Mark acknowledged his victory by holding out his hand to shake his opponent's, but Paul stormed out of the room, with some of the students, including some of his own supporters, jeering his bad sportsmanship.

"Well done," said Ben to Mark when he could get close enough to him to add his congratulations to those of all his friends and supporters. But Mark did not look that happy.

"I think I have upset Paul," said Mark.

"No, it wasn't you," said Ben. "It was losing."

"But everybody loses sometimes," said Mark.

"And not everybody takes it as graciously as they should."

"Should I go out and talk to him?" said Mark.

"No," said Ben. "But perhaps I should."

Ben went out to have a talk with Paul, who was sitting outside in the cold and dark, on the front garden wall by the side of the main building. A few flakes of snow were falling, but it didn't look like it was going to turn into anything heavy.

"Are you alright?" said Ben, and Paul shrugged his shoulders.

"You know, I should be proud of those kids in there, all rallying round Mark after what you said to him. But they had no right to put you down like that."

"I think I deserved it."

"I don't think anyone should ever be put down. Not unless they've broken their ankle in a race."

"What?"

"Never mind. But it feels rotten, doesn't it?"

Paul nodded.

"You understand how rotten Mark must have felt when you called him an idiot?" Paul nodded again, although Ben did not really know if he was thinking about how he had made Mark feel a week or so back.

"Did you know that the word 'idiot' means something, that it is not just an insult? It has a technical definition. An idiot is someone with an IQ of less than 25. There's another word for someone with Mark's IQ. Do you know what that is?"

Paul looked up, still not talking.

"It's genius. Mark has an IQ of over 150. That makes him a genius. Officially. There's no shame in being beaten by a genius, is there?"

"But all the people back there," said Paul, "They were all laughing at me. I can't show my face in there again, can I?"

129

Ben looked back towards the entrance porch of the college. He saw Mark standing at the door, looking concerned, with Shelley standing next to him, looking as if all her planning had gone wrong. Mark looked as if he was dying to come and offer his support to his defeated opponent.

"I'm out here talking to you because Mark is concerned for you."

"He should be laughing at me like everyone else."

"Well, he has this disability called Asperger's Syndrome. It means he doesn't understand some of the things that you and me understand, like bearing a grudge."

"Sounds like it's not as much of a disability as some things."

"Well, there's more to it than that. He doesn't understand poker, for one thing."

"I could help him there."

"It might be a hard job. It would take a lot of patience, and, at the end of it all, he still might not understand."

"Is that what gives him that stutter? This Asperger's thing?"

"No. He stutters because people put him down."

"I'm sorry."

"He doesn't know how to hold it against you," Ben said, and he turned to nod to Mark to come and join them. Again, Mark held out his hand for a handshake. Paul took a look at him, hesitated for a moment, then turned and walked away from them, round the corner and down the hill towards the back entrance to the house where he could sneak back to his room without anybody seeing him.

Mark made to follow him, but Ben stopped him.

"I won," said Mark, "but it didn't feel like winning."

"It should," said Ben. "You did well. I'm sure that Paul will sort it all out in his head, and end up being alright with it. But he needs a bit of time."

Ben took Mark back into the house through the front door, where his friends were still waiting to celebrate his victory. Shelley was also unhappy, because she had intended to give Mark the chance to prove himself, rather than cause this ill-feeling. Emily was with her.

"I messed up, didn't I?" said the student.

"Paul's nose is out of joint, that's all," said Juliette. "Now he knows what it feels like."

"Mark never wanted to hurt his feelings," said Ben.

"He deserved it," said Juliette. Ben wanted to agree, because in some respects he did deserve it, but he decided not to voice his agreement because he was a member of the staff, and was there to help all the students, including the one that called his own star student an idiot.

"I take it you don't approve of what Paul did to Mark," said Emily.

"No, I do not," said Juliette.

"Neither did I," said Shelley, realising where Emily was taking this. "But it didn't stop me doing the same back to him. I did what I disapproved of."

Mark's mother was at the front door. It did not take her long to notice that there was a certain gloom in the front hallway, and, as she knew that her son had been due to play an important chess game today, she feared the worst.

"What happened?" she asked.

"I won," said Mark, miserably.

13.

"So who's Barbara?" Emily Darkchilde asked Ben April in front of his class. She had come down to the cellar because everybody was trying to guess what the parcel was that Ben had received at the school that morning. Was it a new magic trick? It was big, whatever it was. It was about the size of a person. It was rolled up like a carpet, but not quite as heavy. Actually, it was nowhere near as heavy. The return label had said it was from Barbara Stephenson of an address in the north of Birmingham.

"Barbara?" asked Ben.

"The lady who sent your parcel," said Emily.

"Jealous?" said Shelley, who had learned that she could joke with Emily, although she probably wouldn't joke in the same way with Ben. For all his sense of humour, he did not seem to grasp the 'Ben and Emily' comments that had begun to find their way around the college in the last few months.

"I've got a doll in my room, and the pins are ready to go in," said Emily, sharing what Ben could only assume was a private joke that he was not in on. "I just need a name. Barbara, perhaps."

"She's a beautiful woman I know from home," explained Ben with a smile, remembering with fondness the many hours he spent as a child in the company of Barbara Stephenson. "She's nearly seventy now, but she's still handy with a needle and thread. She likes to make some of my props, and over Christmas I gave her something to do. I must say, I didn't expect her to have finished so quickly." It had been nearly two months since Christmas, so the others wondered why Ben thought that was 'quickly'. Perhaps Barbara, being old, worked slowly?

"So, what is it?" Emily asked.

"It's a secret," said Ben.

"B-Ben and I will open it when you've all g-gone," said Mark expectantly, with no idea how lacking in tact he was.

"Actually, Mark, this one is going to be a secret from you as well, at least for the time being."

"Oh," said Mark, looking crestfallen for a few moments, before returning to his big grin and saying, "I like s-surprises."

There was a little more teasing and banter between the students and Emily, with Xander saying something about competition with a seventy-year-old, which made Emily laugh, although Ben had no idea why, or what kind of competition he was referring to. Barbara was not much of a singer, after all, and he didn't think that Emily aspired to making props for him. At the end of the session, Xander stayed for a few minutes to tidy up along with Ben and Mark. Mark carefully started to lift the tall package ready to carry it into the magic storeroom.

"It's not very heavy," he said. "A girl could lift it."

"I hope so," said Ben. "But don't put it away just yet. Leave it there. I'll probably open it later."

"After I've gone home," said Mark.

"You're catching on," said Ben, keeping the humour in his voice so that Mark would take it as a compliment. "But don't let it worry you. This one is a surprise for everyone. Well, almost everyone."

The cellar room was not used for the rest of the day that Tuesday, and Ben was not going to get back there until after the early evening's staff meeting, so he locked the door to his room, just in case.

After the meeting, when Professor Kennington had said something about showing an important visitor around on Thursday, Ben returned to his hideout and unlocked the door. Shelley and her dance tutor, Carolyn Cleese, joined him a short while later.

"I'm fascinated to know what this latest magic trick of yours has to do with me," said the tutor as she floated into the room. She was no longer lithe and fit as she had been in her younger, performing days, but the short middle-aged woman still moved with a dancer's grace as she entered the darkened dungeon to find out why she had been summoned. "I'm hardly a magic type of person, you know."

Shelley followed her in.

"Me, too," said the student. "I mean, not that I'm not a magic type of person, but that I'm fascinated by... you know what I mean."

"Consider this not so much a magic trick as an illusion," said Ben, as he unpacked the parcel and showed them what the old lady had made for them. Carolyn's eyes lit up when she discovered what it was.

"Wonderful!" she said.

"How are we going to keep it a secret?" said Shelley. "We can hardly rehearse in your storeroom."

"We can store it in my cupboard, and you can practise in here until you need to take it up to your dance studio. Then, I suppose, you'll have to close the curtains or something."

"I'm sure we'll find a way," said Carolyn, enthusiasm and delight beaming from her face. She may not have been a 'magic type of person', but this was one illusion she could really work with.

Later that evening, having left the storeroom locked and secure, Ben paid a visit to the pool room, and looked around at the activity going on. Both of the pool tables were in use, and, as usual, there seemed to be quite a queue. Ben had thought he might finally get round to entering a tournament, and he had played plenty of pool in his time, so that might be his choice of game. However, every time he went into the games room it was teeming with students waiting their turn either on one of the pool tables or on the air hockey. Today was no exception.

Paul Harris was there, with a couple of his usual mates around him, and one more person. Mark Tyler was a part of their crowd this afternoon. Paul was trying to teach him how to play pool, and Mark was doing badly. Poor hand-eye coordination and Asperger's Syndrome often go hand in hand. Mark took ages to line up his shots, carefully examining the table and the positions of the various balls on it, before taking his time aiming, and then missing badly. Paul's mates laughed at Mark's appalling effort, but Paul stopped them.

"No, no that's fine," he said, "it'll take a little while for you to get used to the table, I'm sure. You're doing fine."

Ben watched with some amazement. Paul had obviously taken in what Ben had said to him after last week's chess match, and was being wonderfully patient with Mark as he tried to teach him something that Ben was pretty sure Mark would never be able to learn. But the two of them were getting on, that was the important thing.

Paul looked up from his work and saw Ben. He put his arm out to him and thumped him good and hard on the shoulder.

"Hiya, Ben," he said. Since their little heart-to-heart talk last week, Paul had been treating Ben like a best friend, all chummy and first-name-terms. He said 'hello' every time they passed in a corridor, or met in the dining room, or at times like this. Ben found it a little embarrassing. "How's it goin', mate?"

"Very well," said Ben politely, trying not to encourage the young man.

"Ben's got a girlfriend," said Mark.

"I know," said Paul.

"In Birmingham," said Mark.

"Really?" said Paul. "A girl in every port, eh?"

"Birmingham isn't a port," said Mark. "It's inland."

"Oh," said Paul, humouring him, "I didn't know."

"It's not really a girlfriend," Mark went on to explain. "It's an old lady who does some sewing for him."

"Perhaps he likes older women," said Paul, then he turned to face Ben. "I've been wanting to ask you something. There is a rumour going round that the college is closing. Do you know anything about it?"

"A rumour? No, I don't. And I think I would know if there was any substance to it. We had a staff meeting earlier, and nobody mentioned it then. So, if I were you, I wouldn't worry about it."

"Okay," said Paul, apparently satisfied.

"Rumours, especially ones that aren't true, can be pretty damaging sometimes," said Ben. "I think it would be best if you don't spread it unless you know there's some truth to it. In fact, it's probably best if you don't spread it then, too."

This confused Paul. "So there is some truth to it, then?"

"No," said Ben, once again regretting his clumsy mouth. "Not that I know of."

"It's just, well, I heard something else."

"More rumours?" asked Ben, trying to make a point but failing completely.

"Someone said we've got a visitor coming – someone important."

"Someone's coming on Thursday, yes. The principal will be showing him round. We were only told this afternoon. Word gets around."

"And he's coming to close the place down."

"I wouldn't have thought so. I should think it's a parent trying to decide if this college is the right place to send his son or daughter. Professor Kennington didn't say."

"But it's not an inspector or anything."

"An inspector? Any inspector to this college would find sparkling clean kitchens, the highest quality teaching staff and students who are polite, eager to learn, and of above average intelligence, wouldn't you agree?"

"Of course," said Paul. "Especially the bit about the students."

"Students who don't waste their time with unsubstantiated rumours, perhaps?" Ben added, still not convinced that he had got his message across.

The pool games continued slowly. Ben went on his way, once again not getting a game in. He was getting tired anyway, Tuesdays always seemed like long working days, and he didn't want to be too tired tomorrow. In the evening tomorrow he had a show in Norwich. It was a small club, but it was his first club show since last summer, and you have to start somewhere.

He had a long lie-in the next day, although the noise of the college day in action stopped him from actually sleeping. He got up mid-morning and spent a lot of time preparing, and set off early so that he could get to the venue in good time. Wednesday was not the best day for business, even at a town centre night club, so he had a small, relatively unresponsive audience who found his sense of humour slightly more entertaining than his magic. Still, he enjoyed himself, and, he thought as he drove home at 1.30 in the morning, it was a start.

The following day, the visitor arrived. In spite of not having drunk anything alcoholic to drink last night, Ben felt like he had a hangover. He kept a bottle of spring water near him all day to keep himself going – it was really a cure for a hangover, not for going to bed at 2 am and then not actually sleeping until about five in the morning, but it had to suffice.

He was glad that he did not have his lesson until the afternoon, although Mark joined him during the morning in the cellar, and chattered about the visitor all the time he was there.

"I saw him arrive j-just now," he said. "He's very smart, and has a b-briefcase. I think he's f-from the government."

"Because he's smart and had a briefcase?"

"Yes."

"I can be smart and have a briefcase," said Ben. "That doesn't make me a politician."

"Paul says he m-might b-be a spy."

"That sounds interesting," said Ben, wondering how many different stories Paul could come up with.

"Yes," continued Mark. "He says there's someone at the c-college who is a p-politician's son, or d-daughter, and needs p-protecting."

Ben stopped moving the table he was carrying and put it down carefully. He did not like the way things were going.

"Look, Mark," he said, "in a college like this, especially one where there is so much creativity, rumours get made up. Sometimes, what you hear might be true, other times they're just figments of people's imagination. I wouldn't believe what you hear unless there is some evidence to back it up."

Ben hoped that what he said did not constitute a lie. It was possible that the visitor was from the government, and was checking on the security of the college for the sake of Juliette. However, he was sure that if that was the case, Professor Kennington would have told Ben and Emily about it. He also wondered if Paul's apparent inside information, which was relatively accurate about the college harbouring a political VIP, might also have some truth in it regarding the possible closure of the place.

Ben did not want to pursue this possibility. He knew that the college had been running at a loss, and the goodwill of generous local people had helped out in the past. He also knew that not every local person was in favour of the place continuing to run as a college – the local farmer whose land bordered the grounds on the west side, for example. But he always thought that most colleges were not set up to make a profit, and that they were supported by government grants. However, he did not really know where a college's money would come from, and if he asked Professor Kennington about it, he would have to admit that he was following a rumour, and he was not prepared to do that.

The visitor was a short, stocky man with thick dark hair and big glasses that seemed to fill his small face. Ben saw him as he walked the grounds, escorted by the professor, before his own lesson started. Other classes were active; his was not until the afternoon, so he had some free time. However, he did not want to float around the grounds looking like a chicken drumstick at a vegetarian's party, so he decided he would stay out of the way. He spent some time in his room, and then he went down to the cellar to prepare his lesson. Mark was waiting for him outside the classroom.

"Have you seen the v-visitor yet?" asked Mark.

"No," said Ben. "Well, yes, I caught a glimpse of him. I should think we'll meet him later on. He might come and visit our group."

"Oh," said Mark, becoming nervous. "W-what shall we d-do?"

"The same as usual. If he wants to see how the college works, we must do everything we normally do. Business as usual."

The visitor came to lunch, sitting with Professor Kennington and Bryn Jones. Miko and Mark sat with Ben, and Emily Darkchilde came to join them, which was something she had begun to do more often recently. They chatted about the usual things, but Ben also asked if the visitor had been to her class this morning.

"Yes. He was very pleasant, and listened to one or two students sing for a while."

"Did he pay particular attention to Juliette?"

"No. Why should he?" she said. Ben could not explain his theory about the visitor being from the government in front of the students, so he just shrugged his shoulders and let the conversation move on to other things.

In the afternoon, the professor brought the visitor to the magic class as Ben had predicted. He introduced the short man as Mr Francis from London, explaining nothing about who he was or why he was visiting. Mr Francis asked to see something the students had worked on, and the professor quickly suggested that Richard showed them something before Ben had a chance to put an idea forward.

Richard showed his skills with a cup and ball to the visitor. Ben did not know why the professor chose Richard, who was a long way from the best performer among the students. However, Richard was quite brilliant. He put the equipment on his little wheelchair table attachment, and deftly made the ball disappear from his hand and return to beneath the cup several times in different ways, finally making the ball vanish altogether and be replaced by a tennis ball. Richard's patter was nothing special. He did not seem to be very good at making up a spiel for his routines, but his handling skill with the cup and ball was excellent. The visitor was suitably impressed, and moved on to his next port of call. He paid Juliette no attention at all, so Ben's theories were not supported.

That evening, Ben finally managed to get a game of pool in. The winter tournaments at the college lasted for the first two months or so of the year, and January had come and gone, so Ben thought it was too late to join in, but because pool was so popular and there were only two pool tables, there was a complicated and generous scoring system which allowed the better players to play more games, while allowing newcomers to join in the tournament right up to when there were only two weeks left. The scores were multiplied and divided according to how many games you played and with whom, and the highest scoring players played in a knockout finishing round in the last week of February.

Ben played against a couple of people he had not met before, and Juliette. All three beat him. He was mortified, as he had thought that he was really good at the game. Chummy Paul Harris was nearby, ready to give Ben his own kind of moral support.

"Don't worry, Benjy," he said as they racked up for a new game following Juliette's victory over Ben. "They were really good players. They beat me, too, and I reckon I could make the last round."

"Perhaps I stand a chance against Mark," Ben said.

"If he was in the tournament, everyone would want to play against him to build up their scores. But there are rules against that."

"I've got this concern that I'll be the lowest scoring player."

"And they haven't got a trophy for that."

"Thank God."

"That mysterious visitor," said Paul, suddenly changing the subject. "Do you know who he is?"

"I wouldn't say he was that mysterious. Pretty normal, if you ask me."

"Yes, but do you know who he is?"

"No. I didn't ask. I thought I'd mind my own business."

"Meaning I should mind mine."

Ben looked at Paul. He had changed his mind about this lad. "No, I didn't mean it like that. It's natural to be curious. But it might not be too healthy to speculate, if you know what I mean. False rumours going around the college might be bad for morale."

Paul nodded, and called over his opponent for the next game. Juliette made to leave the games room, but before she did she turned to Ben and said in a voice quiet enough to be heard only by him, "'Benjy'?"

And she left.

I will have to have a word with Paul Harris about his over-familiarity, he thought.

As well as questions from people like Paul, some of the staff, too, were curious about the visitor, and one or two comments Ben heard in the staff room might also have come under the heading 'unhealthy speculation'.

Friday night came eventually, and Ben was delighted to get out of the college and down to the Tin Whistle for the week 'staff unofficial' as it had come to be known. He gave Emily a lift, as it was his turn. She had taken to not drinking most Fridays, so she drove on alternate Fridays so that Ben could have a drink if he wanted.

"So who do you think yesterday's visitor was?" he asked her as they pulled up outside the Tin Whistle.

"I reckon it was a guy called Mr Francis."

"Har har," said Ben.

"I wouldn't worry about it," said Emily with a knowing smile. "You see, Bryn knows the man, and will no doubt spill the beans as the evening goes on and we keep treating him to drinks."

There were more of the staff than usual in the pub that night. It seemed they were all prepared to buy Bryn drinks all night in order to find out more about the visitor.

"Jon Francis," he said when he had made sure everyone there had bought him a drink at least once, "represents a charity that works with disabled people, giving disabled students a chance to do things the rest of us do normally. The professor was trying to get a grant out of him."

"And was Mr Francis suitably impressed with what he saw?" asked Emily.

"Well, he was a little disappointed that there were no disabled people in the dancing class."

"I don't think Richard would go for that," said Ben.

"He'd never get into the ball-gown," said Emily.

"But I think he liked the magic show that young Richard put on," continued Bryn, determined that the limelight, now that he had got it, would not be passed over to 'Laurel and Hardy'. He had nicknamed Ben and Emily that and every other comedy duo he could think of because they seemed to banter all the time, especially during the Friday evening unofficials.

"Did he get to meet Mark?" asked Ben.

"I'm not sure," said Bryn. "He should have, shouldn't he? Perhaps the professor feels a little protective about the lad."

"But he is not likely to let that protectiveness prevent him from going for a grant, surely?"

"Oh, Mike doesn't worry about money," said Bryn. "He would certainly protect any student of his rather than accept money. He just believes that everything will turn out alright in the end."

"And will it?" asked Carolyn Cleese, who very rarely came to the Friday evening pub meetings. She, too, was concerned about the college's financial situation. Ben believed that she had moved her entire family to Norfolk to take on this job, so she was concerned, to say the least, to hear that the college's financial situation might put her job in jeopardy.

"He has had some good contacts in the past," said Bryn. "You know that man who owns the house on the other side of the lake? Well, he's a rich businessman who works in London. Well, he works all over the world really. He has another family home in the centre of London, where his two children are educated, and he owns the neighbouring house here to go to for a bit of peace and quiet. He feels guilty, sometimes, about living somewhere else and visiting here for his own convenience, so he puts a lot of money into the community. He's bailed us out a couple of times in the last few years. But his pocket isn't endless. That's why the professor is looking at other sources of income."

"Surely money from a charity like the one Mr Francis represents will only go to supporting a couple of disabled students?" suggested Ben.

"I reckon so, yes. But do you know how many students we would need to break even?"

"How many?"

"Bearing in mind that we have 60 or so at the moment."

"How many?" Emily repeated Ben's question.

"A hundred and twenty."

The room went quiet. A number of the tutors had heard the speculation that the college might be closing down, and now that idea did not seem too far from reality. There was a subdued chatter for the rest of the evening, but one by one the group from the college drifted away to their homes or their rooms at the big house.

Ben and Emily walked out of the heat of the pub's lounge into the cold night air.

"You started at the college at the same time as me, didn't you?" Ben asked Emily, who nodded.

"Yes. You're thinking it might be a short-term appointment."

"I think it might. I'm sure I could find work easily enough, and it's not that I have a family or anything, but it would be sad to see the college go."

"It's been around for years. It's only this last year that the professor has re-invented it to cover the whole range of subjects it now covers."

"It should be given longer to survive," Ben said. "One year isn't enough. We aren't likely to get 120 next year, after only 60 this year."

They got into the car and sat together in silence, thinking it all over before Ben eventually started the engine.

"Would you be prepared to see it through to the end?" said Emily.

"Yes, I would," said Ben, who had been thinking along the same lines. "I can afford to work for less, and for my job to come to an end without having looked elsewhere."

"I think I can, too. Shall we commit to doing that?"

"Agreed."

And they drove home in silence.

The weekend was dull and overcast, which reflected the mood of the few staff still on site. Emily did her bit for the local children, and then she went home. The kitchen and household staff had picked up the general melancholy which had crept in to the staff, and everything felt low. The time of year brought the type of weather which depressed people, and that, coupled with the rumours of the college closing kept people feeling low.

On Sunday afternoon, Ben had an appointment at an old people's home in Franklin, a nearby small town. They were quiet but appreciative, which satisfied him, because he did not want to be exuberant and energetic as he often was in his performances. In the evening, he sat at the meal table with Professor Kennington, who he talked to about the speculation he had heard, both among the staff and students during the last week.

"Most colleges run without any money," said the professor. "Except Oxford. And Cambridge."

"They all get money from somewhere," said Ben, who really didn't know whether the professor was right or not.

"And so do we. I think we can greatly increase our numbers next year. We already have more bookings for next year's intake than we did this time last year."

"And how many is that?"

"Well, last year we had sixteen."

"And this year?"

"Seventeen," said the professor.

14.

Ben heard shouting. There was something distinctive about the angry voice. It was the voice of a male, adult Welshman. Bryn Jones bellowed with a rich, melodic, but extremely loud and irate roar.

"You skulk around the house like you own the place, you walk the grounds like you're hunting for poachers, and you treat the staff as if they did not belong here. Just who do you think you are?"

"I know exactly who I am," said the target of his ire, Helen Bywater. She was not in the slightest fazed by the angry man in front of her. "And I am beginning to get an idea of who you are, too."

"How dare you…" Bryn began, and Ben intervened.

There was a stillness about the early spring air which made the sound carry from the walled garden where Bryn and Helen were arguing across the whole of the grounds. It was cold and it was early on Saturday morning, so none of the students were out yet. Nevertheless, there was no doubt that only the heaviest sleepers would still be in their beds after this racket. Bryn had arrived on that Saturday morning intending to assist some of his students who had work to finish, but he was still a little hung over after last night's unofficial and they weren't up yet, so he had taken a walk to get himself going. He was not in a good mood, and he had nearly collided with Helen on his walk around the grounds.

"I'm sure two adults can conduct themselves in a manner which," started Ben, then he realised he hadn't thought out the rest of his sentence, so he stuttered for a moment, "which wouldn't wake up everybody else."

"You're awake already," said Helen.

"I didn't drink last night. It was my turn to drive."

"You can mind your own bloody business," said Bryn, but he had lowered his voice a little and some of the venom had gone from his voice. At least, his voice was a little less venomous when it was directed at Ben.

"Can I walk with you, Bryn?" Ben asked. He was talking to the art teacher, but his eyes flashed at Helen, who got the message. She nodded, and moved away. One or two curtains upstairs were twitching.

Bryn just stood still for a moment, as if trying to work out why he had got so angry. He was squinting, probably more from the effects of the hangover than the bright morning sunshine.

"Coffee?" Ben suggested.

"Never works for me," said Bryn.

"Water?"

"Already had enough to float a battleship."

Emily came out of the main gate to join them. She had stayed the night in her 'Friday night' room to save going home after last night's staff social. She noticed Helen walking away, so she followed her to chat. Ben and Bryn walked off across the wet, grassy field at the front of the house, towards the trees.

"Are you worried about the college's financial situation?" said Ben. "I mean, you've been here for years. Most of us are new; we only started when the professor reinvented the college. But you…"

"Is that what you think this is?" said Bryn, a little anger still in his voice, but the old Bryn beginning to come back to him. "You think I'm concerned about job security? You're talking out of your…"

"I was just saying, that's all. I mean, Emily and I talked about it yesterday on the way home. We want to support the college to the end. We believe in the professor's vision."

"But you also have to look after your own future," said Bryn. "For what it's worth, I believe in Mike's vision, too. But that isn't what's upsetting me this morning. It's that Bywater woman. She gets right on my nerves."

Ben laughed. Since she arrived in December, Helen Bywater had got on his nerves, too, and Juliette's. Even Professor Kennington seemed less than comfortable with her at times, and he usually accepted everyone. The prank they had played on her at the end of the Christmas holidays helped to lighten the load a bit, but while Juliette was now a little easier with her bodyguard, everyone else was still bothered by her. Everyone had seemed to accept that she was part of the college somehow, although nobody knew who she was. She seemed to do very little, and yet she was always there, ready to annoy or interfere. In fact, she interfered very little, but her presence around people and places made it seem like she was interfering.

"She dominates the scenery," Bryn continued, and his voice began to rise in volume again. "She does nothing, but gets in the way of everything. She hangs around the students in particular, but watches the men as if they were about to molest one of the girls. Who is she, some kind of bodyguard or something?"

"Yes," said Ben, almost without thinking. Then he stopped walking. He had to try and work out what he was about to do, and he couldn't do that and walk at the same time. He knew he shouldn't have said that, and he couldn't take it back. Bryn was not a stupid man, as he had already proven with his deductions about Mark. He had just worked out the truth about Helen Bywater, too, although he was not completely aware of it. Ben thought of trying to cover his slip, but he felt he could no longer hide the truth from this colleague of his who was clever enough to work it out for himself anyway.

"Yes, what?" said Bryn.

"She *is* a bodyguard. Emily and I know about it because we work with Helen's, what does she call it, 'primary'."

"Who?"

"Juliette MacIntyre," said Ben, realising that he could no longer get out of saying it. "She's the daughter of a politician who is currently working in the Middle East in negotiations with religious and political organisations who use terrorism to make their point. Juliette's presence here is a secret to protect her from harm. That's why she needs a bodyguard. The people who were watching her from outside the college before caused some distress among the students, so her father arranged for Mrs Bywater to come here."

"My God," said Bryn, joining all the dots. "The peeping toms. They were bodyguards, too."

"Yes, I'm afraid so. The professor asked us to keep it a secret. I'm sorry."

"You're sorry? Not as sorry as he is going to be. We've been friends for longer than I've been here at the college, and that seems like half a millennium as it is! Well, he's going to get my resignation, as of this morning."

"No, Bryn, wait!" Ben called, but the Welshman turned and stormed off towards the main entrance of the house. Ben followed, realising that, once again, his efforts to help had turned sour. He stopped at the front door, however, because Richard was just coming out as he was going in.

"Hi, Richard, want a hand?"

"No I'm fine thanks, Ben," said Richard. "They'll be here for me in a minute."

"Who will?"

"I get taken to physio every Saturday morning. They arranged it for Saturdays to let me study all week. The day after my physio my legs hurt, so I can get to rest on Sundays, and do nothing."

"That's why I never see you on Sundays. You're writhing in agony somewhere private."

"It's not that bad," said Richard with half a smile. "Mostly."

Ben didn't know what to say next, so there was an uncomfortable silence for a few moments.

"How are you doing in the tournaments?" the teacher asked eventually.

"Fairly well. I might win the poker, and I am in the top ten in two or three other games. Meesh always beats me at Fluxx. She shouldn't, it's mostly a game of luck, but she just seems to know what card combinations are likely to come up next."

"Perhaps she's just lucky," Ben said, when he should really have said 'Who's Meesh?'

A taxi drove through the car park, and stopped at the nearest point to the main entrance that the driveway would allow. Richard wheeled himself towards the vehicle, and Ben accompanied him.

"You do this on your own?" he said, as the driver got out and assisted Richard into the car, which had been converted to make room for wheelchairs.

"I'm a grown-up now," said Richard, as the taxi driver nodded to the tutor, got back into the driving seat and drove down the road. Ben watched him go, and wondered why he did not know that about Richard's physiotherapy before today. The year was half over, and he did not know what was going on about him.

Ben returned to the building wondering about things. The students were beginning to get up, so he might get a game of pool in before the day got busy. He went into the pool room, where two of the students from other classes were playing. He realised that he did not know their names. Six months and only 63 students, and he didn't know most of them. He had made his world smaller than necessary.

Shelley joined them after a few minutes, and proceeded with her game against Ben. He had improved over the few games he had played, but she was still better than him, and won a close game. When he stood up from the table, he noticed Bryn was standing at the door. What must he feel, angry as he was, to see the person who had offered him such support playing games with the students instead of being there for him?

"Okay?" said Ben, rather feebly.

"Yeah," said Bryn, more subdued than usual. "Professor Kennington wants to see you."

"Ooohh!" said Shelley. "In trouble for flirting with the staff?" she laughed, but then she apologised when she saw the look on his face. He might really be in trouble. Ben left the games room.

He knocked on the door of the principal's office. Michael Kennington opened it personally, ushering him in to the room.

"You said you could keep a secret," he started, and then waited for Ben's response. Ben explained the circumstances of this morning's cross between Helen and Bryn.

"I think I had a duty to tell Bryn. He is your most loyal supporter, and he was beginning to work things out about Helen anyway. He's not stupid, you know." Ben thought he was doing alright justifying himself until he said that, and he immediately regretted saying it.

"Yes," said the professor with a thoughtful voice. "I suppose I should have told Bryn. And Carolyn, perhaps. In fact, how many of the staff should I tell? Or more to the point, how many should I not tell?"

"Did Bryn hand in his notice?"

"No, he didn't. I think he had calmed down a bit by the time he came up here. That's the advantage of having an upstairs office."

"He's okay with it, then? I mean with Helen being Juliette's bodyguard."

"I'm not sure he is entirely okay with it, but I think he sees that there is little choice in the matter. No, what upset him, he said, was the fact that I did not tell *him*. She is not in his class, you see, so I felt I did not need to. But he thought I was wrong."

The professor's tone at this point was one of doubt. He seemed to believe that perhaps he had been wrong in not telling more of the staff about the bodyguard situation. He looked Ben in the eyes.

"You would tell me if you thought I was wrong, wouldn't you?"

"I think so, if I thought it was my place," said Ben. "But I'm not sure whether you were right or wrong in Juliette's case. Secrecy was an important consideration, after all."

"I trust my staff, Ben. I should have told them. I was going to tell you off for breaking your secrecy promise to me, but I am not so sure you were wrong, now, after all. I think I shall tell them all."

"Today? They are not all here today, being Saturday."

"But the ones that aren't are available to telephone."

"Do you want me to tell anybody?"

"No, thank you. As the principal, it is my job, and they should hear it from me. Bryn was angry because you told him when it was my job."

Ben agreed, and the two of them stayed in the office and chatted for a while about all sorts of things. As usual, Ben tried to make jokes or tell funny stories of what his students were getting up to in the classroom to lighten the atmosphere a little, but the professor was obviously burdened by what he considered to be his mistake, and, while he smiled politely, he was never going to laugh out loud, not this morning.

Ben departed the office a short while later, and wandered around the premises a bit. He did not see either Helen or Bryn, and he made his way out to the garden wall at the side of the house and sat on it. He felt like putting his head in his hands and moping, but sitting on that low wall as he was would have made him look like a garden gnome.

The sun was bright but not strong as winter was drawing to a close. The flowers were beginning to show in the garden behind him, but they were fragile, and a late frost would kill them if it happened. Ben pondered on the professor and the burdens he was carrying. How did a man with Asperger's Syndrome cope with the financial plight of the college, and the secrecy of Juliette's situation, and the lies he was called upon to tell to keep her safe?

A short while later, a shadow fell across him. He looked up to see the beautiful form of Emily Darkchilde looking down on him.

"Hi," he said.

"You doing anything for the rest of the day?"

"Not particularly," he answered.

"Then you need to be off the premises for a while. Come with me."

They got into her car and she drove. He unburdened himself to her on the journey, leaning back against the head rest. He complained about being the one who had to tell Bryn about the bodyguard situation, about how he thought the professor felt about keeping secrets, and about the students in his class who were just, quite frankly, not very good at magic. He told her about Paul's over-familiarity and his concerns about Mark. She didn't say anything, but listened to his story. Then he ran out of story, and the mood began to change as they continued in silence. It was a pleasant kind of silence, like two people enjoying each other's company without having to say anything.

Eventually, Emily pulled up outside a remarkable little cottage in the country. It was set in its own grounds, barely, and the surrounding garden was overgrown just enough to show that it had been tended, but not much. The house itself, while quite small, was stunningly beautiful, cleanly painted with a deep varnished wooden door. Emily got her front door keys out.

"You live here?" said Ben, amazed.

"Yes."

"But it's a two-hour journey from the college!"

"No, it isn't. It's less than half an hour from the college. We drove for two hours because you needed it. We took the scenic route, if you like."

They went inside the little cottage, and Emily sat Ben down in the living room while she went to make a cup of tea for them both. He sat in one of the two deep armchairs and looked around the room. The old fireplace had in it a gas fire instead of the coal fire that had no doubt once been there, but it still retained its old-fashioned look. On the mantelpiece there were two finely detailed statuettes of dancers, but nothing else. A backwards clock with its entire face reading anti-clockwise, and the hands moving the wrong way, adorned a wall. This was Emily's home and it expressed her personality in the humour of the clock as well as the good taste of the porcelain figures. It was not a full room, there was little clutter and the ornaments were limited to those on the mantelpiece and the wall. But it was comfortable, and warm in spite of the fire not being on, and Ben found that the tension in him that had not quite vanished with the journey was finally dissipating now.

Emily came back into the room with a mug of tea. Ben thought as he took it from her that it should have been a fine china teacup in a house like this, but he appreciated the size of the mug anyway. They sat down and drank together, still silent for a while because it seemed like a shame to break it.

"So, Darkchilde," said Ben eventually. "What kind of name is that? Is it German?"

"It's a stage name," Emily said. "My real name is boring."

"Emily Boring," said Ben. "I can see why you changed it."

"LOL," said Emily, dryly.

"What?" said Ben.

"You spend far too much time with your magic props and not enough time with computers," said Emily. "And for that 'Emily Boring' joke, I'm not going to tell you my real surname."

"It's not Meesh, is it?"

"No, it's not Meesh," said Emily, puzzled at the question.

"So how did you think of the name Darkchilde?"

"It was my father's stage name. He was a rock singer with a band."

"Successful?"

"Within reason, yes. He's retired now, and lives on the south coast. Every now and then the members of the old band get together for a reunion bash."

"Did you ever think of joining a rock band?"

"My dad always encouraged me to make the most of my voice. He's a bit croaky now, from not training properly, he says. I think he puts it on a bit because the audiences like it. Anyway, when I did voice training I discovered where my voice was best used, and I'm pretty certain it's not in a rock band!"

"Ever thought of singing professionally?"

"I already do," she answered. "I've done a few London soul clubs, and there is a night club in Stevenbridge where I sing occasionally. It's good not to be teaching sometimes."

"I suppose it would be," said Ben. "It must be lovely, driving to work in this countryside."

"Except when it's pouring with rain, which is quite often in this part of the world, yes," she laughed. "I imagine it's worse for you, living at the college as well as working there. Except for your occasional adventures into the murky world of children's parties, you don't get out much."

"I love the teaching."

"But you need to take a break from it. Get a life outside your work at the college. You're good for those kids you work with, in more ways than just teaching. But you can't let yourself burn out – then you'd be useless to everyone, including yourself. That's why I decided I needed to live out here."

"It's lovely. And isolated." Ben put his head back in the chair and closed his eyes. "I could go to sleep here."

"Be my guest," said Emily. "Anytime you want to come here, be my guest. Except that I've got a key and you haven't."

"I realised today that I didn't know the names of a couple of the kids at the college. For all the time I spend there, I still live in a very small part of it."

"Locked away in the cellar – the college's dark secret," said Emily, mimicking quite well Juliette's 'mystical' voice and style.

"I walk the grounds almost every day. I have only two lessons a week plus Fridays, so I've got plenty of time. But I haven't really connected with the rest of the college. It took me till February to sign up to the games, and I've only played a few people, mostly ones I already know."

"And it's taken you until now, when you are away from the place, to see what's happening. That's what I meant when I said you need to get away, to have something outside the college to go to. Even if it's only a little spot on a hill under a tree with a beautiful view. I know exactly the place, by the way."

"A tree with a beautiful view?"

"No, a view with a beautiful tree. But it is worth thinking about, isn't it?"

Ben did not sleep as he had said he could, but the two of them chatted about anything and everything. After all, who would sleep in the presence of such a beautiful woman? As they talked, Emily did not reveal her real surname, but they laughed a lot together and Ben felt able to let go of his stresses completely. It was dark when Emily drove Ben back to the college, although it was not late. They said their goodbyes and he watched her drive down the road before turning to go into the house.

Inside, Bryn and Professor Kennington were having a hot drink in the staff room. Ben resisted the urge to say 'what kind of day have you had, then?' The professor told him that he had spoken to every staff member personally, including the kitchen and ground staff, and had told them about Helen and Juliette.

"Everybody was understanding and supportive," he said. "I should have told them before. I apologise for being angry at you for doing the right thing."

"And I'd like to say thank you for supporting me this morning," said Bryn. "I was out of order, and I appreciated your intervention."

"You escaped to get a bit of time to yourself, then," said the professor. "That's good; you spend far too much time here."

"I didn't so much escape as was rescued," said Ben.

"Pursuing your destiny at last, is it?" asked Bryn.

"Sorry?"

"Oh, never mind," said Bryn, looking disappointed that Ben did not understand him.

On Sunday mid-afternoon, Ben received a telephone call. Most of the calls he received were on his mobile and were from friends and family, but for this one he was called to the office.

"Mr April?" the man said.

"Yes?"

"The magic man?"

"Yes, that's me," said Ben with a smile. It had been a while since he had been called that by anyone other than a student. "How can I help you?"

The caller was the fixtures manager from the Shining Star nightclub in Stevenbridge, the nearest large town, about 20 miles away. He invited Ben to perform at the club.

"I'm afraid it's short notice, but we have a cancellation, and we need somebody to do an early evening performance next Wednesday. A thirty minute spot at around 8.30pm. Someone said you were good. Any chance you are available?"

"Yes, I can do that," said Ben a little too eagerly, and the arrangements were made. As he put the telephone down, he smiled to himself. It was about time he got a break like this, and the Shining Star had a reputation for performance quality. He hadn't thought to ask who had recommended him.

He would have to be at his very best for the show, and he did not have much time to prepare.

15.

A battered old vehicle drew up in the car park, and out stepped a casually-dressed man carrying a large suitcase. That is to say, he did not actually step out of the vehicle carrying it; he removed it from the boot of his car, and then he carried it towards the great house, looking about him in wonder as if he had never been to such a palace before. He walked with his suitcase to the front door. Ben and Mark were waiting in the entrance hall for him, and came out to meet him.

"Steve!" Ben said, taking his case and shaking his hand. "It's good to see you. Mark will take your case downstairs, and I'll take you to the staff room to grab a cup of coffee."

"Downstairs?" said Stephen Goss, Ben's guest for the day. "So you are below stairs staff, are you? In the old days, the servants were all…"

"Back when you were young?" Ben interrupted. Stephen was an older man, with wisps of grey hair floating from his nearly-bald head, and masses of laughter lines on his face. His warm brown eyes told people that he enjoyed his life. He was dressed in loose brown trousers and a baggy pullover, but his clothes still looked smart and not clown-like. When he performed as a clown, he dressed differently, so that there was no doubt to his audiences as to who he was supposed to be.

Not many of the staff members were in the staff room, as the staggered nature of the lessons in an average college day did not allow for much socialising, so it had become the habit of the staff to postpone their use of the room to the evening. After a coffee and a 'comfort break', he made his way to Ben's cellar. He was in good time to get ready before the class started at 11 o'clock. He stood in front of the assembled class when Ben's students had all arrived, still dressed in his 'civilian' clothes, as he called them. Without an introduction from Ben, he addressed the group.

"I am Steve Goss, and I am a clown." He paused for a thought. "That sounds a bit like Alcoholics Anonymous, doesn't it?"

"I've done that one," said Ben.

"I can see that it might be difficult to deliver my lines this morning, as we have a heckler in the audience. Today, children, we are going to play a game called 'kill the teacher'."

He went on to describe what a clown is and how clowning would be different from magicianing. He paused at the delivery of that line.

"Magicianing?" he said. "Is there such a word? Well, there is now. Clowns do magic tricks, of course, but a clown would normally pick his tricks differently from a magician. While Ben might work on his sleight of hand, or work with an assistant who does all the real work for him, a clown would look for colourful..."

"Self-working tricks that don't need any skill to operate," Ben finished for him.

"...Yeah, that, and not waste his time trying to learn skills that nobody appreciates anyway."

"I appreciate them," said Mark, interrupting to come to Ben's defence. Ben, from behind where Steve was facing, poked his tongue out at the old man.

"Actually," said Steve, looking straight at Mark by way of an apology, putting on a more serious tone for a few moments, "I didn't mean to undermine what Ben has been teaching you these last couple of terms. I love to watch a skilful magician. I even like to watch Ben sometimes. We are old friends and we often have a go at each other with the old 'clown versus magician' banter, but we don't mean it. In fact, in the world of children's entertainment, skilled magicians who entertain children with magic shows, dressed in their top hats and tails, are still often referred to as clowns."

"I always say I am not a clown," said Ben, reinforcing what his friend had just said, "although I clown around a bit. But I have a great deal of respect for real clowns, people like Steve, who have worked for years to improve their performance skills."

"Who knows?" said Steve. "I might get it right one day."

"Is it true that all clowns are different," asked Xander, "and that no two different clowns have the same make-up?"

"In traditional clowning, yes," said Steve, "although anyone can put a bit of lipstick on their cheeks and call themselves a clown, so not everybody sticks to that tradition. But among the serious clowns, their face is their own, and it means something to have your own unique style of make-up. Many famous clowns have their own face – and some have two."

"So what you're saying is that clowns are two-faced," said Ben.

"I have a full make-up kit for the big clown events, and a quick slap-on for small shows," the clown continued, ignoring Ben's quip. He showed them his make-up kit which included some serious stage make-up, and, as he had already taken up so much time talking without showing them anything, he opened up his case and let them take a look at the clothes and equipment that were inside. He explained that he had not included any magic tricks in his kit today because Ben would have already bored them to tears with that kind of stuff.

After a bit more serious chatter, he paused, getting himself ready for a performance piece.

"I say, I say, I say," he said in a music hall voice, "What's the secret of good comedy?"

"I don't know," said Ben in an equally exaggerated tone, "What's the…"

"Timing!"

He talked to them about comic timing. He talked about the 'rule of three', which Ben had already touched upon in their talks about performance styles.

"The rule of three, as applied to clowning, is where you are trying to do something really difficult, and you try and fail twice, then succeed the third time. It's where you hit someone with a custard pie twice, and they hit you back with the third. It's almost as if you have a musical beat to work to."

He also showed them a little slapstick material which had Mark and Len aching with laughter. He showed them how to trip up in a way that looked convincing, and he borrowed a silk handkerchief which seemed to disappear and reappear all over the place, much to his feigned annoyance. He did a little comedy mime which was clever and funny. And he juggled. He juggled with balls, clubs, knives, diabolo, flower sticks and silk handkerchiefs. Len's eyes nearly popped out of his head with the style and complexity of his juggling skills.

The lesson was full of questions and answers, humour and clowning, and the comedy double-act which Ben and Steve seemed to create when they were together kept the talk sparkling. In fact, they had never been a double act, but when they were in the same room, there was a spark between them which resulted in the funny banter to which the class was subjected.

At lunchtime, Miko, Len and Xander all sat with Steve and the lesson seemed to continue. Something about him provoked interest and discussion about the profession, and how someone would get into a job like this. As Ben observed the students' responses and interaction with his old friend, he realised that Steve was filling a gap that Ben had overlooked in the planning of the year's work – he was telling them about his working life, rather than the mechanics of magic, or clowning, or juggling. Because he had not come in costume or make-up but as an ordinary person, the course of the conversation had been about the profession, not the action, of clowning. On his own table with Mark, Ben revealed that Steve was one of the key people who inspired him to become a magician.

"When I saw him, I knew I didn't want to be a clown," he said.

In the afternoon, Steve decided to go for a wander around the college, except that this time, he took some of his juggling equipment with him. Len followed him, and took a special interest when he went outside and started juggling with bricks. They were not real bricks of course, but 'practical joke' bricks made of sponge, but they looked real. He threw one to the shy young lad, who caught it easily. He passed them all over to him, and watched him juggle for a while. He noticed that Len had no difficulty adapting to different juggling items, so he got some of his other stuff out and Len demonstrated his growing ability with that, too.

"How long have you been juggling?" the old clown asked him.

"I just started last year," said Len.

"And you have never performed in front of anybody."

"No, I don't think I am ready."

"I can assure you you're not ready," said Steve. "And you will never be ready. Not until you've done it when you're *not* ready."

"But Ben, Mr April, he says you shouldn't perform a trick until you are absolutely ready. That tricks are spoilt by performing them too soon."

158

"That's right, if you are performing magic tricks. But not with juggling. You need to learn what entertains people, and you do that by performing. Or, if not performing, at least juggling in front of people to ask their opinions and gauge their reactions."

Steve taught Len to juggle clubs with him, so the two of them made a little double act on the front lawn. When they finished, the old man turned to the house and bowed. Len turned too, a little dumbstruck. There were people in the doorway, looking through the window of the dance studio downstairs and the film studio above it, in fact, it looked like every window had a member of the college looking out of it, watching Len and his sidekick do their act. They all started cheering and applauding. Then Steve put his hands out to indicate that Len was the star of the show, and applauded him with all the others.

"*Now* you're ready," he said.

Steve departed shortly after, leaving a newly inspired Len and a number of the students ready to try something new. Ben felt that his visit had given the class a new lease of life. Shelley was discussing the dance-like qualities of slapstick with Juliette. Miko was talking in his slightly improved English about how he might want to explore mime. Even Xander was inspired to try a new method of overcoming his stage fright. He took Ben aside for a moment, talking to him as quietly as possible so as not to be overheard by his classmates.

"Do you have any masks in your collection of props?" he asked, quietly so that nobody else could hear him.

"Yes, I think so."

"I've been thinking, when clowns have make-up on it's like a mask. Hiding behind a mask would be a good way to overcome something like stage fright, don't you think?"

"It might," said Ben, and they returned to the cellar to find something. He pulled out a 'Phantom of the Opera' style of mask and let Xander have a look at it.

"This'll do," Xander smiled, turning it over in his hands. "Will the theatre be available?"

"The downstairs one will be busy with gamers now that the college day is over. But the upstairs one should be free."

So they went up to the smaller theatre. Xander put on the mask and climbed onto the stage. Ben watched as the lad's knees trembled, saw his body posture change from the confident, attractive 'babe magnet' that Xander liked to think he was to a nervous wreck as he saw, in his mind's eye, an audience watching him. He quickly stepped down from the stage.

"It was worth a try," he said, sadly, to Ben as he returned the mask.

Ben had an early night and rose early the following morning. He had a free day at the college, but should spend the time preparing for that night's performance at the Shining Star nightclub in Stevenbridge. He smiled at the idea that it was Stephen the Clown yesterday and Steven*bridge* tonight.

He got there early, so that he could work out the final details of his act. He had never seen the place before, so he did what he had taught his students to do and had a look at the layout of the nightclub before actually performing there. The stage was a small, raised area against one wall, surrounded on three sides by tables and chairs. There was, offset a little from the stage, an area for the live band. Mentally, Ben dropped a couple of tricks he had brought along from the performance as they were completely unsuitable for this kind of setting. Half of the audience might be able to see what he would show an auditorium full of people who were below and in front of him. There was a chance to move among the audience, and he thought of Juliette, who had moved through the audience at the Halloween concert last year. He should have brought her or some of the class along, and they could have performed one of the tricks which would need a 'beautiful assistant' to do all the work for him, as Stephen Goss would say.

It was 7.30, and the place was just about empty. The man who had booked him greeted him and showed him around, explaining that the evening did not really take off until at least 8 o'clock, which was why they had booked him for 8.30. He went around to the 'backstage' area, a tiny room where performers could drop their stuff, to get himself ready.

At 8 o'clock, still there were only two or three customers. He went to the bar to get a drink. He never drank alcohol on a job, so he ordered a soft drink, for which the barman told him there was no charge because he was performing, and he looked around at the empty room. It was Wednesday, of course, so there would not be that many guests tonight.

Most people would get paid on the Friday, or on the last day of the month, so who would be able to afford to go clubbing tonight? And what better time to try out a new act you haven't seen before than on a night when you are fairly sure you aren't going to be full? The management of this club were good enough to give him a chance, but they didn't know him, so why should they inflict this stranger on a full house? He looked at the four or five people who were here. They were a little spread out, so he couldn't even go and do a little close-up magic with them. While he was pondering his best strategy to impress the management so that they would invite him on a night when they were expecting actual customers, a large party arrived.

In front was Mark Tyler with his mother, followed by Xander and Miko. Then Len wheeled in Richard, and then Shelley and Juliette walked behind, each dressed in their best 'night out' dresses, and each with a man on their arms. The men with them were Professor Michael Kennington and Bryn Jones. Carolyn Cleese followed them in, also in her 'going out' best.

The words 'set-up' went through his mind. Of course, at some stage in the last couple of days he must have mentioned it to the staff that he had this job here tonight. It was Bryn, he thought. He remembered talking to Bryn about it on Sunday evening, and the art teacher had obviously had enough time to arrange for Ben's entire class (all seven of them) to be there that evening. He had even arranged for Carolyn to join them, in spite of the fact that she had told him that she was not too keen on magic, probably because they needed the extra transport.

What was he going to do? Had he already taught them all of the tricks that he had prepared for that evening? No, he thought, he had one or two things that they might not have seen yet. So he prepared to give them a show to remember.

In the next few minutes, more guests arrived, so there was a reasonably-sized audience there by the time he was being introduced. A stagehand put his table onto the small stage, then the same man put his big box carefully onto the centre of the table, following all the instructions Ben had given him earlier. Ben walked onto the stage when the compere had finished giving him a big build-up. Ben slotted in the back of his mind what the man had said about his being 'all the way from Birmingham' and tried to concentrate instead on being the best that he could be. After all, it was better than 'all the way from Lockley in the middle of nowhere'.

He walked onto the performer's area, dressed in the traditional black suit of the magician. Even his little magician's table was the kind of thing you would expect to see a traditional magician use. It consisted of a fairly small board on a single long leg with a tripod-style stand at the bottom. It was covered in a small black red-trimmed tablecloth which covered as little as possible so as not to suggest it was hiding anything.

Ben held a glittering black cane in his hand. He threw it to his other hand. Then he threw it back, and missed. The cane flew around his hand and back onto its starting position. He looked puzzled, and put the cane down, resting it against his table. As he moved away from it, his hand going to his jacket pocket for the next trick, the cane seemed to follow him. It moved faster, virtually flying around between his hands and even around the back of his head, forcing him to duck, as the band played 'In the Mood'. Then, at last, as the band played the final notes, the cane came to rest in his hand again, and he laid it down out of the spotlight on the floor at the back of the raised area.

The music started up again, this time playing their odd version of the X-Files theme, which Ben had asked them to play for this next magical routine when he had arrived. They were playing it badly; it was not, after all, a conventional nightclub band piece. He started to show the audience the box that was on his table. It seemed to be a container inside a container. He lifted up the outer square box, a wooden, ornately decorated box, which, when removed from the table, left behind a white metal tube. Having showed the audience the outer box from all angles, he returned it to its place as a shield for the inner tube, and then he lifted the tube out. He showed the audience the tube, again from different angles. He put his arm through the centre of the tube to show it was hollow and empty. Then he returned it. He looked into the tube, now protected by its box-like shield, put his hand into it, and pulled out a two-metre-long magic wand. After this, he pulled out, rhythmically so that it looked like it was all because of the 'mystical' music, several coloured scarves and streamers.

He knew that the students had seen the 'Square Circle' before, as they had all spent plenty of time practising with it. He was fairly sure that they might not have seen the floating cane, and his next few tricks were a mixture of what they knew and what they didn't. But he did the next lot without the music. The band would have been great if they had rehearsed together beforehand, but, given the preparation time he had, he thought he would just do his stand-up unaccompanied.

"Tonight, I am going to reveal the secrets of magic," he said in a hushed, conspiratorial voice. He leaned towards the silent, expectant audience. "Keep practising."

He moved away from the stage area a bit, but he had not practised with the lighting engineer or the headset microphone they had given him either, so he kept his movements limited and simple. He did a few tricks on the nearest tables, flirted with Juliette as if he had never met her, and asked Shelley to join him up on the stage. He went into a routine they had previously practised together during class, although, among the audience, only the students knew that.

He went over his thirty-minute slot by just a few minutes, but he was sure that was okay, because the audience clapped and cheered and seemed to enjoy the evening. Of course, he thought, having your own 'supporters club' to add volume to the clapping and cheering helps.

He went offstage at the end, and the mc announced the next act, a singer familiar to the club. She was not in his tiny 'backstage' room, so he presumed that they had allowed her to get ready in a more private place. Having noted there was not a lot of room for private places, Ben guessed that would mean the ladies' toilets.

The guest singer started to sing while Ben was still emptying his pockets of the various gadgets and gimmicks he had used in the act, and one or two he had not got so far as using. He stopped dead as he recognised the singer's voice, having stood outside her classroom and listened to her many times over the last six months. It was Emily Darkchilde.

Leaving his stuff untidily piled in his case, he immediately left the little backstage room and joined the college group at their tables. They had reserved a seat for him.

Emily sang several pieces, most of which he had heard before while listening in on her practice sessions. She had the most enchanting voice, he thought, and she had long ago become his favourite singer. However, here in this club, in just the right environment for her, she was at her best. She was dressed in a long blue gown, light in material at the top to keep her cool, but covering her legs to the floor. She moved with a practised grace, her eyes taking in everyone in the room, singing each song as if it was only for the individual listener.

She sang one of Ben's favourite songs, 'Forever Autumn', and, at the end, she sang her own favourite, 'Love Changes Everything', walking around the tables, lingering a little on Ben's group, which was, after all, the largest party in the room.

Ben was not unhappy that he had been so out-performed. This was obviously something she did a lot. She was not only really good at it, but she was also familiar with the club itself, and it looked like some of the other guests in the now crowded room also knew her and were fans. After she had finished her set, she came and joined them at the table, where she received the congratulations and appreciation that she deserved. It took her a few minutes to actually reach them, as some of the other guests stopped her to chat and say how much they loved her performance. A number of them shook her hand, and she paused to acknowledge everyone who took the time to say 'thank you'.

"You were fantastic," Ben finally got to say to her. "Did I ever tell you that 'Forever Autumn' is my favourite song?"

"Yes, you did," she smiled, "that's why I put it in."

"It's even more my favourite now."

"Can something be even more favourite?" she said.

"You told me you had performed here before," Ben said to her.

"Yes," said Emily, "but I think I might have forgotten to say that I sing here quite a lot. You know I said you should get a life outside the college? Well, this is part of *my* life. I've become good friends with the owner."

"So it was you. You arranged for me to be invited."

"Sorry."

"No, I'm delighted. Word-of-mouth, friend of a friend, that's often how we get business."

"I know. I got in here through my father."

"He used to sing here?"

"This used to be a rock club. It still has what they call 'heavy' nights every now and then. But the owner wanted something a little more sophisticated."

164

"So they invited Ben?" said Bryn. "They must have a definition of the word 'sophisticated' that I haven't come across before."

"I think they mean Emily," said Carolyn, not realising that Bryn was joking. Then the penny dropped. "Of course, you were good, too, Ben."

The booking manager came across to the table a little later.

"You were brilliant as usual, babe," he said to Emily, and then he turned to Ben. "We liked what you did, Magic Man." (He had forgotten Ben's name.) "We've been chatting about it out the back, and we'd like you to come back some time soon. We'd like it if you can do some table hopping, and when you're on stage get some of the audience up, too, like you did with the young lady there," he indicated Shelley, who, with her dancer's grace and a fabulous if revealing dress, had obviously caught the man's attention. Ben realised that this man had watched the act carefully, and knew his business.

"So we'll be in touch," he said. "Maybe for a Saturday show next time."

16.

"Can I come in?" said Juliette as she knocked on the cellar door. It was a Monday morning, and Ben had come down to the cellar to tidy up a little for the following day's lesson. In fact, it was more than just tomorrow's lesson which he was tidying up for. With a lesson on Thursday afternoon and Friday's practice and rehearsal time, Ben had frequently spent some of Saturday making the place tidy, but over the past weekend he had been busy with other things. Firstly, he had spent some of the morning outside Emily Darkchilde's room listening to her sing. Later in the day, he had visited Carolyn Cleese's dance studio to find out how Shelley was getting on with her little secret. In the evening, he'd had a small show for the Shining Star nightclub. It turned out to be not so small a show, of course, being a Saturday night. There had been some drunkenness and disruption during his act, which he felt he had coped with fairly well. Nevertheless, it had been an exhausting evening, resulting in his subsequent extensive lie-in and general laziness on Sunday morning. Well, on Sunday all day, to be honest.

That was one reason why the room needed tidying up right now. The other one was that Professor Kennington had informed the staff that he had arranged for the local television station to come and do a piece on the new incarnation of the college, focussing on the more unusual of the arts which he had introduced, which, of course, included Ben's magic class. Ben realised that he had let the cellar room become quite untidy since Christmas, and he had been meaning to get it back to a usable state before now. Now, at last, he had something to work for.

"Certainly," said Ben, looking up from his work at a small presentation table. Juliette looked less bright and confident than usual. If it were possible, she even looked a little troubled.

"Is everything alright?" he asked.

"No, not really," she said, coming in and closing the door behind her. "Someone's found out who my father is."

"One of the students?"

"Yes."

"Who?"

"I don't know," she answered. "But it got to Paul Harris, who is talking about it all across the college."

Ben went across to the door and locked it. "I shouldn't really lock you in with me," he said, "but you want a little privacy, I think. We should tell Helen and the professor that you are here."

"Of course," said Juliette, and she pulled her mobile phone out of a pocket in her neat, dark waistcoat to contact Helen Bywater, with whom she was now, thanks to Ben, on first name terms. Ben went for his mobile, too, but realised that the professor did not have a phone on which he could be contacted, so he dialled the office. He got through to the answer phone, so he hung up.

"Helen?" said Juliette into her mobile. "I'm in the cellar with Mr April, with Ben," she corrected herself. "The other students have found out about me. I don't know if they know about you as well." She listened for a while.

"No," she said to Helen. "I'll stay here with Ben, but thanks for the offer. He's locked the door, so if you decide to come down, please knock and we'll let you in. No, I don't need you right here, it's not as if I'm in any danger and if you are by my side it will finish off any chance of your role in this being kept secret. If I were you I would contact Professor Kennington and tell him."

Pausing from her conversation with the bodyguard, she looked up to Ben and said, with her ear still to the phone, "Do you have tea-making facilities here?"

"No," said Ben.

"Helen," she said back into her phone. "Can you get a message to the kitchen, as well?"

Juliette and Ben worked together to tidy up the classroom and the storeroom attached to it. She was a great help to Ben during that morning, giving the room the benefit of her artistic eye, her 'woman's touch', as he called it. Emily came down with a tray of tea, coffee and cakes, and kept them company for a while, trying to speculate on the effect of this news on the college as a whole.

"Somebody," said Juliette, "is going to call home and tell them the news. It won't be long before the television sends someone here."

"It won't be long at all," said Ben. "They will be here tomorrow."

"What?" said Juliette.

"That's my line," said Ben. "You are supposed to be much more polite." His humour did not have the intended effect, but he was used to that.

"The professor has arranged for someone from the local TV station to pay us a visit tomorrow as a publicity exercise," Emily explained. "It's nothing to do with your little secret, Juliette, but it seems the release of this information has come at an inopportune time. The professor was going to tell us about it at the end of the day. That's why he has called the assembly after class."

"We should try to keep you a secret," suggested Ben.

"We could make her disappear behind one of your curtains and be replaced by Miko," suggested Emily.

"We could let them interview him," Ben thought. Juliette's tension finally broke, and she laughed uncontrollably at the thought of Miko being interviewed. She laughed so much she lost the aristocratic composure she normally carried with her. She doubled up, gasped for breath, and tears ran down her face.

"It wasn't that funny," Ben said.

"Shut up and enjoy the moment," said Emily. "It's not often that someone laughs at your jokes at all."

"So do they know it's you, or do they just think it's one of the students here who is a VIP?" asked Ben when Juliette had regained control of herself.

"They know it's me. Shelley came and asked me directly. She heard it from Paul Harris. They are, you know…"

"Together?" said Ben. "I thought she had better taste." He immediately realised what he had said. "No, forget I said that. Please."

"Not exactly together," said Juliette, "but both of them have their fingers on the pulse of the college grapevine. If you want to know anything, either one or the other of them is the one to ask."

There was a knock on the door. It was Shelley.

"Professor Kennington has called the meeting early," she shouted through the door. "Ten minutes."

All eyes were on Juliette as she entered the larger theatre for the special assembly which the professor had called. In spite of her predicament, she remained cool. Ben and Emily flanked her and did not have to say anything to her fellow students to stop them bothering her with questions and chatter – the looks on their faces was enough. Helen Bywater was nowhere to be seen. It was not her job to protect Juliette from being bothered by her fellow students, after all. When everyone was settled, the professor made his announcement, but it was different from the one he had originally intended to give.

"Some of you have speculated about one of the students being a VIP," he said. "Well, I can confirm that you are correct, and Juliette MacIntyre is, indeed, the daughter of an official who works for the government. We kept it a secret because her father asked us to, and I would very much like to continue to keep the confidence I have promised. Please do not speculate further, and it would be kind to her if you did not bother her about it. If you have any questions, please come to me, and I promise I will be as honest with you as I can be." That was a clever line, thought Ben, because it was the truth, but it was unlikely that anyone would take him up on it. There was some chatter at this point, of course, and the professor waited for it to die down before continuing.

"However, there is something else that I must tell you," he continued after a few minutes. "Tomorrow, we have a television crew coming to do a piece on the college. I invited them before the news of Juliette came out, and I feel it is going to be difficult to put them off now. I would be grateful if you kept her story confidential, and we all concentrated on the issue of what this college is doing and how we have developed a wide range of arts and opportunities."

The professor went on for a little longer about the college and its innovative approach to the creative arts, and how proud he was of his students' creativity, but Ben felt that the students were not paying attention, having just had their rumours confirmed. When the assembly was dismissed, one or two people dared to approach Juliette in spite of her two protectors. One of them was Shelley.

"We're on your side, Juliette," she said, "You can count on us."

"Thank you," said Juliette, displaying just the slightest emotion. Then Shelley guided the other students with her away from the hall. The professor came across to join the three of them as the hall was slowly clearing of students and staff.

"I'm sorry it got out at last," he said, "but I suppose it's surprising that we managed to keep it a secret for this long, nearly two terms. I think my telling every member of the staff may have led to this happening now, I'm afraid."

"My father will be told about this, probably by Helen," said Juliette. "He might want me to leave the school. I like it here very much, and I wouldn't want to leave."

"Neither would we want you to leave, my dear," said Professor Kennington. "We'll do what we can to keep you here."

"Should we go and find Mrs Bywater?" said Emily.

"No need," came her voice from the doorway. She had been watching the assembly from a safe distance. "And yes, Juliette, I will have to tell your father, or at least, my employers. If it helps, I will tell them that this place is safer than many."

"Unless he wants me to hide away in some safe house and do nothing until his work with the negotiations finish."

"How long is that likely to be?" asked Ben.

"He doesn't talk about it much," said Juliette. "It's not going well at the moment, I know that much. It could be years. As long as he doesn't want me out there with him."

"You don't want to be with your father?"

"It's not him, it's the desert. I have a slight skin problem. If I went out to the Middle East to join him, I would be spending most of my time in agony in a hospital – a Middle Eastern hospital, if you know what I mean."

"So the responsibility of keeping her safe, at least for the time being, is mine," said Helen to Ben, Emily and the professor.

"Ours," said Ben.

Ben got together with a few of his students later on, and they got word around that they were going to practise a college-wide magic trick. They were going to make Juliette invisible to the cameras the following day. In order to prevent any curious students from knocking on her door late at night, Juliette secretly moved into the room Emily used on those few days when she stayed overnight at the college. Emily went home reluctantly, but Ben reminded her of what she had said to him about thinking more clearly if you did not spend all your time at the college.

Quite early on Tuesday morning, a large white van appeared in the car park of the college. TV reporter Matt Maunders climbed out with his three-man crew, and they started unloading some of their equipment. Ben went out to greet them. Matt shook Ben's hand. He was a little taller than Ben, but not deliberately imposing. He had short but thick hair, which was so dark brown that it almost looked black, and his eyes were brown and friendly. His warm smile and affable manner had earned him many fans across the county, and had enabled him to get into places that other people had found difficult to broach. His manner on screen was that of the friendly local rather than the digging journalist, although on occasion he was prepared to get nasty in order to achieve his goals. Ben, who had only seen him occasionally on the staff room television, was hoping that he stuck to his friendly local persona today.

"I wonder if we could ask a favour," he said, having been introduced to the other two members of the team. "As you know, we cover a range of different arts, including performance and media. You'll be given a free run of the college, of course, but would it be alright if our own video class shadowed you – filming the film crew, so to speak?"

Matt Maunders laughed with amusement at the idea. "Of course it would. Perhaps we could use some of their footage for part of the broadcast," he suggested.

"That would be fantastic, and very encouraging to the class." Ben wanted to get Matt and his team on their side, to show the college in the most positive light. He led them into the staff room, where he met Professor Kennington. The rest of the staff were teaching in their various classes. Ben excused himself, because he had to set up his own class.

All the tutors had been briefed to show their best stuff, an instruction that was hardly necessary, because every tutor would have wanted to do that anyway. They got out the best performance material that they had produced over the last two terms, and pretended that they were doing it for the first time. Ben had reluctantly allowed Mark to do his guillotine routine because it was one of the best performances he could think of that didn't include Juliette. Mark would pick Len for the part of his assistant, because Shelley was off with the filming team from her video class. Ben had persuaded Emily to ask Shelley to wear her most attractive clothes, especially if it was revealing (as long as it was decent) in order to wrong-foot the team, as well as giving them something pretty to look at. Bryn complained that his class wouldn't get much airtime because they were 'only an art class'. Ben had joked with him about his work being mainstream and always popular, and that he, Ben, was campaigning for minority groups like his own class.

The students were in on the act, too, each one simply eager to have their fifteen seconds of fame. It looked like they were set up to be able to go through the day without mention of Juliette's situation.

When the television team visited Ben and his small class in 'the dungeon', Juliette slipped into the spacious storeroom out of the way, and Mark and Len, who had become good friends over the past few weeks, did a fabulous job of Mark's comedy routine. Len was brilliant as Mark's volunteer, clowning at all the right moments without actually stealing the show. He had taken note of what Stephen Goss had said about comic timing on his visit, and had begun to like the idea of clowning as a profession. Shelley and her crew filmed the mini-show as well as the TV team, and, as she had been in the performance, was able to put the camera in all the right places to get the best footage.

Matt Maunders viewed her team's footage through the video camera's little screen, and nodded his head. He drew alongside Shelley, with whom he had been flirting a little as they had gone from class to class during the morning.

"It's good. Could you send it to us when you've edited it a bit? We might use it on the programme."

"What's through here?" said Matt's real cameraman, pointing at the door to the storeroom where Juliette was hiding.

"That's my storeroom," explained Ben, aware that the students were tensing up a little, and hoping that Matt didn't notice it. "It's got my own magic props in there. The professor gave me this cellar as a classroom because it had a large storeroom attached to it. I'm afraid I can't let you in there, because there are a lot of secrets in there."

Well, *that* was true, he thought.

Matt was happy with that explanation, and the team moved on. They filmed the kitchens, more classes, they spent some time with the dancers and at the end of their time at the college, mid-afternoon, they interviewed the professor. Many of the classes stopped work to look out of the window as they set up in front of the school so that Professor Kennington stood with the imposing old building behind him. It was a beautiful and outstanding backdrop for his speech.

The professor spoke for a few minutes about his vision to extend the range of the old art college to cover many art forms that young people might find interesting. The film crew stood close, and Shelley's team stood behind, filming them. Ben, who had no other class, watched from a safe distance.

Then Matt Maunders asked the question they all thought they had managed to avoid.

"Tell us about the VIP you are harbouring here at the college - the ambassador's daughter who needs a bodyguard to protect her."

"We're not *harbouring* anyone," said the professor, without pause or hesitation. Ben realised that, although he had so wanted to avoid this moment, he had still prepared for it. "Harbouring seems to mean something sinister, like harbouring a criminal. What we are doing is *protecting* the young lady. I think it is important to protect our children. Some people might even say that protecting our children is more important than educating them. At the college here, we are giving them positive experiences, we are setting them up for a future career, perhaps, but most of all, we are protecting them."

"What about your other students, the ones that are in danger because of her presence in the school? How are you protecting them?"

"Actually, we have put nobody in danger – but *you* might have. Nobody was in any danger at all until you came and told the world that she was here. And, of course, you are not broadcasting live, so she, and they, are all still safe, until you show this to your audience. What will happen if you do show it, I expect, is that the ambassador will arrange for his daughter to be moved. So my students will remain safe, but you will certainly have ruined a young person's life. And then you will blame it on me."

He paused for a while, looking over the camera crew's shoulders to the students behind them.

"I expect you will leave that part out of the interview," he continued. "But that doesn't matter, because my film and video students have been following you around, making a film of their own, which we will show in full if you don't."

"I can assure you," said Matt, taken by surprise and suddenly on the defensive, "that we have the best interests of the students at heart. We cannot, in good conscience, hold back this information from our viewers, but we will broadcast it with sensitivity and honesty. However, you are keeping a student at the college. May we speak with her?"

"I'm sorry," said the professor, all smiles and sympathy. "But she has expressed a desire not to be on camera, and we wish to respect that desire. At the moment, the father has not been identified, so she is still safe. We'd like to keep it that way."

"Of course," said Matt.

The crew packed up and started to put their equipment away. Shelley went up to Matt.

"Do you still want a copy of our work?"

"Oh, yes," said Matt, flashing the big smile for a moment. "I think you have done an excellent job."

Everyone in the college got within sight of a television for the following night's broadcast. There was only small footage, including some of Shelley's team's film, shown about the college itself, but most of the professor's interview was shown, except for his threat about showing the full version if they didn't. They focussed rather well on the way the professor justified himself, and the college came out looking good.

However, Juliette's secret was out. For the rest of the evening, there was very little playing of the tournaments, even though most of them had come towards their finish. The rooms set aside to be games rooms were still full of students and staff, but they were all speculating about the future of the college, and Juliette's place in it.

"They might have to close the college down," Ben overheard Paul Harris say, standing up from a pool table that wasn't really being used. "The professor is in his office right now, taking phone calls from irate parents who want to take their kids out of here before we get attacked by terrorists."

"I wonder who told them about her?" said Shelley.

"Someone in your filming class?" suggested Paul. "Maybe someone wants a career in investigative journalism, and wants a head start."

"I don't think it was anyone there," Shelley defended her colleagues. "I know them all, and I don't think they would do this."

"What about you, Paul?" said Ben, interrupting in order to keep the balance of the conversation sensible. "Would your parents want to take you out of the college?"

"I hope not," he said.

"You like it here?"

"Oh, yes, it's great. I wouldn't have thought college life would be so much fun."

"If your parents wanted you out, what would you do?"

"I'd try to persuade them to let me stay."

"How?"

"I don't know. Maybe I'd let the professor talk to them. He was really good on the telly tonight."

"Well, that's what he's upstairs doing right now," said Ben, "for any of the parents that phone."

Juliette stayed out of the way of her friends for the evening, locked away for the most part in Emily's spare room. Emily spent some time with her, and finally came down in order to go home late that night. Many staff and students were still up after midnight, and Ben realised it might take a while for the buzz to die down. The staff did their best to treat the young people as adults, but Ben was pleased for a break in the 'no students' staff room. He flopped into a chair. Emily sat by him.

"How is she?" he asked.

"She thinks it's her fault."

"It isn't, and nobody down here has been blaming her. The general feeling I'm picking up is that everyone wants to support her."

"Except the person who told them about her."

"Word gets out. It's difficult to keep a secret in a place like this. Maybe one of the students called home about it, and a parent or friend from outside did it."

"I suppose so. Juliette thinks she'll be taken out of the college now."

"I hope not. But you're probably right."

"She says she's going to phone her father and tell him how much she would like to stay here. See if there is anything she can do, any idea they can come up with, to salvage the situation."

The professor, also, had spoken to Ambassador MacIntyre, and between them they had come up with a compromise. Juliette's father agreed to let her stay until Easter, and in the meantime, he would take advice as to what to do next. The Easter break was only a week or so away, and the local newspaper and TV station did not leave them alone during the week.

On the Monday afternoon of the following week, as Ben was doing his usual walk around the college grounds, he noticed a large hatchback car pulling in to the car park. He thought he recognised it, but it took him a few seconds to work out from where. It belonged to one of the television reporters who had upset the applecart for Juliette last week. He also saw Helen marching at speed towards the car park, and decided to join her, albeit at a safe distance.

"It has come to my attention," Helen said as she stood at the door of the large car, stopping anyone from getting out on that side, "that you may be a danger to my primary. I therefore cannot allow you onto the premises."

The TV reporter opened his window.

"How are we a danger?"

"I heard Professor Kennington explain to you last week how the protection of the students was best served with privacy, and yet you broadcast the whole of your interview anyway. Therefore I can only assume that you are here to endanger my charge once again." Her voice had a hard edge, and almost sounded threatening.

The driver's passenger prepared his camera to film her. She looked straight at him, with a stare that even a dauntless reporter would find withering.

"Do you want me to say it again, on film? Would you like me to get a court order to prevent you coming here? If I did, I would make sure that everybody knew that it is because you were acting against the country's best interest in a very sensitive political situation in the Middle East. Because that would be the truth."

The man put the camera away. Matt Maunders was less intimidated.

"May we speak with the professor?"

"Do you have an appointment?" Helen asked.

"Are you *his* bodyguard, too? Or just his secretary, perhaps?"

"If you are acting in the best interests of this country, or even of this college, then I am sure the professor will speak with you again. But I seem to remember that last time he felt he needed a back-up of his own."

Ben decided to close the safe distance between them, and not just because he had to strain his ears to hear what the reporter said in response to Helen's challenges.

"I've got an idea," Ben suggested as he got to Helen's side.

"Ah, the magic man," said the reporter, turning on his winning smile. "We loved your guillotine trick." He noticed very quickly that the smile was not going to win over either Helen or Ben.

"Whatever," said Ben. "May I make a suggestion? One that would allow you in to the college to do your interviewing?"

"Go on," said Matt.

"Why don't you arrange to allow the film department here at the college to film you doing your interview? It would be great PR both for the college and for your station, which, I believe, has fallen out of favour with the government over this little incident with our student."

"Fallen out of favour?" said the surprised reporter.

"Yes, didn't you hear? Our student seems to think that one politician wanted to bring a charge of child abuse against you, but that wouldn't work because the young lady in question is over eighteen. But there is certainly the possibility of aiding potential terrorism, and in this political climate that wouldn't be a great career move for the lead reporter of a small local TV channel. And I think your station used to get on quite well with the local MP. You might find that that's all about to change."

"It is?"

"Of course, you could still put it right. Not that you can take back your revelation that she's here at the college, but you might, at least, do something to say you approve of her family's choice of places to protect her? After all, your report on the college, which I thought was really good, was never actually against us."

The reporter said he would think about it, and he nodded some kind of acceptance to Helen, started the car, and turned around to leave the car park. They would no doubt be in touch over the next day or two to follow up the idea of a conversation with the principal, hopefully agreeing with Ben's idea that it should be filmed (and edited) by the college students. Helen watched as their vehicle left, and did not leave her position until they had clearly driven some distance down the road.

"Juliette did not tell me that the government were so angry that the news has got out," she said to Ben.

"Well, she wouldn't," said Ben with a little smile. "I just made it up."

17

The man that Ben had spotted back in September and suspected of being a peeping tom was back. He stood at the entrance to the car park, looking in. Ben looked at him, and realised that his presence now would be more of a comfort than a threat. He wondered how much money the government could afford to throw at protecting Juliette. Negotiations with the Middle East might be fashionable right now, but in a few months' time perhaps the trend would change and the money would not be there any more. What would happen to Juliette then?

He wandered around to the back of the house where he had arranged to meet with Miko. As he walked, he looked around, half expecting to see more guards, but that time had not come yet. Miko was waiting by the lake, a pack of cards in his hands. He was shuffling them with one hand, cutting and spinning the cards around themselves. He had got really good. If only his English had improved along with his card manipulation. Sometimes, Ben thought that giving him card magic to escape to had hindered his progress, rather than helped. Perhaps today would make a difference. Ben was here to help him with his conversational English, as part of the professor's program to help him with his communication skills.

The sun shone brightly down on the two of them, and the early April weather carried with it some promise of warmth. The sky was a beautiful blue, with wisps of cloud, but the weather forecast was still not brilliant.

"Hello, Miko," said Ben.

"Ola," said Miko, because his friends had taken to saying it in Spanish as a way to support him.

"We're here to speak English," Ben corrected him.

"Si," he said, and then he caught on. "Yes, sorry."

"Tell me about the weather."

"It is sunny, but iss not warm yet."

"Yes?" said Ben, encouraging him to continue.

"Yes," he said. So Ben tried another angle.

"What made you come to England?"

"England iss beautiful place to be," said Miko.

"England is a beautiful place to be," Ben corrected him.

"Yes, it is."

"But why are you here?"

"My famil', we have to leave our home in Spain. I used live in Costello Toro, a little town like Lockley."

"Whereabouts in Spain is Costello Toro?"

"Iss near to Seville. My father, he work there. But he get... I don' know how to say. We lend money. He could not pay back."

"Borrowed. You borrowed money."

"Si, yes. My father, he had borrow from bad men. We lost home, get attack', everything. We had run to England."

"How did you get here?"

"We have friend, they very helpful."

"Friends. They *were* very helpful."

"Yes."

"Say it," said Ben, and Miko repeated the sentence. Ben was being drawn into Miko's story, and had forgotten to help him with his English.

"In England, in Bucking-ham-shire, there is big big Spanish, er, family?"

"Community? A group of families?"

"Yes, community. They help us get jobs, get better lend money to pay off men in Spain."

"Get a better loan?"

"Yes, loan. And from friendly bank, not lending whales."

"Loan sharks."

"Yes, I knew it was that. Couldn't remember."

"And have you paid off your loan?"

"We pay off slowly. Then we return to home in Spain."

"When was this? How long have you been in this country?"

"Sin' last year. I could speak no English ever until then."

It was a struggle, but Ben continued to listen to Miko, correcting him occasionally and letting him speak however he could as he told the story of how his brother had been attacked and put in hospital by the loan sharks' thugs, and their house set alight when they decided to run. In England, a Spanish community leader had helped his father get a job and arranged for a loan with a British bank so that the sharks could be paid off in full. However, the family would not be returning to their home in the near future. Their house had been sold off (after the fire damage was repaired) and they had nowhere to go.

While the Spanish community in Buckinghamshire had been a great help, the younger members of the Spanish families spoke a lot of Spanish to each other, rather than English, and that was why Miko had such a problem with the language. Miko's time at the college had been paid for entirely by a grant, and it took some pressure off of his family to have him here. He felt lonely a lot, but still enjoyed the company and support of his new friends here. He was anxious about one thing, however.

"End of the term, we do a show. You ask me if I do performance, and I say yes. Iss mistake. I don' think I can do performance."

"But your card magic is incredible."

"But in English?"

"You have to practise your English, Miko, but why don't you do the performance in Spanish?"

"You will not un'stand me."

"You're good with the cards, I'm sure we'll cope with the rest."

Miko's face lit up at the thought, and immediately Ben could see that he was planning what he should do. They chatted a while longer, but Miko's family's story had affected Ben. When he thought of Juliette's father under threat, Richard having to spend his life in a wheelchair, Mark's condition that would probably disable him from ever getting a job and Miko's family being violently threatened by loan sharks, he just felt thankful for his own life, with his loving parents, and, in fact, his extended family, all of whom were financially stable and supported his unusual choice of career. He knew that his mother was disappointed when he had not taken up teaching straight away, but had not said a word to him because she wanted him to do what he wanted to with his life.

This week was the last week of term, and only two things should have been on his mind - firstly, what to do for Juliette over the Easter holidays, and secondly, more urgently, what to do for the end-of-term show. It was to be a variety show, so there would be pieces from the different classes. Even the filming class had prepared a couple of short films for the college to enjoy, and Emily's singers and Carolyn's dancers had plenty to show, too. Ben had deliberately left Shelley and Juliette out of his plans because they would be involved in other things, so he had picked Miko to perform a magic trick, Richard to do his cups and balls with live camerawork from the video class so that his close-up work was seen on a big screen behind him, and for Mark to do his version of Tommy Cooper's famous multiplying bottles and glasses routine, helped backstage by Len and Xander, who, while they didn't actually have to do much, were included anyway.

Professor Kennington had told the staff and students that nobody was being taken out of the college as a result of the news of the last week or so, and that he had been very pleased with how the parents and students had all been so supportive of the college's situation. Matt Maunders on his evening television programme had gone to great pains to show the college in a good light. The general feeling was that Juliette's bodyguard was just a precaution, and that her life probably wasn't really in danger anyway. So for now, the college was secure. How this was going to affect the professor's attempts at raising money or recruiting new students for next year, nobody could guess. There had been a lull in applications, but often there was a large intake both immediately after Easter, when looming end-of-year exams made people realise that they should be planning what to do next, and in the summer holidays.

Juliette was going to have a holiday this Easter, rather than spend the time at the college with only Helen Bywater for company. Ben's family frequently had a party time in Birmingham over Easter, and Barbara had a spare room which she was willing to lend Juliette for a few days, so it was arranged that she would travel with Ben and join his extended family for a few days. Ben had to return early because he had got another show at the Shining Star, so Emily would take her on for a few days at her cottage. Emily insisted, however, that she only had room for one guest, so she could not take Helen as well. Helen had simply said that she would be around somewhere, and she hoped that she would be invisible and would not bother them.

"No, you can join the family as well," he had said to her. "I'm sure that the government can pay for you to stay at the Dog and you can join in our festivities. Everyone comes home at Easter from wherever they are. Some people don't even know half the others, so you'll blend in, no trouble."

"The Dog?" she inquired.

"I have no idea why so many pubs in the Birmingham area are called the Dog, but I can assure you it's a great place to stay. And you really would be welcome into the family celebrations, as long as we don't tell them who you are. Just one thing, though. How good are you at smiling?"

Juliette's situation having been dealt with for the moment, Ben turned his attention to the show. It was on the last full day of term, with most of the students leaving the following day. There were no actual classes, just lots of preparation. The show itself was a good two hours long, and, once again, included guests from among the families who could make it. Miko's parents were in the audience, as were a few others who had come to collect their children for the holidays.

When it was Miko's turn to do his card routines, he stood up and introduced himself in Spanish. There was something refreshing, something colourful about hearing a different language, so the audience were spellbound, which, of course, is quite appropriate for a magician. He spoke very fast as Spaniards are often inclined to, but he did not waste his time just standing and talking. He proceeded to perform a highly skilled, sparkling show, entirely in Spanish. As his hands flicked through the cards he kept talking as if he was giving a running commentary, and the flow and eloquence of his language added a quality to the performance which astounded Ben, who knew no Spanish whatsoever. His comic timing was so good that, when he cracked a joke, the whole audience laughed, in spite of the fact that only two people in the audience, his parents, actually understood it. His moves with the cards were practised and entertaining, and his style was fast and skilled.

He called up a couple of his young friends to help with some of the tricks he did, all the time speaking in his native tongue, but his body language and gestures told them exactly what they should do. In some ways, Ben thought, he echoed the way Ben had started to teach him by the lake, where language was not necessary, and the cards cut across the barriers. He showed his skills, too, for he had not spent a single day since that day by the lake without taking some considerable time to work on his skills. At the end of his performance, when he bowed, Shelley and Juliette led the audience in a standing ovation.

Xander and Len brought Mark's props onto the stage for Mark's Tommy Cooper tribute. Mark had watched Tommy Cooper's original television routine over and over again, copying every move and word as he performed. He did, in fact, slip a couple of times and reveal a part of the trick that he shouldn't have, but as that was the nature of the trick, nobody noticed. One thing that impressed Ben as he watched was that when he did slip, it did not fluster him and he continued without breaking the flow. This was a far cry from the Mark Tyler who needed Shelley's support just to introduce himself back in September.

There was a break in the show after an hour or so of what Ben considered to be really high-class entertainment. During this time, the cameras were set up for Richard's cups and balls routine. After that, there would be a monologue from someone in the creative writing department, which would give the video crew a chance to remove the close-up camera. Shelley really wanted to stay in to see Richard, but she had to go backstage to prepare for her part.

Richard's handling of the cups and balls was competent, but did not shine like the others had. Ben again noted how he seemed to be lacking in that elusive quality that the experts called 'stage presence'. Luckily, he did not have to say much for his routine, and the cameras did enhance his performance a little, but it was more about the skill of the camera crew than of Richard's handling of the cups and balls.

Next, there was a short comedy film made by the video class, during which Shelley was still not completely ready backstage. In her performance tonight, the secret of the mysterious parcel would finally be revealed. It took both Carolyn and Juliette, who had been let in on the secret, to help her get into costume. She was ready only a few moments before she was announced.

And then, she was on stage. She wore a glittering ball gown, long, flowing and big enough to hide the mechanics of the prop she was using. The parcel had contained a light foam-filled puppet, a life-sized mannequin in a dark suit. There were connecting wires and rods which were attached to parts of the gown that Shelley wore, and, at certain points, attached to her with straps. As she moved across the dance floor, the puppet moved with her. This device had been an idea that Barbara Stephenson and Ben had dreamed up years ago, and the mechanics had been created by a puppeteer Ben had met a year or so back. Barbara had spent two days with Ben going through the design at Christmas, and she had enlisted a number of friends to make the man-sized puppet during the winter months. But it needed a puppeteer to make it look good.

Shelley's dancing skills were the key to bringing the dancing mannequin, who she had named 'Bob', to life. She glided across the stage to music from Strauss, and her every move affected the puppet she wore, making it look like there were two people up there dancing. The model was hinged in just the right way to make all his (its) moves look natural. The hinge mechanisms at its elbows made the arm bend in a very similar way to a human arm, although Shelley had needed some practice to make it move in a flowing, dance-like manner. Carolyn Cleese and Shelley had worked every spare minute they had to make this work, and it had cost a lot of hard work and tiring extra hours, but it was now the highlight of the show.

The feet of the dancing puppet were attached with rods to Shelley's shoes, making them look just a few centimetres apart from her own, so it looked as if Bob was taking the lead. With its knees, chest and shoulders rigged in a similar way to its arms and partly fixed to Shelley's clothes or arms and legs, she could effectively make her foam partner do anything she wanted it to. The only problem was getting its head movements right. The head was well fixed to the shoulders, with a slight looseness to make the head's movements look human, but there was no way to get it to turn and face the right direction. Instead, it seemed to stare into Shelley's eyes like a lovesick puppy.

Ben was spellbound, and, in spite of the fact that he knew what the puppet was, he was drawn into its magic and for a while began to believe it was a real person. All its movements were like human moves as Shelley guided it across the floor, and when the music ended and she took her bow, still face to face with her artificial partner, it was Miko who led the audience in a standing ovation for her.

Ben had loved the way Shelley was always there for other people. She had encouraged and supported everyone in the class, and probably did the same for the other classes she was in. To say her magical skills were not too good was an understatement, but to see her perform this amazing act of dance puppetry may not have been magic, exactly, but was certainly a great stage illusion, and he was proud of her, and pleased that he had been able to do something for her when he had the mannequin made. He hoped that the video class still had their cameras running, because he really wanted to take something for Barbara to see when he went home tomorrow.

When the performance part of the show was over, Professor Kennington said a big thank you to everyone and then he announced the winners of the winter tournaments. Richard and Shelley had won a few of the games between them, which also made Ben pleased. It seemed that his small class had made a big contribution to the life of the college.

After the show, Miko introduced Ben to his parents, and then said goodbye and went off home with them. Mark's mother also came to Ben to say 'thank you' for what he had done for her son. Ben was beginning to think that perhaps he could make a difference for his students after all. However, it was their lives, not just their performances, which needed help and support.

It was difficult to find enough people to help tidy away at the end, as many were doing their last-minute packing before their parents picked them up on the following day. Many of the students who weren't being picked up had to catch an early train in the morning, and a bus had been arranged to take them to the nearest train station, which was several miles away.

It was later in the afternoon of the following day that Ben started the journey back to Birmingham with Juliette as a passenger. Ben was surprised at how little luggage she had, but that was probably because she was used to moving around a lot, so was quite economical with her packing.

As they drove through slow countryside roads towards the bigger major route to Birmingham, Ben tried to make conversation.

"So what's it like mixing with common people like us?"

"Common people?" Juliette laughed. "I wouldn't know, I haven't met any. I've met all sorts of people, rich and poor, aristocratic and what I assume you mean by common, but everyone is different, and everyone has something special to offer."

She paused for a while to think.

"I think sometimes that the people my father mixes with are artificial. I think what I've learned mixing with... mixing with the likes of you, and Mark and his mother, and Shelley and Xander, is that I don't have to put on airs and graces. Sure, I had to keep my secret, but in every other way, I could be me. From what you've told me about your family and friends, I can be me there too."

"You certainly can."

"I think I don't want to be the ambassador's daughter any more."

"Your father is a great man," said Ben, although he had never met him.

"I know, and I love him dearly, and I'm glad I'm his daughter. But I don't mean *his* daughter, I mean the *ambassador's* daughter. I didn't ask to be in this role. I just want to be me."

"I know what you mean. I am so grateful my family is letting me pursue this peculiar career of mine, even when they must have thought I was mad. And I wish I knew what to say to support you now."

"I just had a thought," said Juliette. "When you come home with a girl, your family aren't going to think we're, you know, an item, are they?"

Ben laughed at the thought, and wondered what he would do if they got the wrong impression.

"I hope not. How much of your secret can we tell?"

"That you are looking after me as a favour to my father?"

"That you need protecting, and that I am your designated protector?"

"Perhaps I am your long-lost cousin from..."

"Antarctica?"

"Russia."

"Bognor?" Ben suggested. "Or Wales. Can you do a Bryn Jones impersonation?"

"'Art is drawing pictures, not poncing about doing magic tricks, look you, boyo,'" she attempted, beginning to loosen up a little and show a side of her personality that Ben had not seen before.

"I'd stick to singing," Ben said. "And you don't need to worry about what they think about you and me. My family have had it in their minds that I'm going to marry Mary Donovan since we were both children."

"Mary who?"

"Mary Donovan and I have been friends since we were little. In everyone's mind back home, Mary and I would spend the rest of our lives together."

"Will I meet her?"

"No," said Ben, "I'm afraid not. She's working as an aid worker in Africa. She took up nursing when I went for teacher training, and from there we grew apart. Don't tell my mother, though, she still thinks we'll be married one day."

Ben's family and the extended community at Birmingham welcomed Juliette with open arms. There were parties, reunions, an outing to Cadburyworld, and Juliette was included in everything. Ben's mother embarrassed him relentlessly in front of Juliette, because, as with all mothers, as far as she was concerned he was still her 'little boy'. One or two of the people there did think there might be something going on between Ben and Juliette, and he received one or two remarks about being a lucky man, and what would Mary say? However, it was all light-hearted banter and, as nobody watched Norfolk television, nobody guessed the truth.

At the end of the week following Easter Day, Ben took Juliette back to Norfolk. She seemed genuinely sorry to leave the family behind. In some senses, she seemed more sorry to say 'goodbye' than Ben was. He had always seen Birmingham as his home, of course, and had considered his stay in the college as being 'away' from home, but now he was actually beginning to feel like he had left his roots, and was settling in Lockley. As they drove back, he started to feel that he was going back to his real home.

18

The summer term was here at last. Because of the late Easter, it was to be the shortest term by a long way. Various tutors started getting their students ready for tests, exams and evaluations that would lead to the awarding of certificates at the end of term. Ben had not given much thought to this before now, and felt he should really think about it now.

He had considered giving a certificate of attendance to each of his class, but that did not say they achieved anything, only that they had turned up. He wanted to find a way to evaluate them, but he knew that if he did, some, if not most of them, would fail. Only Juliette and, surprisingly enough, Mark had performed well on stage, at least in English, and he felt that Mark would not achieve the same standard in close-up. Xander and Miko did well with the close-up side, but Miko had not done enough work on stage magic to qualify for that as well, and, of course, Xander's stage fright would stop him gaining any marks there. Len had been too private in his studies for Ben to evaluate him well up to now. Shelley, as fantastic as she was in every other respect, was simply not cut out to be a magician.

Ben thought about his list of students for a moment. He had left someone out. It was Richard Wellington. Perhaps what Richard had said was right, and he really was invisible. It was so easy to work things through without taking Richard into account. He had done some good close-up, but had not performed well on stage. What could he do? The only all-round potential magician among them was the one that needed a bodyguard!

Then he had an idea. Why should everyone have to be good at everything? He could split up the course into different departments, and have awards for achievements in the different disciplines. There could be a number of different sub-subjects covered by the overall name of 'magic'. There was the history of magic, stage magic, close-up, escapology, clowning and juggling, quite a number of different certificates he could give out, and everyone would get something. Everyone, that is, except Shelley, who had not performed any magic at all, unless you counted dancing with a man-sized puppet as a magical illusion. He decided to add 'magical assistant' to the list of awards, because, as poor as she was at being a magician, she had, at some stage, helped everyone in the class do their own part well. Ben could not leave Shelley out of this thinking, because she was a key person in the class, and although Steve Goss had joked about it, the part of assistant was a vital role in a magician's performance.

Ben decided to have a word with Jim Hunter, the teacher of the creative writing class. Jim was married with two children and lived in a village the other side of Lockley, so he was not around most of the time when Ben did his thinking, after the college day or on weekends. Ben knew that Richard was in his class, so he thought Jim might have an idea as to how he should encourage and support his wheelchair-bound student. Ben caught up with Jim after the staff meeting one Tuesday afternoon.

"Jim, can I have a word? It's about Richard Wellington."

"Yes, certainly. Richard. Clever lad. Shame about his accident, of course, but it's woken up a sharp wit in him, I think."

Ben looked at the older man, wondering if they were talking about the same person.

"I have a bit of a problem with him, actually. He doesn't have much of a stage presence, and I don't think I have done much to equip him to fulfil his aims."

"His aims?" asked the English teacher.

"To make a stand for disabled people."

"I think he's great," said Jim, "and I think his work will get him noticed and help him make that stand he wants to make."

"You do?"

"Oh, yes. Richard is good at writing about his situation. He gets his feeling across really well. Sometimes, when I'm reading his work, it really makes my heart ache."

"When I see him on stage, it seems like it's achieving nothing at all."

"Perhaps he shouldn't be on stage then," suggested Jim.

"But he wants to make a difference."

"And you think the only way to make a difference is to become a magician? Think about it. If you asked the average man in the street to name 10 famous magicians, would they manage it?"

"Probably not."

"10 famous writers?"

"Yes, I get your point. It's just that I hadn't seen that in Richard. The lad himself told me that he thought he was invisible."

"The thing is, Ben, you *see* all your students. You have to. You watch their hand movements, where they stand on a stage, how they present to a living audience. I don't. I don't have to see what anyone in my class looks like. They could all be aliens for all I know. In fact, I think Xander Herron *is* an alien. I see them by the work they produce. The only people I notice in my class are the ones that can be a bit of a nuisance. And Richard is anything but that. It's a pleasure to have him as a student."

"You're not keen on Xander?"

"He's a fair enough student. He turns in a decent piece of work every now and then, although he is a bit mouthy in class. I certainly notice him."

"It's strange how what is good in my class is not so good in yours."

"And vice versa," said Jim.

"But Xander is just spirited, that's all. He's not actually disruptive in your classes, is he?"

"Not really. And I thought we were talking about Richard."

"There he is, turning invisible again!" Ben laughed, but Jim's high opinion of the lad set him thinking. Ben realised that Jim was eager to get home, so he let him go. He looked for Emily, who also made a good listener, but she had already gone.

On Wednesday lunchtime Ben was lucky enough to get a chance to sit on the same table as Emily, who was with Juliette and Shelley. Mark was not at the college on Wednesdays, so Ben asked if he could join them.

"It would be an honour to sit on the same table as the three most beautiful women in Norfolk."

"Just Norfolk?" said Emily with a wicked grin, but she let him sit there anyway. Juliette was expressing her feelings about the news that she was still going to be at the college, at least for a bit longer. Although she wanted to stay there, she was still unhappy about the whole situation.

"I talked to my father about my future in this college. He said the decision hasn't been made yet. Hasn't been made! It's been weeks since the television got hold of the story, and they are still sitting in some office somewhere, just talking about it."

"If we're lucky," said Ben, "they'll still be talking about it at the end of term, and you'll still be with us."

"The decision hasn't been made yet?" said Emily. "Did he use those words?"

"Yes," said Juliette.

"Not 'I haven't decided yet'? It sounds like he's not the one making the decision."

"He probably isn't. The people deciding my future are probably faceless civil servants in Whitehall."

"Faceless civil servants?" said Ben. "Do people still call them that? You know, whenever I heard that expression I used to think of people actually walking round without…"

"Ben!" Emily interrupted sharply. Ben realised that he had been exercising his ability for joking at the wrong moment again, and so he decided to shut up. He looked up at Juliette to apologise, but she was smiling at him.

"Every time I've been angry about something, or frustrated, or feeling down because of my father or the situation with the college, you've been there to make a joke. I really appreciate the effort you've made to cheer me up, Ben, honest. Even when it hasn't worked, I appreciate you trying."

"Oh, he's trying all right," said Emily, "*really* trying."

"Thank you," said Ben to Juliette. "And thank *you*," he said to Emily.

"I think you're wrong, Juliette," said Emily. "I don't think Ben was joking for your benefit. I don't think he knows how *not* to joke. I bet if he was at a funeral, he'd be happy to do five minutes' stand-up."

"Five?" said Ben. "I'm sure I could manage more than that."

"See?" said Emily.

"Thanks for taking my mind off being miserable. And Ben's right, I have been at this college for most of the year, nothing serious has happened to me even since the news got out, they have no reason to take me out of the college now. And if they make the decision to move me, between the three of us we can think of an objection that will get them debating for another three terms. Maybe I could even sign on for next year?"

"Next year?" said Ben. "Not in my magic class. I only planned for a one-year course."

"I'm sure the world of magic is bigger than that," said Emily. "I haven't seen any escapology, or ventriloquism."

"My students are already good at escapology," said Ben. "They are always trying to get out of doing any work."

"Seriously, there are areas of magic that you're not into. Perhaps it would be worth looking into those areas as well as the ones you enjoy."

"I think we've covered quite a wide range," said Juliette. "But more stagecraft would be good. Meesh says she'd like to learn about backstage and all the support that goes into different kinds of performances. She says she'd sign up to any course that offered that."

"Doesn't your drama course do that?"

"Only as much as your magic course does. Perhaps the two courses should get together and work on something."

After lunch, Ben went back to his room, and looked at his mobile phone, which he had not brought with him to lunch. There was a message for him from his mother. She very rarely used his mobile phone number, and he was sorry he had not been there to answer it straight away. He looked at his watch and tried to work out what she might be doing right now, early on a Wednesday afternoon. She did her shopping in the mornings, and she would probably be at home right now, so he dialled her number straight away.

"Mum?"

"Benny! Good to hear your voice." Ben winced. 'Benny' was his least favourite name. But it calmed any fears he might have had that there was something wrong. If her reason for calling had been serious it would have been 'Benjamin'.

"Good to hear you, too," said Ben. "I'm phoning back because I missed your call."

"Yes, you did. What's the point of having a mobile phone if you keep it turned off all the time?"

"I hate mobile phones," Ben said, telling her what she already knew. "Anyway, what did you phone about?"

"I've got some good news. Mary Donovan's coming home. We're planning a big welcome home party for her on 30th June. You'll be able to come and join in, won't you? I remember you telling me the college year ends early."

"30th June?" Ben asked, and felt his heart sink. Mary Donovan had been his best friend at school, and he would really want to be there to welcome her home from her stay in Africa, but he did not need a diary to know that he was not going to be available on that day. "Does it have to be 30th June?"

"Yes, it does," said his mother in an insistent type of voice. "We've arranged for her old school friends from all across the country to come to the reunion party. Don't tell me you can't make it. You, of all people, would be the one to persuade her to stay in this country."

"Why would I want to do that?"

"Because you've both had your adventures, and it's time you settled down."

Ben sighed, but not loud enough for his mother to hear. She, along with a number of members of her family and Mary's, had always assumed that the two of them would get married one day. They had been virtually inseparable as children, and had grown up as the closest of friends. What his mother did not know was that they had grown apart when they went off to pursue their separate careers, his in teaching and hers in nursing. Mary had grabbed hold of the vision that she could help people, but was disillusioned by how her qualified nursing friends had found the profession in this country, with more paperwork to do and less respect, and, specifically, less time to actually care for patients. When a chance had come up for her to go to Africa to make a real difference, she had grabbed it with enthusiasm.

He, however, had 'gone the other way', according to Mary. He had abandoned teaching to play with his toys, as far as she was concerned. That special friendship, that closeness and trust, that had enabled them to be such good friends over the years was still there, which is why Mary had found herself able to say such things to him, but she made it clear that being a magician was simply the wrong thing for him to do, and he ought to be doing something better with his life.

"What if she wants to go back to Africa?"

"That's why you should be here on the 30th," said his mother. "So that you can get her to stay. Ellie Donovan and I have been talking about it. She misses her so. We need you here."

"And do you miss me?" said Ben.

"What?"

"Do you miss me and want me to come home?"

"I even missed you when you were at school, and I couldn't wait for you to come home at the end of each day," said his mother with that gooey sound to her voice. "But, no, I'm glad you're happy there, and that you feel you are doing some good for your students."

"I've always been grateful that you let me go my own way. But Mrs Donovan should let Mary go, too."

"She did, and Mary went all the way to Africa for two years. At least you get to visit us every now and then."

"What if Mary has found her place in Africa? Mrs Donovan will need you to help her understand."

"What about you? Would you go to Africa, too?"

Ben took a deep breath. "I'm not going to marry Mary, Mum."

There was silence on the phone for a few minutes. Ben knew he had just hurt his mother, and it nearly made him cry.

"I'm sorry," he said after she said nothing.

"Which reminds me," she said in a cheery voice. "That young lady, Juliette, who you brought home at Easter, I wanted to ask you. Is she the young lady that was on the news? The ambassador's daughter? Is that why you were looking after her?"

"Well done, Mum, and thanks for not saying anything about it while we were with you. Yes, that's her, and she was with me to keep her safe over the holidays."

"Lovely girl. Well brought up. Well, we'll see you on the 30th, then."

"No, Mum, wait," said Ben, only just managing to stop her from finishing the conversation and hanging up. "I can't make that date. It's our big, end-of-year concert then, what we've been working up to for the whole year. I'm sorry, that is the one date I can't make."

"Did you fall out?"

"What?"

"You and Mary. Did you have a falling out when you met, that summer after you both came back from college?"

"No. We're still the friends we've always been. But I'm not sure we were ever going to be married. It's almost, well, it's almost as if it would spoil a good friendship. I think that not many people have the bond we have, and I love her dearly. But not in *that* way."

"Anyway, she thinks your being a magician is a waste of your talents."

"You knew that?"

"Yes, dear. I'm your mother."

As much as he loved talking to his mother, that telephone call spoiled his day. Why was it that the two most important events of the year would fall on the same day? Ben determined that he would rush away after the concert and go back to Birmingham to see Mary, but he knew that, too, would be hard, because many of the students would be leaving the college the following day, and he would want to say goodbye to those young people whose lives he had shared for the last year and to whom he had grown so close.

He walked out to the garden and stood in the middle of the front lawn. He looked at the big house, evaluating in his mind how being here had changed him over the last year. Perhaps a year or two ago he would have gone home to spend time with his family and Mary, but now he knew he would do his duty and support the college, even if it meant making his mother sad.

He turned around slowly and took in the surrounding countryside, the trees inside the college boundaries, and the farmers' fields beyond. The sun shone and a warm breeze touched him. He squinted against the sun, and put up his hand to shade his eyes. To the west, he saw something that glinted in the sunlight.

"Over there," he heard the sound of a woman's voice that he recognised. Helen was issuing orders to a man in a dark suit, one of the other bodyguards whose name he had not bothered to find out. The man crouched low and made for the trees to the west of the premises, hand in his inner jacket pocket as if he was going for a gun. Ben looked out again over the western fields, and he could still see something reflecting in the sunlight. Someone was watching them, only this time he knew it wasn't the bodyguards because they were already on the premises.

He returned to the comparative safety of the big building, away from the openness of the front lawn. He passed Helen, who was standing outside the front of the house like a soldier giving orders. She was wearing an earpiece phone, listening to what her colleague was saying as he made his way off the premises into the farmer's fields, endeavouring to stay out of sight of whoever had the binoculars.

"Is everything alright?" he said to Helen, who more or less ignored him.

"Excuse me," she said, as she moved away to join her colleague. Ben looked up at the upstairs windows of the front of the house. He noticed someone looking out. It looked like Paul Harris. Whatever was happening, it was not going to stay secret.

Ben went into the house, where he saw Professor Kennington, standing looking worried.

"What's going on?" Ben asked him.

"Apparently, Mrs Bywater and her colleagues have been suspicious of something for a few days," said the professor. "I think our relationship with the farmer on that side of the house, which has never been that wonderful, is about to get a lot worse."

"The students have seen that something's going on," said Ben. "I think it would be a good idea to keep them informed, so that there is not unnecessary speculation."

"Of course," said the professor. "As soon as we know what is happening, we will let everybody know."

It was more than an hour later when Helen returned to the house with an explanation of what had happened. It seemed that, with the warmer weather coming, a lot of the students spent their time sunbathing on the lawns of the college grounds. The young ladies often wore skimpy clothes or bikinis to sunbathe, and the western farmer's teenage son had set up a base in a tree house on his father's land, using binoculars to ogle at the girls as they relaxed. Helen and her ever-watchful colleagues had spotted the sun reflecting off of the sunglasses that the lad had been using, and started planning what they were going to do to catch whoever it was who had been watching the college. They had not speculated about whether it was a possible terrorist or kidnapper, or even someone from a local newspaper looking for a story on the ambassador's daughter.

The professor had been wrong about the farmer's reaction, however. He was embarrassed that his son had behaved in such a way, and was grateful that the security team that had caught him were discreet about it and were not going to bring any charges against him. He also thought it was funny that his son had been caught by professional bodyguards who had surprised him in his little tree house with guns in their hands, giving him the fright of his life.

"Shame you didn't take a picture of him I could have shown him every time he misbehaves from now on," he had said to Helen when she had called on his house with the shame-faced lad in tow.

The college was buzzing with the story for a few days, but everybody took it as a bit of fun, and nobody was unduly alarmed by it. It just proved that the bodyguards were on their toes, that's all. However, there were fewer sunbathers out on the front lawn for the next couple of weeks.

A few days after the incident, Helen Bywater arranged to meet Juliette, Emily and Ben in the cellar classroom. She had obviously chosen the classroom because of its association with secrecy, both professionally and unofficially, as that was where Juliette had hidden when her secret had got out. It was as if Helen was making an official appointment this time, and they all, somehow, felt obliged to turn up. When they were together, Helen told them her news.

"My contract with Juliette is over. I am leaving tonight," she said without fuss. She looked at her watch. "In about an hour, in fact."

"Why?" said Juliette.

"Because I am a specialist," she said. "I am an undercover bodyguard. I am supposed to hide in the background while the people in my care live their ordinary lives. Your situation here has changed. From now on, you will be served by a conventional security operative. In fact, there will be two of them, but you will only see one at a time. They will be staying at the Tin Whistle in the village, and take turns at watching over the college."

"Where will you go?"

"I'll go home for a holiday, and sit around doing nothing for a week. Then, my husband gets home."

"Fantastic!" said Ben. "I mean, I'm pleased for you. We'll miss you, of course, but you get to see your husband again."

"No, you won't."

"What?"

"Miss me. You'll be glad I'm gone."

"That's not true," said Ben. "We were just getting used to you. Now we'll have to put up with two new people."

"Will you have much time together before your next assignment?" asked Emily.

"At least six months," said Helen. "The job pays well, and allows some long breaks between assignments. Joe and I will go on holiday somewhere quiet, and…" She looked embarrassed in front of them at the thought of how she and her husband might spend their break together.

"Have some quality time together?" suggested Ben.

"Yes, that," she said with a grin that Ben hadn't seen on her in the six months he had known her.

Juliette threw her arms around her and gave her a big hug.

"Well, I'll miss you even if Ben won't," she said.

19

"I think people are like flowers," said Mark, standing in front of the class in his performance posture. His voice was clear and confident. "Girls are, anyway. I mean, they have flower names, like Rose, Daisy, or Begonia."

"That's brilliant," said Ben while the others laughed at the joke. "You didn't stutter at all."

"I d-don't s-stutter if I practise my lines b-beforehand."

The class was building a routine with a mixture of magic tricks. The exercise was to 'tell a story', that is, to give the trick a reason for being there. They were looking at the flow of the trick, including giving the audience a good reason why your hand might be in a certain position, or why you should open or close a box. Mark was no good at creating his own ideas because he could not evaluate how the audience was likely to respond, so he had used one of Ben's flower routines and was beginning to memorise the lines for his performance. This would probably be the routine he would use at the end-of-year show, the big event that would finish his time here at the college.

Ben was concerned for Mark when the college year was over. There would be no more support from Professor Kennington, and, in fact, there might be no more college here. There was still this disturbing lull in the number of people booking to come to the college next year, and officials responsible for the safety of people like Juliette MacIntyre were making appointments to come and visit – Ben was fairly sure that was not going to be good news.

He told the group that they were going on an expedition soon. He had finally found a local magic shop which they could visit. They had to go on a Saturday afternoon because it needed two cars to take them, and Emily volunteered to drive the other car. That was particularly helpful, as she was more familiar with the town of Stevenbridge than Ben, who was not entirely sure he could find the shop as it was located a littlebit away from the town centre.

Ben had struggled to find a reasonably-sized local magic shop. There was probably one nearby, but he did not know where to look. Shops like that are not commonly advertised, because they are amongst the few business that don't actually want too many customers. He had not visited his magic club since shortly after Christmas, but he had found out that the members there usually bought their stuff from this little shop in Stevenbridge, which was run by one of their members. The shop was really a costume shop with fancy dress hire, theatrical and dance costumes and items for the children. Round the back there was a little den with a reasonable choice of magical props, available only to people who could prove they were magicians.

"You m-mean, p-people have to p-pay to get in b-by doing a m-magic trick?" Mark had asked.

"That's about it," said Ben.

"I promise this will be the first private shop I've ever been in," said Xander with a grin. Mark did not understand why that was funny.

Ben had been used to shopping at one of the two bigger magic suppliers near where he lived in Birmingham, and sometimes in the even bigger shops in London. He had also been supplied, via the Internet, from across the world. He was glad that he had everything he needed for the time being, because he did not think a tiny place like the back room of 'The Glass Slipper' was going to meet his needs.

However, when they all got there, they found that it was quite an impressive place. It was smaller than Ben's storeroom back at the college, but it was an Aladdin's cave of magical delights (it was actually Shelley who coined that phrase). The room had so little space in it that Richard could barely fit his wheelchair in, so he went in on his own, and when he had looked at everything he wanted to, he carefully reversed out and let the others have a look.

Len was not that bothered about the props that might be waiting at the back of the shop, because he saw something in the window that immediately caught his attention. It was a pair of coloured trousers, yellow with multi-coloured spots of different sizes, and he was determined to buy them as the first part of his equipment as a clown. They were not official clown trousers, if there were such things, in that they fitted like ordinary trousers, but Len had given it some thought and trousers with braces and a hula-hoop would just get in the way of his juggling. These trousers were bright and noticeable, and he could wear them comfortably and still perform. He looked around for possible shirts and waistcoats to go with the trousers, but the ones in the shop were too expensive.

"You should ask if Ben's friend Barbara will make something for you," suggested Shelley.

In spite of Ben's encouragement not to spend too much money, they all did. Ben could hardly chastise them for it, however, because he bought a very expensive and sophisticated clear perspex box from which a mass of feather flowers could be produced. Magicians often joked amongst themselves about buying tricks they would probably never use. But Ben was sure he would use this one – he could just see himself on stage at the Shining Star with this glitzy piece of kit.

On the following Sunday afternoon, Ben was lucky enough to find Xander on his own for a few moments. He had been trying to get a few minutes to chat with him. Spring had just about ended and summer was on its way, and Xander seemed to have made no progress with his stage fright problem.

"Some of the stuff you looked at yesterday in the magic shop was big stage stuff. If you want to use that kind of equipment, you're going to have to face your fears."

"I don't know," said Xander with a shrug. "It was great-looking stuff, but just not me. I think I would be happy just to watch the show from the audience."

"I could understand that," said Ben, "if it was anybody but you saying it. I mean, you thrive on being the centre of attention. You've always got people around you, and you love it. Why not transfer that to stage performances?"

"Sometimes, people just aren't good on stage. I'm okay with the other things; surely I don't have to worry about stage fright."

"Wouldn't it be a good idea to face your fears?"

"Why?"

Ben could not answer that one. 'Not everybody can do everything' was a good argument that he couldn't counter.

"Ben, I appreciate your help, but I wonder if there is another way you could help me out."

"You don't want me to fix you up with a girl, do you?"

"No," Xander laughed. "I can do that for myself. Anyway, you have enough trouble fixing yourself up when it's there for the taking."

"What?"

"Sorry, that was out of order. What I wanted was, well, I'm good in small groups. I wondered what would be the chances of me doing some table hopping with you?"

"With me? Where?"

"At that nightclub," said Xander. "You go there quite often, now, don't you?"

"Yes, but it's a professional nightclub. I don't think they do work experience."

"Okay," said Xander. "If they don't I'll accept that. But can you ask them? You never know."

Ben promised to ask, and let Xander go. It was not the answer he was looking for – he had hoped that Xander would want to keep trying to conquer his stage fright. However, if he did some table work in the nightclub, he might just get the urge to do the big performance on stage, so Ben decided he would do as his student had asked and try to arrange an evening's real work at the Shining Star. Who knows, if Xander was any good, they might let him use the place as a testing ground for more of his students.

He put the idea by Professor Kennington later that day. The professor agreed that it would be a good idea as long as it was okay with the nightclub, as it would give real life experience to the young students. However, he had something else on his mind. Some government officials were due to visit him on the following day to talk about Juliette's situation. When they had come back from the Easter holidays, Juliette had returned, too, and nobody had mentioned anything about her no longer being allowed to attend the college that she had grown to love so much. The professor was uneasy about a final decision not being made, but was also not sure about asking, in case his student was taken from him. Finally, three weeks into the term, they got in touch, and made this appointment to speak with him.

Ben offered to sit in on the talk if it helped at all, the meeting being on a Monday when he had no specific duties. The professor was delighted with his offer and accepted. He would have liked to plan what he was going to say, but as he had no idea what they were going to say first, he did not know how to prepare a response.

On the Monday morning, after the start of the college day, the two men arrived. They introduced themselves as Fletcher and Norris. Fletcher was a huge man, approaching two metres high and almost as wide. Alongside the fat man, Norris was a little shorter and thin. The two were dressed in identical black suits. Ben thought they looked a little like Laurel and Hardy, except that they did not wear bowler hats. Norris carried the briefcase that they both used to hold their papers, but he did not open it, at least not to start with. They sat in the staff room, which was more comfortable to use than the professor's tiny office.

"We'd like to say from the beginning," said Fletcher, "that we are impressed with the way you handled the situation with Miss MacIntyre and the television last term. In fact, a number of MP's have talked about sending their children to this college as a result of your efforts."

The professor was taken aback.

"I meant every word of it," he said, after a pause.

"That's the point, or part of it at least," said Fletcher. "There was a cleanness, a certain honesty, about your dealings with the media. In fact, we have noticed since then that the television station in question has been very supportive of the school, almost as if somebody got to them and persuaded them to change their approach."

"I just think they were trying to do the right thing," said Ben quickly, looking at his feet. He was aware that Norris was watching him carefully. Fletcher was doing most of the talking, and Norris was doing most of the careful watching. But Fletcher's words reflected the attitude that Norris was projecting. Perhaps they were psychically linked. Or maybe they were robots with little men in their heads operating them.

"Perhaps," continued Fletcher. "Nevertheless, we are left with this – Miss MacIntyre wants to stay at the school, Ambassador MacIntyre is happy for his daughter to stay, and a number of other high-ranking officials would be quite pleased to have their children stay here while they, too, must go overseas, some of them to areas where they would prefer their children not to join them."

"Surely most MP's send their children to Oxford or Cambridge, or some other mainstream universities," said the professor.

"Indeed," continued Fletcher. "But not all of the young people in question are university material. Some of them would prefer to study performing arts, for example."

"There are performing arts colleges all across the country," said the professor, and Ben wondered if he was trying to talk himself out of getting the business.

"And this one is far enough from London to be away from it all, and near enough to drive here and home again in a single day. And in addition, and this is the main point I want to address, it would be a good idea to post all our security personnel to one location, rather than to have them scattered across the country. It is a question of communication and economics."

Ben did not know what to say. He had the faintest idea in the back of his mind that the professor had actually seen that one coming. He did not know whether the professor would throw them out straight away for even suggesting it, or welcome them with open arms. There was silence for a while as they mulled it over.

"How many bodyguards are we talking about?" asked the professor slowly. "Will each student have their own?"

"We don't know for sure at the moment," said Fletcher. "We think six officials will want to send their children here as from September, and we think three security personnel will be sufficient."

"And how prominent will they be on site?"

"I think the professor doesn't want to make this place appear like a prison camp," said Ben.

"Of course," said Fletcher. "Well, we would want them to be housed on site, but they would be instructed to be as discreet as possible. We would like you to consider this as a possibility."

"Of course. We would be delighted to have new students at the college," the professor said. "However, I am concerned about the presence of security personnel, as you can imagine."

"May I say my piece now?" Norris spoke for the first time. Fletcher nodded for him to continue. Norris took out some paperwork from the briefcase and laid it on the table in front of him. It looked like it was full of accounts. If it was the college's accounts, thought Ben, then something dreadful was about to happen.

And it happened.

"My part in this procedure has been to look in to your finances. This college has been running at a loss for quite some time. It has, year on year, been relying on the generosity of wealthy locals to bail it out. This says a number of things. Firstly, that the local people love and support what you do. Secondly, that the future of this facility is in doubt. And thirdly, that your prices are too low. There are some colleges that charge ten times what you are charging."

"I will not make this place into a college only for the rich."

"Some of your students pay nothing to be here – rather, they are subsidised."

"We still receive payments, whether from them or from charities that help them."

"What I am suggesting," continued Norris, "is that you charge a much higher fee to those who can afford it."

"I am very unhappy about a two-tier pricing system," said the professor.

"It doesn't have to be two-tier, exactly," suggested Ben, interrupting to try and get the professor to see that these people were trying to help. "If you set the price high for everyone, then allow concessions. You already charge different prices for boarders and day students."

"That is to cover the cost of housekeeping," argued the professor.

"But the boarders, in general, can either afford it or are subsidised by someone else," continued Ben. "By charging higher prices, you can run your own subsidy fund. If your local rich friends no longer have to 'bail you out', as Mr Norris put it, they might be happy to contribute to a special fund which supports less privileged students. And there's one other thing – charging bed and board for bodyguards, sorry, 'security personnel' to be there would be a reasonable solution, and the price could be high because of the inconvenience factor, and the possible negative publicity to the college. I mean, If you don't like the thought of them being here, you could charge an *enormous* price to cover inconvenience."

He shot a glance at Norris, who didn't flinch.

"I am sure there would be no negative publicity to the college," said Fletcher. "I seem to recall that when you gave that television interview, you said something about the safety of your students being even more important than their education. Surely having a few members of auxiliary staff whose responsibility was nothing but the safety of your students would achieve exactly what you said you wanted on television."

"Well, that is what I said," said the professor, looking very much like he was feeling the burden of his position right now.

"I think we have put a lot on you," said Fletcher.

"But we have also offered a solution to your current financial situation," said Norris. "What we are offering must be good news to you, surely."

"What about the other students?" said the professor. "The ones that are not so privileged?"

"It seems to me that they could only benefit from the presence of professional security," said Fletcher.

"I think the professor was talking about some people with money or high standing possibly feeling they are above their children mixing with commoners," said Ben.

"No, I wasn't," said the professor.

"I know what you mean," said Fletcher, "and I think that those people too snobbish to see the advantage of a place like this, that mixes able and disabled students, rich and poor, well-educated and…"

"…not so well-educated," said Ben before Fletcher could say something less kind.

"Yes," said Fletcher. "The point is, the mix is good. Our young people need to see the rest of the world in a situation which is, shall we say, unbiased. Some of our children may be the next leaders of our country, and, although you don't have a politics class, spending some time here might be useful."

"Possibly *because* we don't have a politics class," suggested Ben. "They can learn their politics elsewhere."

"Precisely," said Fletcher. "And they can learn their life skills here. Not to mention some performance skills that might come in handy on a more serious level."

This hit the note for the professor, who had struggled with people in authority who did not know how to relate to him in the past. Attitudes towards disability had improved a lot since his school days, where he was frequently punished for being who he was, but there was still much to be done to support people like Mark. People like himself, in fact. Here was an opportunity to contribute towards that process. In a moment, all his questions had been answered, all his anxieties dispelled. In spite of being poor at reading people, he had also worked out something from Fletcher's words that Ben had missed.

"I accept," he said in a tone that sounded like triumph. "I will write to you with some inflated prices, and I will include Ben's suggestion about charging extortionate prices for bodyguards."

"I didn't say *that*," said Ben.

"And your own daughter, Mr Fletcher," continued the professor, revealing his observation. "Will she be coming?"

"Son," said Fletcher, delighted that the professor had been sharp enough to work out where he was coming from. "He wants to act. Nothing else matters to him."

"We will be glad to welcome him," said the professor with a beaming smile.

"Yes," said Ben with a resigned sigh. "And if he wants to do nothing but act, he'll probably end up enrolling in my class just to fill his sheet."

"And what do you do?" asked Norris.

"I make ambassador's daughters disappear," he said.

Final details were arranged, and the two government representatives went on their way. The professor resolved to tell the rest of the staff at their Tuesday meeting. Increased prices would mean that they would not need so many students to enrol in order to break even next year, and the arrival of VIP children might increase their reputation, therefore recruiting more students over the summer. The professor was determined not to use this as an advertising point, but, as he had already discovered, word would get out anyway. The possible success of the professor's re-invented college would lift the whole community, too. The people who had supported this venture financially would be relieved that it was finally going to pay its own way. At least, that was the plan. There was still the actual recruiting of students to do.

The management of the Shining Star, encouraged by Emily's support, were pleased to allow Ben to bring Xander to perform around the tables on a number of conditions. Firstly, Ben had to perform as well, although he did not have to watch over Xander, so he could do different tables. Secondly, they would only pay one fee – this was a work experience spot, not employment. Thirdly, and best of all as far as Ben was concerned, Emily had to come and sing, too. Emily agreed as long as she could bring one of her students to sing with her. If Ben could do it, why shouldn't she?

The date was set for a Wednesday evening, which was often the try-out night for the club anyway. There were not too many customers on Wednesdays, and the ones that came were fairly sympathetic, and so not too hard on the performers. The four of them all went in Emily's car, because she was best at getting a parking space near to the venue. On the journey, Ben gave a bit of a briefing to his young apprentice.

"Don't stay too long at any table. About eight minutes would be good, but don't keep looking at your watch to check! You should be able to judge whether they are having fun. If they don't want to see magic don't inflict it on them."

"Are you trying to make me nervous?" said Xander.

"Sorry," said Ben, eager that Xander should not suffer stage fright when he was not even on a stage. "Be yourself, have fun, do whatever it is you normally do that gets everyone on your side. You're good at being the life and soul of the party – that's what you'll be doing tonight."

Early in the evening, shortly after the first few customers had come in, but before it got busy, Xander and Ben did a few tables, and Ben noted that Xander was really quite good. His main talent was in getting everyone on his side. He had a cheeky banter which was warm and welcoming, and as it was early in the evening, he set the mood for the guests to have a good evening. He did get one or two tricks wrong, and he laughed along with the table he was with at his mistakes. As the evening went on, he loosened up and was enjoying himself at least as much as the guests he was entertaining.

Once or twice Ben signalled him to move on as he was dominating a table a little too much, and he did tend to focus on the attractive young ladies of any given group, but he still did well. They stopped when the 'stage' show started, and stood at the bar to listen to Emily singing her duet with Juliette.

They sang 'When You Believe', and their harmonies were spellbinding. Juliette's voice was the perfect match for Emily's, and the mood that Ben and Xander had created with their magic deepened with the singers' performance.

"I could do this for a living," Xander whispered to Ben at the bar as they applauded their colleagues. After the show the bookings manager came and gave his comments at Xander's performance. What he said was helpful and complimentary, but honest. When Emily joined them, they discussed the possibility of having a student night, where people from the college would get the chance to perform to a 'real' audience, and the nightclub would pay a small fee to the college for their troubles, mainly to cover transport. Emily thought it was a great idea, and they agreed to ask the professor about it in the morning. One evening's fee once or twice a year was never going to solve the college's financial problems, but anything that helped further the college's growing positive reputation was going to be a good thing.

On the way home, Xander commented, "My feet are killing me."

"I forgot to tell you that bit," said Ben with a smile.

"You get used to it," said Emily.

"Do you?" said Ben. "I don't think I ever have."

"The secret is to sit down when you're not actually performing," said Emily, "rather than standing at the bar."

The professor was happy to negotiate with the Shining Star nightclub about work experience, and the reputation of the college did grow, quite quickly. Seven students from wealthy families connected to politicians in the city signed up for next year, and four security officers also booked for the residential services of the college. From that, word got around and the office was dealing with a number of enquiries over the next couple of weeks.

Even the local television station got in on the act, highlighting the new success of the college, and, of course, taking some credit for putting it on the map with their own stories. The professor was content for them to do this, but encouraged them to steer clear of publicising the bodyguard aspect of their next year's intake. Rather he pointed them to their deal with the Shining Star as a work experience venue, which satisfied them for the time being.

"The number of students we have coming next year is approaching fifty," he announced with some triumph to everyone at the first staff meeting of June.

"Fifty?" said Ben. "That's not so good. We needed 120, didn't we?"

"It was half that number this time last year," said the professor. "Most of our students joined us over the summer holidays. Not to mention the increase in fees, particularly for bodyguards, has almost tripled our potential income. I think we can say we are heading for success. And I would like to thank everyone here for your support, particularly when things looked grim."

Ben wondered if the professor's delight at the way things looked was a little premature, but he acknowledged that Professor Kennington was always optimistic and positive, and that it was that attitude which had got him so much support in the past. Ben also wondered about his own future. He had agreed to teach at the college for one year, and that year was almost over. He had to decide very soon whether it was time to move on, perhaps even to decide if Mary Donovan had been right and that he should do something more useful with his life, or whether, as he had begun to feel over Easter, this place was really becoming his home.

20.

"Mum?"

Ben was sure that he had dialled his mother, but the line was crackly and there was some considerable background noise.

"Mitchell?" his mother's voice sounded through the interference.

"No, it's Ben."

"It's been what?"

"Ben. Your son. You don't have a son called Mitchell."

"Sorry. I've been expecting a call from Mitchell."

"Mitchell? New boyfriend?"

"You must use longer sentences," said his mother. "I can't understand you if you talk in fragments. Not with this noise."

"What noise?"

"Can't you hear it? I thought it was loud enough to hear even all the way to Lincolnshire."

"Norfolk."

"Scotland even," said his mother. There was definitely something loud going on his mother's end of the line.

"So what is this noise I can hear all the way over here in Belgium?" Ben said.

"Are you in Belgium, now? I can't keep up with you."

"No, I'm still at the college in Linc... in Norfolk."

"Then why did you say you were in Belgium?"

"I was, never mind. What's the noise?"

"It's roadworks. Right outside the house. Anyway, it's good to almost hear your voice."

Ben had thought he'd better talk to his mother to try to explain, again, why he couldn't make the party she was arranging for Mary's homecoming. He had missed a couple of calls from her because of business. Also, he had missed them because he wasn't sure what he was going to say to her.

"I'm really sorry I can't make the 30th," he said. "I can do the 31st, it's just that this end-of-year show is what we've been working for all year."

"I know," she said. "I spoke to your professor chappie."

"You know what it's like. It's a commitment of the job." Then he realised what she had said. "You did what?"

"Professor Kensington," she said.

"Kennington."

"Him too. Lovely man. I could understand why you'd want to work for him. He explained everything. In fact, he invited us all to join you there."

"You spoke to my boss? Over my head?"

"No, on the phone."

"Why couldn't you just talk to me?"

"Because you keep your phone turned off most of the time."

"Oh, yes."

"Anyway, I thought we would book in at your little pub in that village."

"You and?"

"All of us. The family, Mary, her family, her..." and then the crackling on the line took over.

"Coming to visit us?"

"If you won't come to us, we will have to come to you."

"Oh, great," he said, losing all his performance skills for a moment.

"That's what I thought you'd say," said his mother, just as the noise stopped and the line went clear.

"How many of you?" asked Ben, clearing his voice.

"About thirteen."

Thirteen for dinner, thought Ben. It was a good thing this wasn't an Agatha Christie story. Having said that, he thought, he still might not come out of this alive.

"You might want to phone Mary in Africa," she suggested.

"I might? I mean, I might."

She gave him the number, and they were able to talk about some

213

of the details of their visit to his college before the workmen outside her house started up again and they decided to finish their chat. Then Ben sat in his room looking at his telephone for a while before finally getting up off his bed and getting on with the rest of his day.

He had spoken with the professor over the last two weeks or so about awards and certificates. Professor Kennington agreed that departmentalising the magic course was a good idea, and that would mean giving out several certificates to some individuals, but everybody on the course would receive at least one. He also talked about running the course over two years, and bringing in short-term specialists in certain areas to cover some of the things he was not so good at.

"The subject is bigger than you, is it?" asked the professor.

"I think we should cover a much wider range than just magic. That's in line with your original vision of changing the college from an art college to one that covers many different forms of art. If you really are going to double the numbers of students, you'll probably want to increase the range of material you are offering them, too. And I think performance arts associated to magic would need two years, rather than one."

"I agree with you. But who would deliver this two-year course? You still haven't told me for certain that you will be staying on."

"I apologise for keeping you waiting," Ben said. "And I would love to continue working for you, although I might consider living off-site sometime in the next year or so."

"That would be agreeable. We would be pleased to have you. We can sort out the details of the actual content of the course later."

Ben had known for some time that he would say 'yes' to another year or two at the college, but he had simply tried to resist the inevitable. The difficult thing would be telling his family. Somehow, he thought, everyone back home had got it into their heads that Mary and he would be getting married now that she had come back from Africa and he had got this 'magic thing' out of his system, and that he would get a 'real' job. He had wondered, while waiting for them to arrive, if Emily would mind masquerading as his fiancé or something to make his task of telling them easier. He knew, of course, that he would not ask her to do such a thing. To start with, she would tell him not to be such a wimp and just get on and do it. However, he was aware of how, although his parents had supported him in everything he did, they also had expectations of him which he had not met.

He decided to have a go at calling Mary on the African number his mother had given him. He tried to work out what time it would be there at the moment. Where in Africa was she? Was it two, three hours ahead? Or behind? Perhaps Miko could help, he came from another country. Oh, well, it can't be the middle of the night there, it's not like it is Australia or New Zealand after all. Nevertheless, he failed to get through.

He was walking through the corridors looking at his mobile phone, and he nearly bumped into Emily and Juliette going the other way. They were talking about an issue which had come up in the residential students' common area.

"Sorry," he said when he looked up and saw them.

"Imagine him not noticing you," Juliette said to Emily as if he wasn't there, but Emily decided not to pick up the joke.

"Are you alright?" she asked him.

"Not exactly. I could do with another drive out in the country, if you're available."

She smiled one of those smiles which attacked the gloom and drove it away. "Of course. But I take it you don't mean right now, a few minutes before your next class?"

"Oh, no, of course not," said Ben, suddenly inexplicably flustered, like a schoolboy asking a girl for a date. "Er, what were you talking about?"

"Some of the lads have taken to placing a bet on just about anything," said Emily. "It started with who is going to win a tournament game, and the winnings were paid in chocolate. Then they started betting money – just a few pence here and there, it was harmless enough. But over the last week, they've been betting on which teacher would go into the staff room first, whether it will rain tomorrow, what type of magic trick you'll be teaching them next."

"My class?" he said, astounded.

"I'm afraid so," said Juliette.

"Who?"

"I don't want to get anyone into trouble," Juliette said.

"This is about getting them *out* of trouble," said Emily. "Ben is going to think of a way of letting them know that he knows about the gambling thing, and that he won't take further action against them if they pack it in straight away."

"What she said," said Ben.

"It's mostly Xander and Len," said Juliette. "I think Miko goes along with it sometimes, but I'm not sure. He might be trying to persuade them that it's not a good idea."

Ben agreed that it was likely, with Miko's family's experience of money-lenders, that he would advise caution and encourage the other lads to take gambling a little more seriously. Still, he thought, if it was just a bit of fun that ran the risk of getting out of control, he thought he might try and deal with it in a light-hearted way and hope that might be enough to temper the lads' ideas and prevent a bit of fun from becoming a serious problem. He decided to quickly change the start of the lesson.

"Did anyone put any money on who would win the winter tournaments?" Ben asked his class a few minutes later. Nobody answered. Len and Xander were looking at the floor. They obviously knew that he had found out, and were expecting a lecture.

"I've got a secret here that will help you win at gambling." Everyone's attention became focussed on him. He had, in the past, taught them how to bring the aces in a pack of cards into your hand to win at poker, and he had also warned the rest of the college students never to play poker with any of his students. But now he had four different coloured boxes in front of him.

"Pick a number, one to four," he invited them.

"One," said Shelley.

"Okay. You can have one. I want two more people to pick numbers, leaving me with whatever is left. Xander?"

"Three."

"Four," said Mark.

"Do you want to change your minds?" he asked them. "Or are you happy with the minds you've got?"

None of them laughed at that joke. It must have been the twelfth time they had heard it this year. None of them changed their choices, either. Ben rummaged around for a small cloth purse, and showed his audience. Inside the purse were the numbers one to four, each number on a different coloured disc. Shelley got the green one, Mark's was blue, and Xander's was red.

"I haven't touched these boxes, so it might be a good idea to get one of you to hand them out. They must match the colour you've chosen. Len, would you?"

Len handed the boxes out to each of the students who had called a number, and gave the last one to Ben. One by one, Ben had them open their boxes and read the note that was inside. On a slip of paper in each box was the word 'loser' in Ben's handwriting.

Ben opened his box last of all. Inside it was a crisp, new fifty pound note. He turned it over in his hands.

"Fifty pounds! I don't get to see a fifty pound note that often. I didn't know they were that colour." He then made an issue of putting it away in his wallet. He got a polite round of applause.

"To win at gambling, you have to be the banker."

Over the rest of the week, he found out from Juliette that the gambling had stopped. He was sure that it wasn't the trick that had achieved that result, just that he had gently let them know that he knew about it.

As the warm days came on, he found Emily, one Friday afternoon, talking to Mark. Ben was a little surprised, because Mark didn't talk to girls very easily, and he knew that Emily did not feel entirely comfortable around him, either. But he was energetically trying to explain something about the difference between playing chess on a computer and playing a human opponent, and she was listening as if she was interested.

Ben wondered if he should interfere and rescue her, as sometimes he got very enthused on a subject and did not realise he was boring his listener, but she really was paying attention to him. He stood at a distance. She flashed him one of her 'melt your heart' smiles and he came and sat with them.

"H-hello, Mr, I mean Ben," he said.

"You weren't going to call me Mr Ben, were you?"

Mark looked embarrassed.

"It's alright, Mark," said Emily, taking his side. "He knows about the Mr Ben references."

"As if by magic," Ben grinned.

"So are you here to give your opinion on chess on the computer?" asked Emily.

"No, I wanted to ask you something," said Ben.

"At last," she said. "I've been waiting all my life for this."

"Er, no, I mean, I was going to take you up on your offer for a break at your cottage. I mean to unwind."

"Good idea," she said, eyes still smiling. "How about tomorrow for lunch?"

So it was agreed, and they met at her house for a light snack around noon that Saturday.

"It was good you chatting to Mark yesterday," he said to Emily as she brought in some food for them both, "or rather, listening to him."

"He's a good lad. You know why I went out of my way to talk to him, don't you?"

"You're not completely comfortable with him, are you?"

"It's not really him. He's great. But he personifies people with his condition in general. You remember I told you I was attacked by someone with Asperger's, a violent young lad in the school where I taught, and the system favoured him over me. That's why I'm at the professor's college instead of teaching in a mainstream school. I couldn't hack being attacked by someone like him again."

"Mark's not like him. He's not violent."

"I know. But as soon as I heard the word "Asperger's" I went cold. I wanted to face Mark and try and like the lad, but I didn't know how."

"Did it help, getting to talk to Mark properly?"

"Yes, I suppose it did. Mark's a lovely lad, in his own way, but I still struggle with people like him. You know, he has no idea what *I'm* feeling while he's talking at me."

"I know what you mean," said Ben, feeling a little defensive on behalf of the lad, "but he is a peaceful type. So peaceful he wouldn't know how to deal with violence if it came and hit him in the face."

"People kept telling me that the lad who attacked me was just frustrated with the way the world didn't understand him. But I didn't care about that – he attacked me, and nobody wanted to take my side."

"I think if Mark was there he would have taken your side."

"I think you might be right."

"How do you get on with Professor Kennington?"

"He's great."

"You don't have a problem with him?"

"No. Why?"

"You only have a problem with people with Asperger's," Ben said. Emily said nothing for a moment as she worked out what Ben was trying to say.

"The professor?" she said eventually, incredulous that she had not noticed anything about the principal's manner which left a clue that he had Asperger's Syndrome.

"I couldn't say. If he hasn't told you, then maybe I shouldn't."

"Does Bryn know?"

"I would guess he doesn't. I think he told me by accident."

"That would explain why he helps Mark, and why he doesn't want to turn away anyone with any kind of problem, any misfit, so to speak." She stared into space for a moment, then she started laughing. She laughed with tears running down her face, but the tears weren't from the humour of the situation. He let her laugh and cry her feelings away. He wanted to put his arms around her to comfort her but he suddenly felt clumsy and even a little embarrassed.

She calmed down and stared into space for a while, her emotions now apparently sorted. The warmth came back to her eyes, and she looked at him in that giving, generous way that had been customary for her up to today. He was aware that he had been staring at her. Well, what man wouldn't?

"So what about you, Ben? Why did you want to get away for a while?"

"I had a childhood friend, Mary. Everyone thought we'd eventually get married, we were that close. We fell out when we went away to college, and she ended up going off to Africa to do aid work. I'm not sure where we stand now. It feels like there's a distance between us."

"Well, there is. Africa's a long way away," said Emily. He glared at her.

"Sorry," she said, "I've been with you too long."

"It's just that, all this time, I've failed to make up with her. And all this time, that's the one thing I've needed to do."

"Needed?" said Emily. She was normally so understanding, so

sympathetic, that Ben felt he could come to her with anything. Today, however, she seemed a little different. She was not as comfortable with his story about Mary as she had been about other things. He thought, perhaps, she had not completely settled about Professor Kennington having Asperger's. But he continued with his story anyway. He explained how she had thought that teaching was a good thing, but when he had gone for magic as a career she had not liked it, and thought he should do something more useful with his life.

"Like her?"

"Yes, like her, I suppose."

"Going off to Africa to save the world?" she said, and there seemed to be a little sarcasm in her voice.

"Or at least to save a few lives over there."

"She should get off her high horse."

"What?"

It seemed to Ben that she had formed an unkind picture of Mary from what he had said about her. He apologised for making her look like that. She was a really nice person, really. He found himself saying 'really' far too much. There was something not quite comfortable between Ben and Emily for a moment. Normally, when they were together, he felt so relaxed. He could do anything, or nothing, and they would be good together. But now that he was talking about Mary, it was different.

Emily suddenly composed herself.

"So what are you going to do?" she asked, politely. "I mean. Have you tried to 'make up'? I know she's in Africa, but you can contact her, surely?"

"I can't get through. But she's coming back to England at the end of term. She, they're all coming to see our end-of-year show."

That last comment was badly timed, because Emily had a cup of tea to her lips at the moment he said it. She nearly spat it all over his lunch.

"Well," she said after she recovered, "you'll get a chance to make up then, won't you?"

"I suppose. The thing is, I think everyone expects me to marry her. You know, the whole family. Both families. We've all been such good friends for so long, and Mary and I were really close, but as friends.

Nothing more. I want to make peace between us, but I don't want anything else. I'm afraid that if I go out of my way to build the peace between us, my mother will start making wedding arrangements."

At that, Emily laughed her musical laugh again. She sat back in her chair and relaxed, and that special atmosphere returned to the room again.

"I don't think it works that way," she said. "You have to make up with Mary because you need to, not because anyone else needs you to. And I think that when she sees you here at the college, she will know you have done some good in your part of the world, like she has in hers."

21.

The week ending 30th June was a blur of activity. Everyone was getting ready for the big show on the Friday. There were last minute rehearsals, props to prepare, the outdoor stage to construct, sound, lighting, access, risk assessments; it was a wonder any of them had any energy to actually perform on the day.

On the 29th, guests would start arriving. Among them would be a group of Ben's family and friends. They had booked all the remaining rooms in the Tin Whistle and planned to descend on Ben for the first part of their celebrations of Mary Donovan's return to England. Ben, who was normally confident in front of an audience, began to realise how Xander must feel when he had to stand on a stage. It was not being on stage, however, that concerned Ben, but the family-and-friends reunion, and to top it all, that it would happen on his home territory.

On the Thursday afternoon, Ben's family, friends, and, in particular, Mary, all turned up at the college in three cars. There were thirteen of them, as his mother had said. Unlucky for some, he thought. He smiled as he greeted them, hugged and hand-shook everyone, and finally got to see his old best friend again.

She looked fantastic. The African sun had certainly darkened her skin, and appeared to have aged her a bit as well. Her light brown hair was cut seriously short and had bleached in the sun to take on an almost blonde appearance. There were lines around her eyes, and whether they were worry lines or laughter lines he could not tell – probably the former. She looked altogether more serious than he remembered her. Best of all, he thought, she had brought a friend. He was a tall, African man of about the same age as Mary.

"Hi, Ben, it's good to see you," she said. "I want to introduce you to Doctor David Bala, my fiancé."

Fiancé! Why had his mother not warned him? He had wasted good worrying time for nothing. Or had she told him, and he had not heard? What with the roadworks outside her home and interference on the line, she might have thought he heard her tell him when her list of who was to be here was interrupted by interference. That's why she gave him her African telephone number, so that he could call her to congratulate her. That's why she hadn't gone on about them not getting married the last couple of times they had spoken on the phone.

"David!" Ben said, more enthusiastically than he had intended. "It's good to meet you." They shook hands, and Ben wanted to say how grateful he was that the African had got him off the hook, but he thought it might be better just to be nice to him. He did risk a little glance around at the rest of the family, however, to see if he could gauge from their expression what they felt about this bombshell from Mary. They all looked suitably pleased for her, but Mary had come home a couple of days ago, so they'd had the time to get used to it.

"David," he said again, "Is Mary bringing you to settle in this country, or is she going back to Africa with you?"

"We're going back at the end of the summer," said Mary, answering for the tall African. "We'll be married there next year."

"I'm really pleased for Mary. And for you, too, David. You've caught yourself one special woman."

"She says lots of great things about you," David said. "I thought for a while that I might have a rival."

"No chance," Ben assured him looking up into his face, because David was several inches taller than him, not to mention broader and more muscled. "Mary and I have been good friends since, well, since probably *before* we were both born. Our friendship is far too valuable to spoil by getting married. Oh, I didn't mean..." he stuttered, realising that he might have just offended the man. David just laughed.

"I am glad to hear it," he said. He had a rich, deep, fruity voice, his English a little accented but lucid.

Ben gave them a tour of the college, and they seemed to find it funny that his classroom was in the cellar. Mary's younger brother, James, made some comment about it being 'suitable accommodation'. He was always a smart alec. Ben was interrupted by Mark and one or two of the other students who were panicking about being ready for the show tomorrow, but his family were gracious and let him deal with them before continuing with their excursion.

Mary slipped away from the bunch early on to have a chat with some of Ben's students. Ben noticed, and could not help feeling that she was going to embarrass him with stories about when they were younger, or, more likely, the students would embarrass him with stories about him now. Still, he had twelve other guests to worry about, so he let her go.

Later, he gave them directions to the Tin Whistle in nearby Lockley, and they settled in for the night. He joined them as soon as he was sure all of his duties at the college were done, and they enjoyed a big family time together. As the evening went on, everyone went to bed except Ben and Mary, who chatted into the night. They talked about old times; about growing up together, and about how they had both changed. Mary talked about how she felt fulfilled doing her nursing work in Africa and how she had met David while she worked in a tin-hut hospital over there, and Ben talked a little, but not much, about the college.

"Do you approve of what I've done?" Mary asked him rather unexpectedly.

"Approve of what?" asked Ben. "Hitching up with that good-looking doctor of yours, or going to Africa in the first place?"

Mary laughed. "The last time I spoke to you I felt we didn't quite finish right. We've always been the best of friends. We've never fallen out. But when I said goodbye to you two years ago, I was a bit full of myself. I was going off to save the world, and I wondered why you weren't. I think I said what you were doing was silly."

"What I was doing *was* silly," he said. "But in a good way."

"And now you're back to teaching."

"But teaching magic," he reminded her.

"You've got a student in a wheelchair, and one with Asperger's Syndrome."

"I noticed you went off to meet them earlier. You'll get a chance to see them both perform tomorrow, in the show."

"But you are doing some good."

"You don't have to go to Africa to do some good," said Ben. "But you asked about *me* approving of what *you're* doing. You know you never needed my approval, but I always admired you for going out there. And I'm pleased for you and David. Let me know the details of your wedding plans, and I will do everything in my power to get to the wedding."

"That would mean a lot to me."

"You know that your mum and mine have been planning for us to get married for the last few years."

"Yes," said Mary. "But I think our friendship was never going in that direction. Like what you said to David earlier. We'll be friends forever, I'm sure, but..."

"I know what you mean. I value our friendship, but..."

The conversation faded, and they just enjoyed each other's company for a while. Ben let himself out of the pub's lounge at around two o'clock in the morning. He felt satisfied that he had made his peace with Mary. In fact, he felt that they had renewed their old friendship. He was genuinely pleased that she had got engaged, and that their friendship was back on a non-romantic track. He hoped their respective mothers were satisfied with the way things had turned out.

The following morning, the family got to the college in time for the awards ceremony, and stayed for the huge spread that the kitchen staff had laid on for all the visitors. Most of the village were there, as well as many of the parents and friends of the boarders. The awards ceremony was quite long, bearing in mind that there were only 63 students at the college, and the alfresco buffet that followed went on for nearly three hours. The whole day was held outside using chairs from both of the theatres and a number of classrooms, and tables from the dining room and anywhere else they could be found. It was to be followed by the show, a display of the skills and talents of many of the students, also using a makeshift outdoor theatre. The college year was just about over, and this was the last big event.

Juliette found Ben, and managed to draw him away from his family group. She had with her an older man. He was smartly dressed, and had a tan that looked like Mary's. He had obviously been abroad recently, almost certainly in a hot country. His facial features reminded him of Juliette, so he worked out quite quickly that he was a member of her family, but had not quite decided which member. Surely it wasn't...

She introduced him to Ben.

"Mr April, I'd like you to meet the Right Honourable William MacIntyre, my father."

Ben was taken aback. The man who was saving the world in whatever part of the Middle East he was supposed to be saving the world in was here in England. More to the point, he was here in the college.

"I'm honoured to meet you," said Ben, taking his hand. He had a firm, solid handshake. He was obviously a man of resolve and determination. But Ben did not work that out just from shaking his hand.

"You've done a lot for my daughter here," said the man in a deep, rich voice that was almost musical. Perhaps a good voice runs in the family, Ben thought. "I must thank you for all your time and trouble. I know it must have been an inconvenience having security around you all the time."

"We managed. It took some getting used to, but..." Ben let his voice trail off, not sure how much Juliette had told him about what they had got up to at Christmas.

"I heard about the disappearing act," said the ambassador. "Your joke got a laugh as far away as Teheran."

"My father's finished his job in the Middle East," said Juliette with a huge smile. "He's back in England for a while."

"A while?"

"I am retiring," said the ambassador. "I was beginning to feel that I was being unfair to my daughter, not allowing her to step into the public eye when she wanted so much to be a performer. We have had a number of conversations over the last year, Juliette and I, and I feel it's time for me to step out of the spotlight so that she can step into it."

"What about your work?"

"It's come to a natural end," he said. "It would be nice to believe that I have made a difference. Perhaps I have, but right now the Americans are making moves that would seriously compromise my work if I stayed out there, and we don't want to be at odds with them, so I was going to be moved to the Jordan. I decided early retirement would be better than having to start again somewhere else."

"He'll be on call to Downing Street as an advisor," Juliette said with some pride in her father. "But that's changed things for today."

"How?" asked Ben.

"I wasn't going to perform today, being a fairly public occasion, but now that my father is home, I don't have to hide backstage any more. I would like to sing, but the performances have been set, and I haven't prepared anything."

"You've prepared all year," said Ben, "and I am sure the professor will allow you to be flexible. If your father has given up his career to be here today, the least we can do is let you sing for him."

"Well, I haven't actually given up my career as such," started the ambassador.

"Why did you 'retire', as you put it?" asked Ben, looking him in the eye. He paused before answering.

"There are a number of reasons. The American involvement, to start with. And many people are working in Jordan already. They don't really need me."

"And the *real* reason?"

"Do you know religious activists are easier to deal with than magicians?" he said with a laugh. "Very well, I'll tell you the reason you're looking for. It's only one of the reasons, not the whole picture, but whenever I spoke to Juliette, I could hear the anguish in her voice. I could hear how much she worried for me, how much she hated the bodyguards she was given, and how much she wanted to perform in public. I am a politician, but I am her father first. What else could I do?"

Juliette stood dumbstruck. She knew that her father loved her, but it was almost a shock to the system to see that love in action in such a way. She threw her arms around him and hugged him tightly in a way unbecoming for an ambassador's daughter, and her tears stained his expensive tailored jacket. Ben slipped away, because it was no longer any of his business. Before he returned to his own family, however, he paid a quick visit to Emily, who he asked to arrange one extra spot on the performance roster for the show.

The show was to be filmed in full by the video department, and so Ben dropped in on Shelley and Paul, who were involved in the filming of part of the show, sharing the task with other members of the class.

"Juliette is going to be singing," he said. "You can film it. She doesn't have to be kept secret any more."

"That's great news, isn't it, Meesh?" said Paul to Shelley.

"Meesh?" said Ben.

"Yes," said Shelley. "Me."

"You? Meesh?" said Ben.

"Yes. Me Meesh; you Ben," said Shelley, bewildered.

"Meesh!" he said with a sudden realisation. "Michelle. Shelley. You're Meesh."

"I know I am," she said, and then it suddenly dawned on her. "You've heard people talk about 'Meesh', haven't you, but you didn't know it was me?"

"Sorry," said Ben, a little sheepishly. "You were always Shelley when you were in my class. But it's good to know, at last, who everyone is talking about."

Eventually, Ben's mother caught up with him, and he sat in the audience with his family and friends. The indoor theatre was far too small for the huge audience that had come for the last performance, so a makeshift stage had been put together out on the front lawn, and, as people finished their food, the chairs set out for the morning's awards and the meal were rearranged for the show. As people were settling down, just before the show was due to begin, Xander Herron walked among them with a few close-up tricks to show them, and Len Berkley juggled and clowned around wearing his new, brightly coloured trousers.

The show was good and long, with excellent performances from singers, dancers, actors and magicians - the best of everything anyone had produced during the year. When any of his students came on, whether it was to take part in the drama, or to sing or dance, or actually to do magic, he was nervous for them, like a mother at her little child's first performance.

Miko wheeled Richard onto the stage for his bit. It had been decided that his written work in the creative writing class was so good that he should simply read some of it out to everyone. So he sat, alone on the big stage area, with a sheet of paper on his lap.

"I used to move on legs," he read. "I was six feet tall, and I had aspirations to be in one of the big football clubs. That will never happen now. Thanks to the gift of alcohol, I now move on wheels and I have shrunk to two thirds of my former height. I need the help of mechanical devices in order to go to the toilet, and people no longer notice me like they used to. In bulk I am bigger, partly because I have not been able to exercise off the excess fat, and partly because of all the extra metalwork I carry around with me, but people still fall over me when they are walking down the street. They apologise, of course, but they still look at me as though it was my fault.

"The man who did this to me survived the crash unscathed. Because I did not die, he did not go to prison, and in a few months' time he will be driving again, free to get himself drunk and do this to someone else. Perhaps I should have died, then at least I would have done some good and he would have been locked away.

"But instead, I am still suffering from the hangover of *his* night out. People treat me as if I was useless, as if it was my brain that had been damaged, and not my spine. I find my head full of hatred for everyone who ever drives home from the pub."

He looked to the sky.

"How could you let this happen to me? But it is not God who has caused me this suffering. It is a man. When I close my eyes to sleep, I see this man. I imagine him driving his car. He knew what the drink could do, he is told all the time, in adverts, in magazines and newspapers, on the television. But he was so sure it would not happen to him.

"Well it didn't happen to him. It happened to me."

Richard paused in his reading and looked directly at the camera.

"I know the address of the man who did this to me. I am sending him a copy of this. I hope it hurts. I hope it really, really hurts."

Richard's reading was met with a stunned silence. Then, as Miko started to wheel him down the specially made ramp, people started to clap. The applause got louder, and one or two stood up to encourage him. Before long the whole audience was standing, and, as he was wheeled back to his seat in the audience, the people nearest him patted him on the back or shook his hand.

Mark's magical piece started the second half of the show. He had a small music-stand table on which stood a vase in which was a small bunch of feather flowers. By the side of the vase there was a red velvety bag with a wooden handle.

"I think people are like flowers," said Mark. "Girls are, anyway. I mean, they have flower names, like Rose, or Daisy," and he paused for exactly the right amount of time, "or Begonia."

He allowed the laughter as if he hadn't really noticed it, and he picked up the vase, and took out the flowers.

"But boys can be like flowers, too. The heads of the flower are like the talents that we have. It might be football, or public speaking, or acting, or dancing."

As he examined the little bouquet of flowers he was holding, he looked up as if he had just noticed the audience there. He made to show them the flowers. All his movements were precise and confident.

"It's all right," he told the audience, "they are only fake flowers. They are made of feathers and wire. Which is just as well, because there is a hole in the vase, so I can't water it." He picked up the golden-coloured metal container and showed it to the audience. There was a hole in the bottom. The audience politely laughed, and he put the vase down again next to the bag.

"But sometimes, people can be so hurtful, can't they? They can call you names," he said, plucking one of the heads off of the flower stalk. He let it drop to the floor of the stage.

"Or they can tell you you're rubbish." He picked off another flower head and let that drop, too.

"Or you can be horrible to yourself – you can believe you are no good because you…"

He stopped, and Ben felt his heart beat faster. So far, he had got all his lines right and his timing had been perfect, but now that he was on stage, it was as if something had just entered his mind, distracting him. Ben knew that feeling, because it had happened to him. But he could handle it, and he was not sure that Mark could put the diversion out of his mind and get on with what he had rehearsed.

"…because you stutter, or because you d-don't always understand what people say when they d-don't say exactly what they mean." The lines he had prepared were real to him, and he started to remember past experiences that had taken the heads of his own flowers. Ben thought he could almost feel Mark's hands go clammy. He noticed a panic, or a look of despair appear in Mark's eyes. He was starting to remember some of his own experiences when people had plucked away a few of his own flower heads. He needed to get past this, thought Ben, to realise where he was and get back to the performance.

Mark looked at the audience, a group of people who cared about him, who wanted him to succeed. He took a deep breath, and composed himself. He pulled off another two flower heads. He recovered from remembering what people had done to him in the past, and got on with the performance.

"Even people who understand and want to help, like our parents and teachers, can get it wrong, say the wrong things and hurt us." He pulled off the last flower head, and let it drop to the floor. His hesitation had gone, and he delivered his lines without a stutter.

"We don't look like beautiful flowers any more, just like weeds," he said, looking at the bunch of green stalks he still held in his hand. He returned the bunch to the vase, placing them in carefully as if they were damaged and he did not want to harm them any more.

Len came on stage to pick up the bits of the flowers that had fallen to the floor, and Mark picked up the bag for Len to use as a rubbish bin. Then Mark looked into the bag, and a well-rehearsed look of surprise crossed his face. He showed the bag to the equally astonished Len, whose acting skills were great as long as he didn't have a speaking part. Then he put his hand into the bag to take out a large silk cloth. He turned the bag inside out to show that there was nothing else in it.

"What we need is a blanket of love and encouragement," he said, picking up the stalks from the vase and covering it with the silk cloth. "Then, with patience and support, we can help people who have been hurt and discouraged to grow new flowers."

He whipped the cloth away from the flowers to reveal that the bunch of stalks had grown new flower heads, more colourful that the ones that he had pulled off. He waited for the applause to begin to die down, and said, "And if we all work together, we can be a great big bunch of flowers together."

At that, he pulled off the lid of the vase to reveal a huge bunch of flowers there, too, and he added the bunch in his hand to the flowers in the vase to make a great display of colour. He took his bow and people started applauding.

But he did not move off straight away. When the applause had completely died away and there was silence, he said something that he had not prepared in his so-careful rehearsals.

"P-people who know m-me know that I have Asperger's S-syndrome. It's a strange sort of c-condition. I'm n-not stupid, but sometimes I look like I am. It's b-been a p-problem for me all m-my life. I just want to thank Mr B-Ben April, my t-tutor, for all the t-time and t-trouble he has t-taken looking after me this year. The thought that I c-could do this sort of thing on stage was, well, out of the q-question. But he has encouraged me, supported me, and helped me to start growing new f-flowers."

He paused for a moment and looked up, finding Ben's eyes among the sea of faces in front of him.

"That was a figure of speech."

He bowed, left the stage quickly, and the applause lasted until he was out of sight around the back. Ben looked at the ground, aware of his family looking at him and how hot his face had become, and not wanting anyone to notice the tears in his eyes.

Mary, who was sitting next to him, leaned across to whisper something to him, but she couldn't, for a moment, think of anything to say, so she just put her hand on his shoulder.

Emily Darkchilde and Juliette got up to sing a duet. This concert was not the place for the tutors to sing normally, but Juliette had not rehearsed a piece specially for the occasion, so they decided they would sing the duet they had performed at the Shining Star nightclub. They performed 'When You Believe', which was well received, and perfectly well-placed in the show thanks to Mark's performance.

The concert was well over two hours long, but seemed to be over in no time. At the end, Ben left his seat in order to congratulate his class, but was stopped by a strong arm grabbing his shoulder. He turned to face his mother.

"I know I've told you this before, but I need to say it now. Ben, I'm proud of you. I might have doubted you in the past, but not now. I hope you have decided to stay here."

"Yes, I have."

"That's good," she said, and she looked as if she was going to say something else, but changed her mind.

Emily Darkchilde came up to say her piece.

"Mike says you're staying on."

"I think there's something you should know about Professor Kennington," Ben said to her.

"What's that?"

"He doesn't like being called Mike. It's Michael."

"Thanks for telling me. I might have got it wrong – for the last year."

"Should I have said that sooner?"

"It's been good working with you this year. I'm really pleased you decided to stay on," said Emily, and she gave him a kiss on the lips. It was a sweet, beautiful kiss which spoke more eloquently than words. It awakened emotions in him that must have been there for a while, but he hadn't given the time to nurture them. Or even notice them.

All of a sudden, he worked out what everyone else had known about him and Emily since before Christmas, and had been trying to hint at ever since.

About the Author

Peter Cooper is a magician, puppeteer and award-winning ventriloquist. He is a founder member of the King of Hearts Creative Outreach, which serves to build up confidence in children and young people, and is engaged in community development and Christian communication.

Lightning Source UK Ltd.
Milton Keynes UK
23 April 2010

153223UK00002B/2/P